A Kinder City:
A Market World Novel

A
Kinder
City:

A Market World Novel

Peter Taylor-Gooby

Matador
Unit E2 Airfield Business Park,
Harrison Road,
Market Harborough. LE16 7UL
Tel: 0116 279 2299
Email: books@troubador.co.uk
Web: www.troubador.co.uk/matador
Twitter: @matadorbooks

ISBN 978 1803131 290
British Library Cataloguing in Publication Data.
A catalogue record for this book is available from the British Library.

Printed and bound in the UK by TJ Books Limited, Padstow, Cornwall
Typeset in 11pt Minion Pro by Troubador Publishing Ltd, Leicester, UK

Matador is an imprint of Troubador Publishing Ltd

I wish to thank David Evens, David Pick, Nick Riding, Simon Thompson, Terry Pratt, Tim Armstrong, Linda James, Pat Marsh, Gary Studley, Trevor Breedon, Greta Ross, Charlotte Cornell, Tony Osgood, Gill Laker, Mike, Derek and the members of the Save As writers group and of the Curtis Brown Creative class of 2019 and many others for advice, encouragement and tolerance, but most of all I want to thank Sue Lakeman.

Also by the Author

Blood Ties (2020)

Ardent Justice (2017)

The Baby Auction (2016)

What crimes will men not sink to, from the
sacred hunger for gold?

Virgil, Aeneid

David

David Ashwood lies sprawled across his bed. He could sit at a desk in the study room, but he prefers it here, by himself. He turns the pillow endways on the headboard, punches a hollow in the stuffing and lies back. He needs to think.

Volume One of the Standing Orders is propped up on his lap, open at the One Law, but he is numb with exhaustion and the clauses seem to merge into each other. He knows he should care. He has sworn before the City to enforce the Law, the one thing in Market World that you can never trade. He is an oath-bearer, an Enforcer new-minted, he wears the black uniform and he must never break his oath.

The light clicks off. The long room is in darkness, lit only by the moon shining silver through the window above him. He should raise his hand and wave it at the motion-detector but he doesn't move.

Sarah, that's her name. He wonders what she's thinking of now. He remembers the great horse that pulled her cart, black as boot-polish and bigger than any horse he has ever seen, with a great yoke of muscle across her shoulders and scarlet flowers plaited in her mane. Juno, Sarah's horse, and he'd stood with his hand on the bridle, talking softly, calming her, with the Enforcers all round them holding their whips ready and Adam reading Sarah the One Law.

Sarah hadn't understood what was happening. She didn't take any of it seriously. He guesses she'll be in a holding cell, sitting on the bed, like he is. Perhaps she'll have a blanket round her. She'll be a bit nervous now. He could help her.

She'd look up with that curious, slightly mocking expression when he tapped on the cell door. He thinks of the way she smiled at him and raised her eyebrows at the same time. He'd sit there, maybe next to her on the end of the bed. He'd go through everything carefully, make her understand that smuggling was a serious charge, but it would all be alright, she'd have a friend, someone in court who was on her side.

They never understood, the villagers, you can't give stuff to your friends when you have a good harvest, you have to trade with a willing buyer and that means money and a bill of sale. Why does it matter? The One Law, no exceptions. You let people do what they felt like, that way led to chaos, the Great Hunger, the time before he had any real memories. People told him his parents had been good, honest people, but they always looked sideways when they said it. One of his uncles had snorted and sighed at the same time: 'Too honest for their own good.' Anyway, his job was to enforce the Law, but you can explain it, why it's there, show people some respect.

He wonders what it is like, sitting on the seat of a cart with the reins held loosely in both hands, the touch of a breeze on your cheek. People would look up at you as you passed by, some of them would wave and shout greetings, maybe you'd give someone a lift. Your horse would pull at an easy pace, thinking of the stable. You'd call out some words that the horse understood and it would trot a little faster for a bit. You'd be sure to reach your village before sunset.

The manual slides down onto the floor and the light clicks on. How can he help her? He slips back his sleeve and touches his wristband, the wristband that everyone in Market World wears, with the tiny screen that flashes for every transaction, that shows how much you have, how much you owe. Seven hundred and fifty-two credits. You are your account. That's what he's worth.

He blinks and reaches out, then hesitates and gets to his feet. Nothing stirs in the room. He moves silently past the beds, grey blankets all neatly folded, according to regulations. He pauses by the half-sergeant's cubicle. Curtis. He has a way of twisting his mouth when he's accusing someone, Denny's got a moustache just like his and takes him off brilliantly.

No echo of boots on the spiral iron staircase. He passes down to the main notice board and checks tomorrow's Audit Schedule again. Her name is "S. Cordell". First case, Court Three: 11.15 am. He pauses at the lower landing, then moves on, keeping to the side of the passageway. He turns a corner into the Holding Corridor. Yellow ceiling and walls, grey floor and strip-lights that glare at him, the stink of new paint in his nostrils.

He pauses and hears voices and the stamp of a boot in the corridor. He turns back and passes through the side-gate into the courtyard. The moon shines out, full and brilliant, from behind dark clouds. The cobble-stones and the low buildings

3

in front of him are silvered, weightless, enchanted. His spirits rise. He breathes the hot, raw smell of horses, sweat, shit and leather, and enters the stables. The stalls stretch out to his left, just like the row of beds in the dormitory. The straw rustles as a horse shifts from one leg to another.

He's never been in the stables before. The mounted patrol keeps to itself. You only see them at ceremonies. Word is, they despise everyone, even the Entrepreneurs.

Something heavy thuds against the side of a stall and he pauses, silent. A lantern gleams to the right. Words he can't make out, then a voice says, quite clearly:

'Easy there.'

The horse whickers softly. David nods.

'That's Juno.'

The lantern swings up out of the stall towards him and a voice calls: 'Who's that?'

The lantern blinds him for a moment and he holds a hand in front of his eyes. 'It's alright. I just came to check on the horse they brought in today, the black one. She's called Juno.'

A broad-faced lad comes forward, holding the lamp out to the side. He wears corduroy and his hair is dark and tangled.

'So that's her name. You here for a bet?'

'She was scared. I just want to see how she's doing.'

The boy looks up at him and puts his hand to the side of his face, as if it helps him think. For a minute neither of them speaks.

'She's big, ain't she? She yours?'

David nods.

'Sort of.'

4

The lad hangs the lantern from a hook set in the wall.

'She's not easy here. I got her away from the others.'

David nods again and swallows. Juno's hindquarters are taller than he is. She almost fills the stall. He takes a deep breath and holds his belly in and eases himself in beside her. After a moment she leans away from him and he slides past her, the warm flank pressing against his chest. She turns her head and gazes at him.

'Can I talk to you?' he says. 'Just wanted to see how you're doing.'

Juno blinks and moves her head and he has the feeling that she understands him.

'You're going to be alright. We'll look after you.'

He leans against Juno's neck for a moment. The blood pulses in her body. She watches him as he pats the yoke of muscle across her shoulders.

The boy hands him something.

'She'll like this.'

It fits snug in his palm, a brush. He presses the bristles against the back of his left hand.

Juno lowers her head and he rubs it down her neck, then again and again. She gives a soft whinny, just on the edge of hearing. The boy chuckles.

'You ain't done this before, have you? Here, you got to push when you brush her down, put your strength into it. And do it in circles, round and round. She loves it. And this one's to keep the brush clean.'

He balances a metal square with tines set in it on the edge of the stall.

David leans into Juno's flank and rubs the brush down against her coat and round and feels a shiver run through her. The rich sweet scent of her rises up all round him. He brushes her again, bending towards her, his free hand reaching up onto the curve of her back. She whinnies with pleasure and her coat gleams where the brush has been. He works his way slowly along Juno's flank, learning the curves and bulges of her muscles, the power that is in her. She stamps her feet just once. He moves slowly past her and she shifts over and he leans into her other flank. The lad stands back, holding up the lantern, his eyes on David.

David straightens and stretches both arms upwards. His back aches. He stands by Juno's head.

'Try this.'

The lad holds out another brush. He rubs it against the back of his hand. It's softer, it almost tickles him.

He rubs it all the way down Juno's flank and on down the hind leg and feels her lean towards him.

The boy grins:

'She likes that.'

He works round with the soft brush, long even strokes, all the way round to her head. Juno closes her eyes and holds herself absolutely still.

The lad hands him a felt cloth.

'Gently, now. She likes to have her face cleaned. I'll get you a stool.'

He folds the cloth and strokes Juno's face with it, her forehead, her cheeks, her nose. She turns her head for him and her eyes meet his and don't look away.

The boy holds out a comb.

'Now you make her beautiful.'

'But she's lovely already', he thinks. He pulls the teeth of the comb evenly through the forelock, lifting it away from her eyes, and then through her mane, dividing it. The red flowers have gone.

'You haven't got anything I could tie in it, have you? A bit of ribbon?'

He slips out his wristband, then slides it back under his cuff. The boy doesn't notice.

'You'll make a stableman yet. We don't go in for that kind of thing. You could plait it.'

David reaches up to the mane, bunching the coarse fair hair in his hand.

'I'm not serious. You'll be here all night.'

''Salright.'

'Hang on, I'll get you some steps.'

The step-ladder creaks and sways sideways as David climbs up. He leans into Juno's neck. She stands stock-still for him, like a sculpted horse, and his heart calms. He needs both hands free to plait.

He works at the task, at peace. The stable-boy shifts his weight from one leg to the other and scratches himself. He hears the movements of other horses, like fenders, bumped against a quay-side by a quiet sea.

He leans back. The ladder totters and the lad grabs it.

'Not a bad job.'

He doesn't say anything. The plaits are dark tassels dangling evenly against the sable of her coat.

He's finished now. He doesn't want to leave, he could maybe stay there with Juno.

'Adam does an inspection later. You'd better get going.'

'Thanks.' He turns to Juno. 'You'll be out of here tomorrow.'

'One way or another. Franklin's buying up horses. Any he can get.'

He can't see the lad's expression. He doesn't say anything, just runs his hand down the side of Juno's face, and edges backwards out of the stall.

'She likes apples. Can you get her some?'

'No problem.'

'Look, about the horses, I need to have a chat with you. Tell me about Juno.'

'One thing I know, she ain't right for Franklin. Sit yourself down.'

He fetches out a couple of stools and they squat in the circle of light, in the warmth of the stable, with the noises of resting horses all round them.

'She's a Percheron, what we call a "heavy horse". She's strong as two ordinary horses and she keeps going, but she's got a mind of her own.'

David listens as the lad tells him about the different breeds of horse, how to look after them, how to treat them. He feels he's entered a different world, somewhere warm and kind, not ruled by order and the law, where his oath is a small thing, no longer the loadstone and burden of his life.

When the lad has finished, he asks:

'Have you got anywhere a bit out of the way where you could maybe put a horse like Juno? So Franklin's crew don't see her?'

Martin grins and rubs at his wrist as if his wristband's too tight.

'Might have.'

He flips back his cuff and they click. David knows he's paying three times what stabling usually costs. The lad wipes the back of his hand across his mouth, spits in it and grips David's.

'Done. I'll look after her. Franklin don't know the difference between a Percheron and a cross-bred pony.'

They both catch the sound of boots stamping across the yard.

'You'd better get out of the way. That's Adam.'

The door starts to open and David slips behind it.

'How's it going, Martin?'

'Nothing to report, sir.'

Adam sniffs the air and peers round. He stares at Juno.

'You been prettying that horse up?'

'Sir.'

'Well don't. She'll only go to Franklin.'

David hardly breathes. He waits until the sound of Adam's steps has faded, then edges round the door and creeps out into the yard, into the silver light of the enchanted world. No sign of movement anywhere. He sneaks across to the side-door and looks back. Adam stands three paces behind him. He has a white scar running from the corner of his right eye to his mouth and a way of looking at you as if he's judging you.

David shivers.

'Ashwood. What are you doing out here?'

'Couldn't sleep, sir.'

'Don't push it. I've got my eye on you.'

Adam strides off on his patrol round the barracks.

Everyone is in bed when David enters the dormitory. As he passes the end cubicle, Curtis shifts in his sleep. The half-sergeant's cold eyes glitter and then close. David freezes and tiptoes to his bed, lies down, takes a deep breath and is instantly asleep.

Rachel

Paul Ferris, Commander of the City's Enforcers, checks his hair in the mirror, smooths the smile from his face and tucks his gold-braided cap under his left arm. His black uniform is crisp and perfect, the silver lanyard looped across his chest, the gold stars on the epaulettes brightly polished and a double-row of ribbons above the breast pocket.

He steps out of the office, crosses the landing, taps on the Chair's door and pushes it open.

'Come in.'

Rachel West, Chair of the City Council, rises to meet him. Her hazel eyes are warm and direct with a faint smudge of tiredness above them. She wears a fitted dark linen suit, tailored to resemble an Enforcer's military uniform. A thin gold chain encircles her neck with the city crest, the balance with the two tiny scale-pans, at her throat.

She holds out her hand. 'Always good to see you.'

'And to see you, Madam.'

He grips her hand and bends forward. She smiles and pauses, her eyes on his, and shakes her head, ever so slightly.

'Business. The Council will make a decision on the Development Programme this morning.'

She points to the model on the table behind them. It seems like a child's toy, everything neat and orderly, brightly coloured, miniature, clean. You could imagine playing with it, rearranging everything until it satisfied you and no-one would mind at all. Lilliput towers, the strongholds of the Entrepreneurs, rise up at the heart of it all, clustered to the west of City Square. Opposite them and much smaller, are the Halls of Justice.

If you knew the City well you might notice that the massive sheds of Franklin's factories next to the Pit, the great rubbish dump, the no man's land between the southern boundary of the City and the Old Town, have all been left out. You'd be more surprised that the vast forests that lie beyond the farmland have vanished. Great fields stretch out to the edges of the table. Silos and barns and sheds, huge and made of metal, not timber and thatch, cluster in identical farms laid out equidistant. Wide straight roads run North, South, East and West into the city, smooth as paper, where now there are only trackways and paths. The Old Road, that has linked the City to the harbour from the time before the Great Hunger, has disappeared.

Ferris runs a hand along one of the roads and inspects the grey mark on his thumb.

Strange machines harvest the crops, each with a tiny figure in white overalls and red helmet piloting it. He leans down and touches one. No horses anywhere.

At the edge of the model, the geology is labelled. Arrows point to coal seams, lead, tin, and oil for lighting and a metal called aluminium on the northern margin. A new structure, something he's never seen before reaches up, like a fortress but not a fortress, gleaming steel sheds

11

and towers and gantries, pure, silver and glistening. Pipes snake round the sheds and silos, branching into off-shoots and re-joining. They fuse into a massive bulge, like a tumour, out of which a chimney rises higher than any of the forest trees. Great wagons enter and leave, laden with minerals and devices and crates.

He points:

'No horses, everything powers itself. This is Franklin's dream.'

'Franklin's no dreamer.'

Smaller roads run between the four great roads, binding them together, like a net cast over Market World. Metal castles stand at the junctions of the highways and the lesser roads. A wisp of cotton-wool smoke issues vertically from one of the chimneys. The forest is gone and with it the villages. Just one remains, thatched cottages, an ancient windmill and women queueing to draw water from the well. Children chase ducks into a pond and labourers rest on the bench at the door of the public house on the other side of the village green.

Rachel reaches down and touches the tip of the church spire.

'Franklin's dream has the potential to enrich everyone in the entire City, that's what he says. They leaked it months back and the final report has been circulating for at least a week. There's no denying that people like him.'

'You don't trust him, do you?'

She touches the balance at her throat. 'Does anyone?'

'I don't trust this model.'

'No-one trusts it. They just think it's the way forward.'

'It's the Entrepreneurs – they always want more.'

She smiles and places her hand on his sleeve. 'Times are changing, Paul. Maybe it's time to change with them.'

'Perhaps. Perhaps Franklin has over-reached himself. Popular or not, we should never have given him the contract for security and re-education in the Old Town.'

'He offered the best value for money. There have been no complaints. Like I said, people like him, and it is election year. He has a silver tongue.'

'No complaints. No news at all, only rumours. When did you last receive a report you could trust about what goes on in his factories? He has some scheme underway. I trust him no more than I trust his smile – or his plan.'

Ferris fixes his eyes on hers. She returns his gaze.

'I have my duty to the people of Market World. If this proposal makes us all richer I must support it.'

'Of course. And I have my duty to enforce the One Law. I hope the meeting goes well.'

Rachel pauses outside the entrance to the Great Hall. Weariness drags at her. She unwraps a miniature chocolate truffle without looking at it, slips it between her lips and crushes it with her tongue. The coarse sweet relish of it overwhelms everything for an instant. She touches the other chocolate in her pocket with her finger-tips.

Footsteps patter towards her.

'Madam?' Esther, her assistant, holds out the wine-red folder. 'The meeting papers, and the proposal.'

She stands back respectfully. Her dark hair is tied back and she wears no jewellery.

'Esther. I trust you, you know that.'

'Madam?'

Rachel puts the back of her hand against her mouth. 'No matter.'

She closes her eyes for a moment.

'Madam, they're waiting for you.'

Her eyes snap open. She straightens her back.

'Excellent.'

She sweeps through the double doors into the Great Hall. The room in which the City Council meets is high-ceilinged, with oak panelling and a glass wall on the right. She glances out over the city, her city. The only buildings taller than the Halls of Justice are the great towers of the Entrepreneurs, stretching upwards – the Dagger, with the gold-plated hilt, balanced on its impossible point, the Swan with its graceful tower curling over to the helipad, and the red scaffolding where they're rebuilding the right wing, and the others in the haze behind them. Franklin's Tower, tallest of all of them, stands directly opposite, black steel-clad concrete studded with myriad windows. Sometimes she thinks she sees tiny figures in those windows staring down at her.

The boulevards stretch out like canyons between the boutiques and stores and market halls of the centre, out to the residence blocks and shops and supermarkets of the suburbs and beyond, to the yellow and brown of the fields and the green of the hills and the dark fringe of distant forest. Only the Enforcers go beyond the cultivated land. That's where Franklin's dream lies. That is the world over which he would cast his web.

The southern suburbs are only visible if you open a window and lean out – the first city, the Old Town, as people call it now, residence blocks, sheds and mean timber housing jumbled together with alleyways and paths and cobbled streets snaking among them. Franklin's factories are there, somewhere among it all, crouching behind their metal ramparts with their giant chimneys, and, although no-one talks of it, his Security Centre.

For one instant she feels the weight of it all.

She slaps the folder down on the oak table that runs the length of the room. The golden balance at the right-hand corner of the table, the emblem of the City, quivers. The Council members rise to their feet, the Citizen Delegates to her right, six of them in work clothes, neat and decent, all watching her, and the representatives of the Entrepreneurs' Guild on her left. The Entrepreneurs wear pin-striped business suits. Their hair is neatly trimmed. Guild pins sparkle at their lapels. They spread their elbows and let their notepads and folders sprawl across the table. Their assistants sit on upright chairs behind them, along the wall.

She keeps her eyes on Franklin at the far end of the table. He pulls himself to his feet. His jowls sag to a double-chin and his blond hair is combed forward over a bald patch. He's built like a barrel and he watches her with the eyes of a hunting dog.

You're out of condition, she thinks, but you're still dangerous. No-one knows how old he is or which generation of Franklins he comes from. There has always been a Franklin, since Franklin long ago made the first trade and set up the first market. Trade and the market lifted Market World, alone of all humanity, out of the Great Hunger, and the One Law enforces the market and only the market. Franklin, chair of the Entrepreneur's Guild, owner of the largest chain of food shops and market-halls and most of the residence blocks and the factories and the sports and entertainment centres and academies and the main TV channel and newspapers and who knows what else. Franklin, who will buy your land at a fair price, won't he, who pays you the wage you're worth, who charges a reasonable rent, who sells you the food you eat at market price, not a cent higher, not a cent lower. Franklin, the richest man in Market World, our friend, our guide and our benefactor, by the One Law.

I will watch you like a hawk. Her mind runs clear as water. Her fingertips tingle as they always do when she takes the chair at the head of the table.

'Good morning, ladies and gentlemen. Please sit. We have a packed agenda.'

Chairs scrape, drowning out the murmured 'Good morning, Madam.' Franklin's lips do not move. The pin he always wears, the ornate silver $\mathcal{F}$, glitters in his lapel.

She cracks open the folder. Someone speaks in tones rich with success:

'There's only one item.'

She knows Franklin's voice without looking up.

'Mr Franklin, you are here to present your proposal. I chair the Council.'

'Madam, I am sure you understand me. The rest is detail, I'll leave you to sort it. I have to go in thirty minutes.'

'Mr Franklin…'

'I'm making an exceptionally generous offer to my City, something that will benefit all of us. We all know our minds on this, I trust.'

His mouth opens in a smile, showing his teeth, and his cheeks crease. He glances at the Guild representatives.

One of them, Noah, flabby-cheeked with a drooping moustache he should trim, pats his hands together in applause. He's never been photographed without a bottle of his trade-mark sauce somewhere in shot. The newscasts refer to him as the "ketchup king".

Rachel braces herself.

'I chair this meeting.'

Franklin leans forward.

'Emergency resolution. I have other commitments. Time is money.' He raises his hand, palm forward. 'All in favour?'

The Entrepreneurs raise their right hands as one. The Citizens glance round at her, frowning.

She sighs.

'Mr Franklin. You are not a member of council. You are a senior Entrepreneur and we permit you to present your proposal.'

Randal, the Citizen at the far end, next to Franklin speaks:

'Oh, let's get it done.'

Good-looking, a smooth skin and a way of folding his hands together, he's a grocer in a moderate way of business. Ever the optimist. He opens his hands and raises one.

Franklin grunts.

'Passed, Madam Chairman.'

'Very well.' She glances at Esther. 'Minute it.'

She puts her finger to the balance.

'Item Seven. The Development Programme. Mr Franklin, you have a presentation.'

'Thank you. I don't need slides. I'm sure you've all read my proposal, consulted your colleagues, advisors and mentors. People have been talking about nothing else for weeks.'

He pauses and raises a hand as if deprecating applause.

'In essence, it's simple. Will we stride forward into the future, our future, or will we diminish, and become part of history? Every kingdom, every empire, every civilisation has faced that question. All have failed at some point to seize the next opportunity – and they have fallen, to be replaced by more vigorous nations. Market World must not fail.'

He strolls to the window and waves his hand as if he owns the view.

'Raise your eyes. Look beyond the city. Look beyond the fields. You see green hills. You see the great forests. There's the one paved road built in the time before history. My wagons are the only ones to travel that road. We bring you the food you eat.'

He spreads both arms wide.

'Have you ever asked yourselves: who owns that land? Everywhere off the Old Road where you can only travel on horse-back? Who has the right to use it? Who owns the produce we could grow there? Who owns what is under it?'

No-one speaks.

'I have the answer. My scriveners have examined the records.'

He pauses.

'No-one owns it. Terra Nullius.'

'Excuse me.' Jack Simmons breaks in. Cropped red hair, cheekbones and tight lips, she's the most assertive of the Citizen Delegates.

Franklin ignores her and addresses Rachel.

'The normal courtesy is to allow the presenter to finish.'

A numbness weighs at Rachel's temples.

'The question is allowed.'

Jack rises.

'As I understand it the forest is peopled. The villagers own the land. The people who sell you the food that is on the shelves of your stores, Mr Franklin. Labelled organic I believe, premium price.'

'If I may.'

A very young woman, by her face little more than a teenager, with a startled expression. She coughs. Rosie Collane, President of the Scriveners' Guild.

'If I may. Extensive enquiries in the archives, by myself and my associates and deputies, demonstrate that there are no deeds, wills or mandates that grant title to the forest to any one person, agency or body corporate. Indeed there is no possibility and no procedure for granting such title. There is no legal process for villagers to obtain title, collectively, severally or individually, to any land beyond the houses, dwellings and curtilages of the villages themselves.'

She sits and a scarlet blush extends up her cheeks.

'But, if I may,' Jack continues, 'the villagers have always lived there. They collect the produce of the forest, they hunt the creatures that live there and they manage the forest. They are the custodians of the land beyond the City.'

Franklin glowers and flexes his shoulders.

Collane rises. 'May I point out that disparagement of my professional judgement is a direct erosion of my standing and value as a scrivener and could entail extensive compensation, unlimited by statute?'

Franklin smacks his hand on the table.

'Terra Nullius,' he repeats. 'No-one's land. If your point is that the forest people use it, I retort that I will use it more efficiently, and I will do so for everyone's good, I and the other Entrepreneurs of the City. I've proven what I can do. Law and order in the Old Town. Jobs and re-education in my factories. It all works. If necessary, I will pay the villages for the land. Market price.'

He spreads his arms and even Rachel feels how compelling his voice is.

'Can you not conceive what I, what we, could do with that land?'

He looks along the row of Delegates, fixing his eyes on each of them in turn.

'We could sell the timber, plough up the ground with modern machinery, use proper fertilisers, grow wheat and vegetables and build sheds for cattle. Do you know what is under that ground? Coal, oil, metal – so much more than we have now, so much more that we could use. To benefit all of us – even you Jackie Simmons.'

He coughs and pulls a handkerchief from his breast pocket and snuffles into it.

'Those poor, untaught villagers. Can you not imagine what I will do for them, just as I have for the city? All through the market, all through fair exchange. They will work in my factories and I will pay them a proper wage. No longer at the mercy of the seasons, they will be able to pay school-fees for their children, buy proper health insurance and rent decent housing.'

'Mr Franklin. I really must protest.'

Jack is on her feet again. A gust of fondness for her fills Rachel's breast. She smothers it, but it's still there, deep within her.

'Let us hear the comment.'

Franklin glares at her.

'Just because you don't understand their wisdom, doesn't make them ignorant. Their way of life has endured from before the Great Hunger. My great-grandmother was a villager. She had lessons she could teach us.'

'I do apologise. My enthusiasm runs away with me. Very well. Let me pursue my project and they will pursue theirs and we will see what they chose – my comfortable weatherproof homes, my schools, my clinics, all at a fair price, and an eight-hour day in clean overalls in my factory. Or would they rather have the tumbledown cottage, the filth, the disease, the ignorance, the famine when the harvest fails and the wild animals howling in the night? Shall I tell you the answer? Why don't you let me ask them?'

'But…' Jeremy, a retired upholsterer, is the oldest of the Delegates. His jacket hangs from his shoulders and his voice trembles. 'But why? We don't need more, we have enough, if we share it.'

'Nonsense. We are Entrepreneurs, we are Market World. We alone of all humanity found the way back to civilisation and order and we didn't do it by sharing and having nothing left for ourselves. We did it through the market. We work, we trade, we make more and we invest. The country and the forest, they are our first step.'

He lowers his voice.

'The villagers, all the people out there, they're lucky, they're in on the ground floor. When the Programme is completed we will move on. We will trade across the circling sea, with the people of lands yet unknown. The market, progress, endless growth, limitless trade, civilisation – that we will give to the world.'

He thrusts his chin forward as if challenging each of them.

'I move we accept the proposal in full.'

Collane looks round, takes a deep breath, and starts clapping. Rex Moran, the smooth-faced young man next to her, joins in, and the other Entrepreneurs start to applaud, one by one. Franklin's glance sweeps along the row of them and he nods. The Delegates stare at Rachel. Jack waves her hand to show she wishes to speak, her face hard as granite. Amos also raises his hand. Rachel ignores him. He's a citizen-delegate, a vendor of coal and lamp-oil. No-one knows his background but word is that he's the son of Julia Porran, one-time President of the Transport Guild. He has a way of glancing sideways when he talks that inclines you to mistrust him.

She lifts the folder and bangs it on the table.

'We do not applaud at Council meetings. We consider. Please conduct yourself appropriately.'

Franklin folds his arms.

'And the motion? Do I have a seconder?'

The Entrepreneurs raise their hands as one.

Rachel shades her eyes. 'I believe Ms Simmons wishes to speak.'

Jack rises to her feet. She fixes her eyes on Franklin's and does not look away.

'This is a momentous decision which will decide the whole direction of our city. We cannot make it in half an hour on the basis of one proposal. We must investigate and research. We must consult.'

She pauses and draws breath.

'We do not know what minerals lie underground in the forest. We do not know what the impact of mining them will be, on the air we breathe and the water we drink. Make no mistake. This is not about farming or about trade or about civilisation. I note that your plan', she nods to the folder on the desk in front of her, 'includes factories, roads and warehouses. This is about raw materials for your manufacturing complex. This is about industry, about pollution, about destroying the environment on which we depend for life. This is about profits for you and misery for the rest of us. We will never be able to go back. We cannot take the risk.'

Franklin ignores Rachel. He looks only at the Entrepreneurs. If you heard him talk from behind a screen, only the words, you'd think of he was doing you a favour.

'This is our opportunity. We will each become rich and we will make each other rich. That is what the market does. Do you wish the historians of Market World to say we turned our backs on our great opportunity? Do you deny our villagers, the most backward of our citizens, the chance to move forward as they ardently desire? Our world will grow. Do you have so little confidence in what we have achieved that you think that a bad thing?'

'But the factories. We all know about air quality in the Old Town...'

Moran leaps to his feet. 'My turn. Air quality is a distraction. The problem is exaggerated and we have the

23

technology, we will solve it. This is our future and we must seize the opportunity.'

'Very well. The vote.' Franklin gathers his papers. 'I have to go very shortly.'

Rachel stares at him and shifts her gaze to the Delegates. Four of them look to her with spaniel eyes. Jack glares at Franklin. Amos, his chest puffed up, strokes one hand along his neck. The Entrepreneurs grin at each other. Rex whispers something to Collane, who looks away.

Franklin stands, gripping the edge of the table. His assistants gather round him. Rachel glances at Esther who shakes her head. Her throat constricts and she speaks with an effort.

'The vote. In favour?' The six Entrepreneurs raise their hands. 'Against?' Five of the six Citizen Delegates vote against. Amos glances at Franklin, then at Rachel. He raises his hand half-way.

Esther leans forward:

'Casting vote, Madam.'

'Thank you.' Rachel pauses. 'The proposal contains much excellent material. But there are issues. We need to consider the environmental impact. We will give Mr Franklin's proposal the consideration it merits. I cast my vote against – for now. We will adjourn the debate, commission a further report on the impact of the proposed development and establish a working party.'

Franklin inclines his head.

'Very well. I am respected throughout Market World because people know that I stand for progress.'

His glance sweeps across the Delegates and fixes on Amos.

'I have noted all your votes. You may delay my Programme but you will not prevent it.'

Rachel stares at him, her face without expression.

'Thank you. As I stay, I will establish a working party to examine how to put this ambitious programme into practice, taking into account the interests and opinions of all stake-holders. In due course.'

'Good day, Madam.'

Franklin smiles at them all, the smile of a popular man who knows that he deserves his popularity. The Entrepreneurs crowd round him, shouting their congratulations. He shakes hands, throws his arms round Rosie Collane and holds her briefly against him, waves to Noah and strides out of the room with his assistants behind him. The Delegates huddle round Jack, talking in hushed voices. Amos remains seated, his head in his hands.

The Third Court

In an overheated semi-basement, seven storeys beneath the Council Chamber, David awaits Sarah's Audit Hearing. The windows are horizontal slits high up the walls and the overhead strip-lights are still on, although it's before 11.00 am and bright sunshine outside. The room is barely wide enough to hold the dais with the wooden table for the Assessor, her Recorder and the clerk, with the chair for the witness to the right and the dock for the defaulter to the left. He feels stifled and wonders if he suffers from asthma.

He has found a seat at the back of the courtroom on an upright chair that grates when he moves. He shouldn't be here. He crept in with the public through the main door, and was squeezed against a young man with inky fingers, a notebook, and furtive eyes. As soon as he sees the uniform the young man introduces himself as a TV reporter, but doesn't give a channel. He slips his cuff back to show his wristband.

'We pay for your stories. Do you think Franklin has the answer to lawlessness in the Old Town?'

David touches the insignia on his sleeve: 'No comment.'

A group of young women and men in blue uniforms without badges fill the benches at the front of the room. David guesses they are cadets from the Academy. Not so long ago I was one of you, he thinks. A cadet whose hair seems unruly despite the regulation cut looks back at him and says something to the young woman next to him. She glances round and giggles.

The Assessor enters at the door behind the bench, a spare black woman in a navy blue trouser suit with the badge of office – the Golden Balance – on her breast pocket. Her clerk follows her. Everyone rises with a scraping of chairs and David is forced back against the main door.

The Assessor surveys the room through metal-rimmed spectacles, sighs, and sits down.

'What have you got for us today?'

The clerk bows his head. He's short, plump-faced and his hair needs combing. He reminds David of a pocket spaniel.

'Long list, Madam. First case, Major Breach of the One Law. Conveying a cargo without contract. Intent to supply said cargo without payment.'

'Bring the defaulter to scrutiny.'

David is forced to stand as the main door opens and the Court-Serjeant enters, a square-shouldered older man in a gold-braided uniform, who scowls at the Bench, the Assessor and the audience. He leads Sarah into the courtroom. She glances round the room, as if noting the details for when she tells her friends the story.

The Serjeant grasps her arm and the clerk slaps his hand on the desk:

'Proceed.'

She nods to him, picks the officer's fingers from her arm with her other hand and strolls forward.

'Take her to the dock.'

'Please. I'll find my own way.'

The clerk snorts.

'Silence.'

She takes her position to the left of the bench, the Serjeant behind her, and looks round. David feels she is searching him out. The journalist licks his biro and scribbles at his pad.

The Assessor leans towards her.

'You are Ms S.Cordell, known as Sarah. You are called to scrutiny for a serious Audit transgression. I have reviewed the evidence and am minded to order full compensation with costs. Have you anything to say?'

Sarah frowns, and for an instant David feels dizzy, as if everything is back to front. She is the judge and he stands accused in the dock. Then her face lights up.

'Not really. I was taking some fruit and other produce from Coneystone to our cousins and friends in the Old Town. First time I've done the trip, we had a great crop this year. These people,' she waves a hand towards David, 'him and his mates, jumped out on me, all dressed up like comedy policemen. Pity it was muddy, they kept falling over. He'll do it now if you're lucky.'

Someone sniggers and the Assessor fixes her gaze on the cadets.

Sarah keeps talking.

'It's not funny. They scared Juno.'

'That's of no importance. The question is: have you a valid contract?' The Assessor pauses a moment, then raises her voice. 'You have no contract, it's idle to deny it. Answer a simple question: who pays you for the apples?'

'But it's a good act, you really should see it. Then they frightened Juno and upset the applecart.' Her face darkens. 'So to speak. Then they took me here and kept me in and I'm worried about Juno. The apples will spoil. So will the blackberries.' She turns to the court: 'You haven't seen where they've put Juno have you? Lovely beast, heavy horse, red ribbons in her mane. You wouldn't miss her.'

The Assessor thrusts her face towards Sarah.

'You will address the question. The longer you waste the court's time, the more it will cost you.'

Sarah smooths her forehead with her hand.

'Oh no, I'm sorry, didn't I say? The apples and everything, they're all presents. Brilliant harvest this year. You can have some.'

She looks round at all of them, smiling at her good fortune.

The Assessor straightens her back. She glances at the clerk, who nods.

'Thank you. Transfer of commodity at zero price: major breach.'

'I'm sorry? Would you like some apples? Don't you want witnesses? Look, one of them's over there.'

David colours and hunches down in his chair, but he can't stop himself gazing at her. He feels as if everyone in the court is craning round to look at him.

The clerk slaps the desk again.

'Silence!'

Sarah raises an eyebrow but says nothing. The Assessor sighs.

'Breach of the One Law. Full confession. Witnesses are unnecessary.'

David feels the tension flow out of his shoulders.

Sarah shakes her head, her face comical. Her eyelid flutters. David can't tell if she just winked at him.

'I'm sorry?'

'The One Law directs that all transactions must be between willing buyer and willing seller at an agreed price. Law of the Market. You do not give people things that you could sell to them. There are no exceptions.'

'But....' Sarah stops, her mouth open.

'Be quiet. You have incurred substantial expenses.'

She gestures to the clerk, who reads out staccato from a thin strip of paper:

'Deployment twelve Enforcers, 1 captain, 1 sergeant, 1 half-sergeant for 4 hours: 300 credits: Item: deduction for value of training exercise: minus 110 credits.

Uniform cleaning: 10 credits.

Accommodation, item: basic cell by one night: 200 credits; item: stabling and incidentals: 4 credits.

Security during accommodation: 50 credits.

Incidentals: toothpaste, soap, towel etc: 5 credits.

Courtroom, third grade, by one hour, staffing and incidentals: 100 credits.

Compensation: inconvenience of arrest to the detainee, standard rate 2 credits an hour by 18 hours: minus 36 credits. Item: proceeds, sale of 1 horse: minus 17 credits. Item: proceeds sale of cart and contents: minus 32 credits.'

David keeps his eyes on Sarah. She raises her eyebrows again and shrugs her shoulders.

'Total 474 credits.'

'Thank you. Ms Cordell, your breach cost Market World 669 credits minus 110 credits value of training provided, 36 credits citizen compensation and 49 credits sale of confiscated items. Your civic recompense is set at 474 credits. Next case.'

Sarah stares at her.

'You must be joking! What is a credit anyway?'

The Assessor blinks.

'Next case.'

'But what about Juno?'

The clerk remarks to no-one 'Additional court time may be purchased at 1.4 credits a minute.'

The Court-Serjeant seizes Sarah by the arm and hustles her towards the door. David rises and pulls his chair out of the way. She catches his eye as she passes and looks back at him and grimaces. It strikes him to the heart. He grips the door and stops it from shutting. The next case, a market trader accused of short weight, in a shabby suit with the jacket too tight under his shoulders, is brought in.

A buzz of conversation rises from the cadets. The young man who stared back at David tilts his head towards the young woman next to him and whispers something that is terribly important to them both. He takes the young woman's hand, ignoring the others. The Assessor glowers at them

'Silence! Or I shall clear the court.'

The journalist flips to the next page, sucks at his pen and writes.

David slips round the door and pulls it shut behind him. He leans against it for a full half-minute, his eyes closed.

He knows that the staircase in front of him leads up to the main hall where fines are paid. He turns left and strides down the corridor towards the barracks block. Voices

31

sound from the guard room and he dodges left again into a narrower corridor with raw concrete walls lit by unshaded light-bulbs, then up an iron spiral stair. He listens for footsteps, then creeps across a metal landing as softly as if he were on a close surveillance exercise and it was Adam assessing him. He listens again, and passes through a side-door into the Process Room. He blinks in the daylight that streams in from tall windows overlooking City Square. His heart feels tight in his chest. He has never in his life done anything like this. He doesn't know why he is doing it now. He is a fool.

The duty Enforcer sits at the metal desk with the band-reader on it and the empty metal chair opposite, examining her finger nails. She slips something into her mouth. David clenches his fist, relaxes it and lets the door slam shut. The sound echoes across the room. She jerks upright and glances towards him, and pulls her jacket straight.

He knows her, they did their basic training together. Six weeks of square-bashing with Curtis shouting at you.

'Hi Jan. Your lucky day. I'm to take over.'

He didn't plan that. Where did it come from?

Jan frowns.

'Who says? I'm here 'til 18.00 hours.'

She chews at something.

'Curtis. Extra duty – for yesterday.'

'I heard. Curtis doesn't like you, does he?'

'Yeah, well. It's a long story, I think he was a bit scared of the horse. Guess he likes you.'

'Sure he does.' She studies his face. 'Are you alright?'

'Yeah, well. I'll be OK.'

'That bad, is it? You've got friends you know.'

'Sure… Thanks.'

She touches his hand.

'All yours. I'm off.'

The side-door clicks to. David expels the air from his lungs and breathes in slowly to calm the throbbing in his head. He touches the band-reader in front of him. He's used it a thousand times. You key in the amount, touch your wristband against the screen and it deducts or adds on the credits.

No citizen in Market World is ever without a wristband. It's fastened to your wrist at the citizenship ceremony when you pass eighteen and goes with you to the grave. You get lessons on it in "Lifeskills" at school. It only works if the buyer assents to the deal and that is infallible. Willing seller, willing buyer. As the signs in the street say: 'You're not dressed without it', 'No pay, no get' and 'You are your account'.

He swallows and pushes the hair back off his forehead.

The door is thrown open and the Serjeant enters, still gripping Sarah by the arm. He marches her up to the desk and releases her. He reminds David of an elderly bullfrog.

'All yours. Watch her. She tried to chat up my deputy in the Guard Room.'

'I did not. I just said he had nice eyes for a comedian.' She stares at David. 'Nice to meet you again.'

She holds out her hand.

David reaches out, then lays his hand palm-down on the desk.

'The defaulter will maintain discipline,' barks the Serjeant. 'Sit.'

Sarah looks round her, pulls out the chair, sits and crosses her legs.

David squares his shoulders.

'Alright. I'll take over from here.'

'The court placed Ms Cordell in my charge.'

The Serjeant keeps his hand on Sarah's shoulder.

'Until her debt is discharged. Which is now.'

He looks the Serjeant in the eye. After a pause the officer drops his hand and pulls on a leather glove.

'Very well.'

The door slams behind him. David licks his lips and looks at Sarah and tries to smile. He has the script by heart, he learned it last night.

'You understand that you must pay civic recompense as decided by the court. 474 credits. Touch your wristband to the reader.'

'Where's Juno? I don't care about the cart, but she's not used to being away from me.'

'Your possessions will be auctioned to defray expenses. Just touch your wristband here. See that number? That's your account: "Debit 474". But you must have a wristband. It's always issued at the citizenship ceremony when you leave school. You could buy that cartload ten times over with that many credits. Twenty times.'

He taps the reader. She grins at him.

'We don't bother with those things in the villages, waste of time.' She starts to get up. 'Let's go and find Juno. I need to get on my way.'

'She's OK, I sorted it. She's being looked after.'

'Are you sure? What do you know about horses?'

'She's OK.'

'Tell me about Juno.'

She rests her chin on her fingertips and fixes her eyes on him. He places his hands together on the table.

'She's a black Percheron. 18 hands.'

She nods and her cheeks dimple.

'She's being fed OK?'

'All the hay she wants – and crushed oats. And apples, but not too many. I tell you, she's OK. Trust me. Now touch your wristband to the reader.'

She's puzzled. Her brow furrows in tiny creases.

'What wristband? I told you we don't go in for them. My sister'll plait you one out of wool. She's only nine.'

'You really don't understand do you? You are in Market World. You pay for everything, you have to. You've taken up the time of the court and the resources of the Enforcers. No-one is going to lock you up for free.'

She giggles and the tiny dints dimple her cheeks. She places her hand over her mouth.

'Sorry, but you just said...'

'I know. Everything is for sale here, you get nothing without paying for it. The One Law – law of the market. It's what gives us a well-ordered society, why we're so much better off than you are in the villages.'

'Sort of "All for One and One for All?" Free for All?'

'Sort of – but it works. Don't you see it?'

He craves for her to understand, to see how his world is better, to want to be part of it. That's why he's here. For her. He will be her guide, her mentor, her friend and she will trust him.

She shakes her head.

'You really shouldn't take these things so seriously. It doesn't make you happy, does it?'

There's a sharpness in her glance, as if it's in her mind to say something else, but she continues: 'Anyway, I don't have a wristband.'

He shows her the numbers on the screen set into the black band on his left wrist. 'There. See – all my credits: seven hundred and fifty-two, until I get paid. It's all connected up to central computing – they keep the records. It's how we do things.'

He feels a flush of pleasure at teaching her. She's so confident and, at the same time, so wrong, so much in need of help and he can give it. His left leg trembles against the desk. He wills it to be calm.

She folds her arms.

'Yeah, I heard stories about that. But I told you, we don't bother with that kind of stuff – it's no fun.'

'Listen. In the past was the Great Hunger. Didn't they tell you about it in school? Everything was terrible, people fought for food, children starved and warlords ruled the land. So many died they could no longer bury the dead.'

She shivers. 'Sounds nasty.'

He finds it hard to concentrate.

'Look out of that window.' He points over City Square. 'Can't you see? Everyone going about their business. The shops, full of food and clothes and everything you need. The residence blocks where everybody lives.'

The words come more easily as he remembers the lesson. She mutters something to herself.

'What's that?'

'Don't look as if they're having much fun.'

'Clinics where you can buy medicine, schools and training colleges where you can pay for a degree, markets where citizens buy and sell at a fair price. Above them, the towers of the Entrepreneurs. And everywhere the Enforcers watching over us all, trusted by everyone, making sure we follow the rules.'

She peers out through the window.

'They're not happy. No-one's smiling, nobody stops for a chat. Why aren't there children playing? Or animals? And their clothes are so drab. Don't you like to see trees?' She spreads out her arms. 'They're so lovely this time of year.'

'Everyone's busy, they're going about their business. That's what you do in Market World. Children are in school or training or working. No time to waste. We keep the beasts in their sheds and the trees in the park. What's the profit in bright clothes?'

He watches her as if, at that moment, she matters more than anything to him. The thought comes to him: I am an Enforcer. She will understand, without the Enforcers there is no market, no Market World. I am worthy of respect.

She needs to see Market World as it is, but he can't let her go out there. She'll be as lost as he would be in the forest. How desolate it would be, to be alone on those streets with no wristband and the night coming on.

'When did you last eat?'

He has her full attention.

'I don't know.' She pauses and tiny creases appear between her eyebrows. Her face clears. 'I had some dried fish on the way. They wouldn't give me breakfast back there, they kept saying didn't I know "No pay, no get". They didn't like it when I asked if that was the chorus and could I sing along? I keep telling you, you people have no sense of humour.'

David stands and at the same time flips his left hand forward onto the reader without looking down, hears the click as it makes contact and checks the screen. "Account cleared". She doesn't notice. He's in command for once like he's in a novel.

'Come on. We'll find a café. You need someone to show you what Market World's really like. And I'll tell you my dream – why I'm an Enforcer.'

Her eyes light up and she rubs her hands together.

'And I'll tell you about how we live in the villages. And we'll find Juno, won't we?'

'Of course.'

She trusts him. He knows that she trusts him.

He leads the way, through the lobby and the double doors and down the flight of steps from the Halls of Justice into City Square. Happiness bubbles within him. She laughs, mouth open, the dimples in her cheeks each side of it. He remembers he's on extra duty. He'll deal with that later.

The Social Capital

David feels the pride swell in his breast as it always does when he strides down the broad stone steps of the Halls of Justice into City Square. He casts his eyes up to the Towers of the Entrepreneurs and thinks of them, busy in their offices, watching over Market World. Behind him stand the Halls, seven stories with the Governor's Suite on the Top Floor. You wouldn't know they weren't one of the residence blocks, apart from their size and the stone steps to the double doors of the main entrance. The emblem of the golden balance is set into the wall above it, and the words in golden letters a foot high:

No Deal but a Fair Deal,

No Law but the One Law

He is an Enforcer, an oath-bearer, he wears the black uniform and the insignia of the City. When he descends these steps he is about his duty and everyone who sees him knows it instantly. He bears the one rank among the citizens who may not buy and sell, the one who pledges to serve the One Law, regardless of interest or reward. He is the bedrock of Market World.

He lowers his gaze to the citizens pouring into the square from the boulevards at each corner, everyone about their own business. A slim black women in a maroon and indigo headdress passes in front of him. The baby in the sling across her shoulders stares at him with round eyes. Immediately behind her, an older woman on a grey pedal bike with a basket on the handle-bars brakes and swerves to make room for him. Everywhere people fall back to let him through.

A cheery voice behind him calls out: 'Hello. Lovely day.'

A ripple runs through the stream of people. They pull back, waver, then eddy into their former courses. No-one smiles at Sarah, apart from the baby in the sling. No-one returns her greeting.

He calls over his shoulder.

'Just follow me. Do as I do. We do not waste words.'

'OK boss.'

There's an unnecessary music in her tone.

He loves the way people stand aside to let him pass, the way the crowd always parts for an Enforcer. Today something is different. People look past him, over his shoulder. He swings round. The stripes on Sarah's jacket and the bright yellow of her neck–cloth stand out like plumage. Standing close to her he can make out silver scroll-work, like writing in an antique script, worked into the cloth. He thinks of the finches in the aviary in City Park. Her clothes glow at him, set against the dark worsted and serge and flannel of business suits and the denim blue of work-clothes. Somewhere she's found a patterned scarlet and white scarf to bind round her hair. Her face lights up and she smiles at him against the backdrop of faces glancing up, then away, as intent on their business as all the citizens of Market World.

'Can't you take that bit of cloth off?'

'Oh it's just for fun.' She unties it, flicks it at him and stuffs it half into a side-pocket. 'I bet all your butterflies are grey. When are we going to find Juno?'

The lock of hair hangs forward and she smooths it back.

'Thank you. We'll just get some food first.'

She raises her face and looks round and wrinkles her nose, and the image of a squirrel floats into his mind.

'So good to be outside. I didn't like it in there. But your air smells of people crowded together and things I don't know. Tell me.' She sniffs again. 'It's like we're downwind of a sulky bonfire. But you don't have any trees or leaves.'

He frowns at her: 'Nobody wastes time smelling the air.'

'I can think of someone who does.'

He comes to a stop and holds out his arm.

'This is Eastern Boulevard, the balance point, neither North, where the mansions of the richer citizens cluster, nor South to the dwellings of the poor, sloping away towards the Pit. That's the ancient rubbish tip, older than the City, older than memory. No one owns it, it's where those with no income live by scavenging. The city sells them licenses – fair's fair.'

'Why don't you just give them stuff?'

'I've never been there, it's Franklin's domain. His factories are on the edge of it, he runs Re-education and Security there. The Old Town, where you were heading, is beyond it.'

But she's looking at the shop-windows with their huge displays and bargain prices. She chuckles and the dimples are back.

'It's mad. People want things, why don't you just share everything out and have a feast and dancing? Look!'

She gestures to Eldorado, Franklin's luxury market on the corner. A display of giant cheeses, framed by olive branches with the leaves still on them, fills the main window.

'Too much, it would go off before you ate it, but doesn't it smell lovely? Not like that stink back there. That could choke a child – ugh!'

She breathes in the ripe smell, eyes closed in enjoyment, and he can't help smiling with her. Then he frowns and she continues before he can think of a response:

'But those poor trees – how can you tear off living branches? Don't you like trees?'

'Why not? You own a tree, you make use of it.' He thinks: that's not an answer. 'Listen: the only thing you can't own is a person. Everything else we buy and sell. Do you see? It all fits together, everything works.'

The street widen out and traders line the pavement on both sides. Some stand behind stalls, semi-permanent booths of canvas and plywood, dull green, blue-grey, beige, maroon, one with amber stripes, all of them showing the emblem of the scales of justice. They stroll past a food stall, "Fairer Fare", with bowls of bean salad and pumpkin porridge and suet-pudding lined up for inspection.

'Look, doesn't it make you hungry?'

She seizes his arm and points at some apple cakes. He lets her fingers grip his elbow for a moment and wonders at the pleasure welling up inside him. He swings away from her and she lets him go.

'Come on. I'm trying to tell you things. I want to take you to a proper café. Show you Market World.'

Between the stalls are the lesser traders. Some of them hold out trays stacked with brushes, toy cars, old comics, cooking pots, second-hand clothes and rusty tools, all of them battered, things you might find in the Pit if you got to the carts coming in from the Northern suburbs in time. Others squat with sheets of cardboard in front of them. An old man, his beard grizzled and straggling, crouches over a child's shoe on a bit of newspaper. *Where did you sleep last night?* David thinks. He spots the crutches, slid in under one of the stalls.

Sarah beckons to him.

'Come on!'

A display of home-made fudge is spread before the next trader. David swallows the saliva in his mouth. He glances along the row and checks they are all offering something for sale, then remembers he's not on pavement duty. The traders lean forward as soon as they see his uniform:

'Combs for sale! You won't find cheaper – 20 cents.'

'Everything for sale, make me an offer.'

'Don't you deserve a treat? Best fudge in the City! Home-made.'

She halts and tugs at his arm.

'Fudge, don't you love it?'

He was a child when he last ate something like that.

'I don't know. Look – it's fair exchange in action.'

'C'mon.'

She snatches up a piece and crams it into his mouth, ignoring the trader's shout of 'Oi!'

David opens his mouth to protest but the burst of sweetness overpowers his yelp. He clamps his lips shut and tries to swallow the cloying lump, splutters and starts to cough. The traders snigger. Someone offers him a sugar doughnut with red jam dripping out of it, another trader shakes his lemonade to make it fizz. Sarah thumps hard on his back and he straightens, coughs properly, and the fudge tracks syrup down his gullet.

'Alright?' She laughs at him again.

He nods, not looking at her, reaches out, clicks wristbands with the trader, straightens his jacket and strides away from that place. Shame and anger boil inside him. He swallows again and pauses as they reach a cobbled side-street.

'Up here, it's not far.'

Sarah is still chatting to the man. He's small and lean, as so many of them are, with dark hair and something silver round his neck. He gestures as he talks. She reaches out and David is sure she touches him. She waves and comes over as if nothing has happened.

'He's from the country, his name's Jerry. I know his village.'

'Street people. They sell rubbish, stuff from the Pit. Steer clear of them, that's my advice. Are you eating something?'

She swallows and spreads her hands and opens her mouth.

'How could I be? No wristband. Come on, I'm hungry.'

There's a faint smell of sugar, but he's not sure it isn't the fudge in his own mouth. Her face is like that of a child caught with her hand in the biscuit-barrel.

He pushes open a door set next to a bay window and the familiar rush of warmth, the feeling that here he is among friends, that no-one will judge him, sweeps over him.

'Come on. *The Social Capital* – no idea what that means but it's my favourite café.'

A plump older woman with a pleasant face, wearing a dusky red apron, comes forward to greet them. Her greying hair is scraped back to a bun.

He takes off his cap.

'Good morning Emma.'

Emma smiles and bobs her head. The café is crowded, people talking and eating all round them, but she ushers them towards the window, takes the *Reserved* sign off a table, draws back a chair for Sarah and dips her head again, smiling all the time.

Sarah draws her chair forward:

'Love the name of the café. Did you think it up?'

Emma stands back, still smiling at them.

David looks up at her and speaks clearly.

'Full breakfast with coffee. Cream porridge, bacon sandwich. Second breakfast.'

He rubs his hands together and glances at Sarah.

'Porridge sounds great. Definitely no bacon. Have you any fruit?'

Emma dips her head for the final time and leaves them.

David leans forward.

'She's deaf and dumb. From birth. Lip-reads. She's built this business from nothing. In Market World you can do that if you work at it. Isn't it splendid?'

Emma sets down a flask and the smell of hot coffee surrounds them.

'Wow! That is so wonderful.' Sarah raises her mug with

45

both hands and sniffs at the aroma as if it's perfume. 'So long since I've drunk coffee.'

'We trade. Pay and you get the best coffee. Market World. It's mainly people from the North Suburbs come here.'

Sarah is busy with her porridge and cream. Emma places pots of honey and blackberries on the table.

'It's lovely.' She takes another spoonful. 'So many flavours in one mouthful!'

'I wanted you to taste it. Three blends of oats, all from different farms, mountain honey traded down from beyond the hills, cream from cows pastured on the meadows south of the City. In Market World you're free, you can have anything you want, so long as you pay.'

He can't think why, but it matters to him that she grasps what's so special about his City, about the Enforcers, about himself. She needs to know, to understand that here you can choose what you want in life, you don't have to live the way you've always lived, like you do in a village.

'Do you see? We are a serious people and we make progress. We don't waste energy on fancy clothes and trees and chatter. We have rules and everyone follows them. I've been on patrol, I've seen life in the villages.'

David pauses. It's only once on a dawn exercise that he'd observed a village but he's attended sessions on "Village Life" on the training programme.

'There's mud everywhere, you have disease, lice, rickets, half the year there's no work in the fields and you're huddled in your huts. Time sidles by, every day the same. You meet the same people, you eat the same things. Your diet is beans and millet and water, you never know whether the food will last the winter. When anyone's ill there's only you to care for them, you must feed your horses or eat them.'

She spoons porridge into her mouth and shakes her head slowly at the same time.

He continues:

'No wonder people come to the city, to Market World. Ah, here's the fruit.'

Emma places a dish of fruit on the table between them, apples, gold and red, grapes, black and luscious, pink slices of melon, segments of orange arranged round them, and more blackberries. He closes his eyes for a second. The smell takes him to a place long ago, so long that he has no real memories, just of a slice of apple in his mouth and warmth all round him and someone who would always look after him, just the way Market World looks after him.

She scrapes her porridge bowl clean and licks the spoon.

'I did love that. But you don't believe what you said do you? We do know how to cook and use herbs. We do look after people who are ill. The air smells clean. We respect our horses and we never, never eat them. You don't like trees. You don't enjoy dressing in nice clothes. That's sad.'

'You haven't been in one of our shops. You haven't seen our factories, our residence blocks, our improvement centres, our academies.'

He feels his cheeks redden. He wipes his lips with the napkin.

'Don't get worked up. Maybe I'll show you my village one day – maybe not.'

'I'd like that.'

'Come on, finish that porridge. Then we'll find Juno and I'll get on my way.'

She pauses for a moment as if thinking of something, and for a moment there's the sudden flicker, as if everything was back to front and she was explaining things to him. She tucks one of the apples into her pocket.

'This is for her.'

She takes up another and bites into the crisp flesh.

'I love apples, so many different flavours, so many varieties we have.' She gasps, her eyes flash and she spits out the pulp. She bends forward and sniffs once at the half-eaten apple in her hand and says, without inflection, as if reciting a catechism:

'This is my apple. It's from my cart. I would know it anywhere.'

'It's just an apple. We'll buy some more. Like I say, in Market World we have the tastiest apples money can buy.'

She repeats with emphasis,

'It's my apple from my cart. I love those apples. You stole them. You and Market World and your fine words about buying and selling, fair's fair, and everyone's free, they sound so good, but you stole my fruit. Do you know how much work it takes to grow an orchard?'

'Sarah, it's OK. They probably auctioned the apples to help pay your compensation. Have an orange, I bet you've never tasted anything like it. I'll take you to see Juno soon.'

'You stole my apples! Why would I trust you? I'll find Juno by myself.'

'Who's getting upset now?' He reaches out to touch her wrist. 'I'll help you, I want to help you.'

She shoves the table hard at him, snatches up his porridge-bowl and hurls the contents at his face. The bowl smashes against the floor. Porridge, warm and sticky, drips down his chin onto his uniform.

The other diners stare at them. Emma glares, mouth open, hands spread.

He wipes the porridge from his eyes.

'Sarah! Listen to me.'

She ignores him and leaps to her feet. Her chair clatters backwards. She strides to the door and wrenches it open.

'All of you!' she shouts, 'You're parasites! You've never grown anything for yourselves.'

She slams the door and it judders back ajar. David raises a hand but there is no strength in him. He hauls himself to his feet, holding onto the chair like a beaten boxer and whispers:

'I broke my oath for you. I bribed the stable-lad. Juno's safe.'

Emma hands him his cap, her mouth clamped shut. A dullness presses behind his eyes. He can't face her.

He blunders through the door. People press towards him like a solid wall. He catches sight of the yellow scarf against the greys and dark blues of the crowd as she swings round onto the Boulevard without slowing, one hand on a street sign. He jumps up to spot her over the crowd and forces his way through, but everyone's so tall and they stare at the porridge spreading down his uniform and won't get out of the way fast enough.

A porter with a roll of carpet on his shoulder steps sideways and he glimpses another flash of the golden neck-cloth at a street-corner and burrows into the crowd.

A young man with black hair shoves at him and he barges through.

When he reaches the corner, she's gone. The breath catches in his throat and he has to pause for a moment, panting. His lungs ache and he gulps at the air.

He follows more slowly, but the street ends in a small cobbled square with a café where five ways meet and he knows he'll never find her. Her words buzz in his head.

'My apples!'

But they were impounded. She must understand, she owed the City credits and they were auctioned to offset her account.

'Are you alright?'

A young woman in blue work clothes and a check apron stands in front of him. He tries to answer but the words stick in his mouth and he nods. He straightens his back and flicks porridge from his jacket. She offers him a damp cloth. She's from the café. He clicks wristbands for the courtesy and sponges at himself.

'Never better.'

She stares at him.

'It's in your hair.'

He needs to sleep. He needs to find her. He looked after Juno, he paid her fine. Why did he do that?

He turns to make his way back to the *Social Capital* and sort out the reckoning.

A round-faced child, a boy, in a ragged brown jersey and corduroy shorts, stands halfway down the street.

'She dropped this.'

The boy holds out a scarlet and white striped cloth with a muddy stain across it.

'Where? Where did she go?'

'Twenty credits, mister.'

He sighs and clicks and the child lets go of the cloth. A jagged tear runs across it.

'Where?'

But the boy has gone. He rubs at the cloth with his thumb and folds it and places it in his breast pocket.

Juno

The first person he meets back in the Halls of Justice is Curtis. He's leaning against the wall, eating an apple, just inside the side-entrance. Behind him stone steps run down to the yellow corridor with the strip-lights and the notice-board. He tosses the core out of the building, past David's ear.

'You're in trouble, Davey-boy. Better clean yourself up.' He grins and shows the teeth jumbled in his mouth. 'They want you on the top floor.'

'OK.'

David pushes past the half-sergeant and hears Curtis' voice echo behind him:

'Address me as "Sir". And wait 'til I dismiss you.'

David turns the corner up the iron spiral. The dullness spreads like fog behind his temples. He stops to draw breath.

Footsteps clatter on the stairs above him and he stands back as a squad of Enforcers stamp past, in street patrol order, visors, stab jackets, whips coiled at their belts. The last of them pauses. It's Jan. She rests her hand on his forearm.

'Something's up. Full alert and they want you upstairs. You be careful.'

'Thanks. And you.'

'And your uniform's a mess. Gotta go.'

She rushes on down the stairs. For some reason his heart lightens. He pushes through the metal door into the wash-room.

He snaps to attention and salutes, right forearm across his chest. Ferris nods and leans forward. His office is smaller than David expected and furnished with a plain deal table, the golden balance at the corner, and two upright chairs. The window that spans the wall behind him looks out over the City. From where David stands only the Towers of the Entrepreneurs are visible, set against a dull sky heavy with rainclouds.

He's aware of Adam standing to the side, scrutinizing him as if this were an inspection.

'Ashwood, at ease. We have a problem.'

'Sir.' He swallows and continues. 'I regret strongly, I'm sorry, I broke barracks, I…'

Adam sniffs.

'I wanted to help, sir. And the business of the horse. I thought I could help the defaulter understand, she would see what we do in Market World, how it all works and she would, well, like me – us …'

Ferris raises both eyebrows. He falters and stops. '… Sir.'

'I see. That wasn't actually why we asked you to come up. We thought you might be able to help us.'

'Help us,' echoes Adam. There's no emotion in his voice, no warmth. David glances at him. He smiles, thin-lipped, and Ferris continues:

'We have a problem in the Southern City. As you know, Franklin's people,' Adam grunts, 'have the contract for security and re-education there, where his factories are. Something is underway, something big, bigger than anything he's done before. It's all linked up with the villages and his projects. None of our usual contacts will talk to us. He pays them or they're frightened. You'll be our agent.'

'But…why me? I'm not a spy.'

'To the contrary. These people don't trust Enforcers. You've shown that you can gain their sympathy. The woman, Sarah Cordell. She likes you, and she knows her way round the Old Town.'

· 'But she….'

Adam takes a pace forward.

'She would have been our link to the Old Town, but you took her out of the Halls. She can help us find out what Franklin's up to. The factories, Franklin's mills, and his Security Centre, they're his main base now, and they're off-limits to Enforcers. That was a mistake.'

Ferris holds up his hand.

'We'll discuss that later.'

A frown crosses Adam's face, but Ferris fixes his grey eyes on David and doesn't notice it:

'We need a full report, as full as possible, on Franklin and what he is doing there and we want you to do it. It involves close liaison with the people in the Old Town. That woman, cultivate her, get to know her. I know you'll do it. For the City.'

As Ferris gazes at him, David senses a nugget of calm within his breast. His pulse quietens.

Someone in the room, very close to him, says: 'Yes I'll do it,' and he knows that this is his task. He will build trust between the people of the Old Town and the people of the New City. And he will find Sarah and she will understand what he has achieved.

'Good. Now to details. You will report to me. Adam will explain about your dress, identity and recompense. Travel by bus, like a street-trader. Whatever you do, don't go near the Pit. Find your way round it.'

Ferris holds out his arm and flicks back his sleeve.

'Thank you. I place my confidence and that of the City in you. This is your great opportunity.'

They click wristbands and salute.

Ferris tugs at his right ear and watches the door close behind David.

'What do we know about David Ashwood?'

'I'll fetch my register, sir.'

Adam lays the volume on the desk. It's as large as a family bible with annotations and crossings-out in a number of different hands, and additional pages interleaved into it. He runs a finger down the index and flips back through it, nearly to the front cover.

'He came as a Hunger Orphan. In the Academy most of his life.'

'I see. Not many of those make it to Enforcer.'

Adam peers at the script.

'These records go back a long way. His mother was a travelling preacher.'

'An unsettled time.'

'Nothing more. She disappeared.'

'Thank you.'

Ferris turns and stares out of the window at Franklin's Tower. His lips move.

'Beg pardon, sir?'

'I said "I don't know how we can stop him".'

'Sir?'

'Franklin, his programme, his security guards. He wants everything. If no-one stops him, he'll be king in Market World.'

'Above my pay grade. Sir.'

Ferris turns to him.

'Come off it, Adam. I've known you a long time. I always thought it was a big mistake when the City gave him the security contract in the Old Town.'

'Sir.'

Adam stiffens to attention. He stares straight ahead, past Ferris at Franklin's Tower as it pierces the cloud layer beyond City Square, and further, to the Pit and the factories hidden in the fog hanging over the Old Town.

David strolls down the main corridor. If I could whistle, I would, he thinks. He can't remember a word of the briefing. He pauses at the courtyard door and listens. No-one has followed him. He checks again, then crosses swiftly. The coarse sweet smell of horse and straw and leather rises round him and he breathes it in.

He raps on the first stall. Martin steps out, his arm round a bundle of hay. 'Thought you'd be back. You can help me muck out this lot if you like.'

'How's Juno?'

'She's safe. I just been giving her feed. Take a look.'

He runs his hand down Juno's haunch. She shifts aside and he squeezes his belly past her. Her large eyes are fixed on him. She gives a soft whinny.

'Hi Juno. Time for some exercise. Maybe see Sarah. OK?'

He leans into the warm rough hair of her neck and closes his eyes. After a minute he straightens and runs his hand down the contours of her cheek. Juno inclines her head and raises it again. He edges back out of the stall.

Martin hands him a shovel and yard-broom.

'We've got mucking out to do first.'

David starts on the first stall, shoving the raw-smelling straw and shit backwards into a pile, then forcing the shovel under it and heaving it into the barrow. Martin watches him.

'You'll find it easier if you don't try to take such big shovelfuls.'

He leads the way to the midden out behind the stables. David hoists up the handles of the barrow and the muck pours out and spreads. A grey rat dashes out, hesitates with one delicate foot raised, blinks up at him, and scuttles into a hole in the wall.

'People pay to take it away,' says Martin. 'The market gardens.'

David rests on the broom-handle. His back aches, down to his loins. He enjoys the work.

Later they take a break. Martin offers him tea from a yellow thermos flask with an orange band and a cork for the stopper. Footsteps sound outside in the yard. Martin catches his eye and moves towards the door, the thermos still in his hand, a wisp of steam escaping from it. After a minute he returns and carefully sets the thermos upright on the edge of the stall.

He won't look David in the eye.

'You'd better say goodbye to Juno. I'll give you back the credits.'

He pulls his sleeve back and offers his wristband.

'What? We had an understanding.'

David springs to his feet, and leans forward. The thermos falls to the ground with a tinkle of glass. They both ignore it.

'Franklin wants her, they've already sold her. Highest bid. Here. Let's click and be friends.'

'But…'

Martin looks down. 'I get orders. Franklin takes horses sometimes. I don't know why.'

'Sarah wants her.' Ideas flood through his brain. 'She's special. You can't let her go.'

'It's how it is. I'm sorry.'

He's an Enforcer. Law of the Market. They said travel by bus, don't draw attention to yourself. They'd sell Juno for seventeen credits. Besides they'll find out he paid Sarah's compensation as soon as they audit. He has to find her, to sort things out, bring back the information they need.

'I'm here for Juno.'

'You?'

'I'm an agent for Commander Ferris.'

He takes the letter that Adam gave him out of his inside pocket and holds it out. Martin moves to take it and he catches it back.

'Just read it.'

Martin colours. 'I do horses,' he mumbles.

'Look at the signature, the seal.' The golden balance, embossed on the paper. 'Ferris authorised expenses.'

Martin touches the seal with his fingertips.

'OK.'

David flicks back his sleeve. *This cleans me out,* he thinks.

'Deal.'

'I'll say the Enforcers took Juno. Franklin can quarrel with your lot. You'll need a saddle and tack, oats, a blanket, that big one. You'll have to get hay.' He chews at his lip. 'There's a gate round the back. Good luck.'

He soon gets used to the rocking motion, forwards and backwards, but he can't get rid of the fear that he might topple sideways if his foot slipped out of a stirrup. He is high enough to see into first floor windows. He swallows again and the overpowering taste of sugar and the image of a lump of fudge swim into his brain. He has no way of making Juno go where he wants her to.

He shakes the reins. She continues to plod forwards. On Southern Boulevard people pull away from him and stop and point and look up. They've never seen a horse this big before. A young woman clasps two children, a boy and a girl, against her skirts, her face white. He stares straight ahead, his face tense, his mouth straight.

A high taut voice shouts:

'Get back, it's coming through.'

He's wearing the brown corduroy trousers and old khaki jersey with leather elbow and shoulder pads that Adam gave him. He wishes he had something to protect his head. He grips the reins and pulls at them.

Juno halts. She doesn't do anything, she just stands there. People move in closer. She snorts and shakes her head and the bridle rattles. David looks round at them, faces turned up to him on all sides, and straightens his back. He raises a hand and waves and someone cheers. A man on horseback. He shakes the reins and Juno steps forward at the same time.

The road starts to slope downhill away from the heart of the City. He feels Juno's gait change, a tighter bunching of the muscles in her neck and shoulders, a lengthening of her stride. He focuses harder on his bearing, blending in with the movement of the mount beneath him.

The buildings change round him. The shopfronts grow less frequent, and smaller, less brightly lit, apart from the store from Franklin's "One Shop" chain he passes at a junction. The crowds thin out and he travels into a meaner district. On his left is a residence block with a crack running up the front wall, propped up with a lattice-work of timber. A pile of rubbish spills out of an alleyway, cardboard, garishly coloured, rotten cabbages, corrugated metal poking up. Children in ragged clothes climb on the heap and pick at it and one of them chews at something. The downward slope grows steadily steeper and the air becomes darker and colder.

The air smells different here. It's staler and heavier, not just the fug he's used to in the barracks, the sense that it's been breathed by too many people, but something else, harsher and sharper, that he can't place. The clouds thicken above him and the light grows dim. He can only see a few hundred metres ahead of him.

The residence blocks end and he senses the space opening out about him but he can't see to the edges. Juno halts and shifts from side to side and he leans forward and runs his hand along her neck and feels her trembling. The stink is almost over-powering, the raw sweetness of decay and filth, like the midden a hundred times over. As his eyes become used to the light, he makes out a great mound of rubbish in front of him, higher than a residence block, vegetables, paper, rotten fruit, offal, cardboard, plastic, rusting metal, a dead dog, bottles, boxes, rope, tins, jars, wooden poles, netting, a broken television, a cartwheel, a cracked tarpaulin, nameless things with metal innards ripped open.

He has blundered into the Pit. Something moves on the mound, glimpsed dimly at the corner of his eye. People are here, children and adults, in ragged jeans and sweaters and jackets, bits of material across their mouths, some of them wearing goggles. They move with a crouching gait, sideways, like crabs, they scuttle, all of them coming towards him, more of them with every moment. Some of them emerge from tunnels in the great mound, others sidle in from the edges.

Without thinking he jerks Juno's head to the left. She lets out a sharp whinny and moves off at a trot.

The nearest figure straightens and shouts something. He can't stop looking at it, a man or woman, with tangled dark hair in a stained cloak, once yellow and green. It shouts at him, inarticulate sounds, like an animal, and reaches out with bony fingers to Juno's neck.

He can't see the face, just an impression of eyes glinting between the mask and the hair. He wrenches himself away and bends forward and urges Juno into a canter. He rises and falls in the saddle as if he knew what he was doing, and they're on a street with residence blocks on either side and the air's brighter. They slow to a trot and he turns Juno to the right and the muscles across her shoulders ripple as they climb up the slope towards the Old Town. He glances down side streets as they pass the Pit. He makes out a metal fence as high as three men against which the rubbish is piled in great mounds, and behind it buildings. Franklin's Security Centre and his factories, massive, squat, with tiny windows, lit up although it's mid-day, and metal shutters.

The pain in his back spreads up into his shoulders and neck. It sends hot spikes down the insides of his legs. He needs this to come to an end. He passes over a cross-roads and turns his head from side to side. The streets stretch away empty. A group of children rushes out of an alley he hasn't noticed. They jostle and tumble past each other, like tame squirrels at feeding time. One of them, a boy, stares up at him. He has a broad, sun-tanned face with unkempt black hair and bright eyes. He grins at David and reminds him of Martin. He's dressed in denims, washed pale and patched on knees and arms. He turns and puts two fingers in his mouth and whistles.

David listens. The whistle echoes against the residence blocks. Someone takes it up, the same tone, and others repeat it, off to one side. The boy waves and runs into an alley. David glances round. Pain jerks down his spine. The street behind him is empty. He pulls at the bridle and Juno halts. He waits. A shiver runs along her from mouth to tail. He has no plan whatsoever, and no idea how to dismount from a heavy horse onto cobble stones.

The Old Town

He hears a pattering noise, like heavy rain on a tin roof, from far in front of him and off to the right. It swells and separates into the scamper of feet, the babble of high-pitched, excited voices and an occasional thud he can't place. A football bounces out of an alley, followed by a crowd of children. They mob round him, looking up, fidgeting, chattering, not one of them standing still. A girl in blue and white football strip runs forward, traps the ball, flips it into the air with her toe and tucks it under her arm.

A tall figure in a striped jacket follows them, and stares at him from the mouth of the alley. She pushes the lock of black hair back out of her eyes. His throat tightens, he can hardly breathe.

She walks towards him and reaches up to touch Juno's cheek. The mare gives a long whinny, and she places one hand on each side of her face and kisses her on the tip of her nose.

'Oh Juno. I've missed you.'

She closes her eyes. David sits tall in the saddle.

'I brought her back to you.'

Someone in the crowd cheers and is hushed.

She ignores him. She talks softly to the horse and he leans towards her:

'I bribed the stable-lad, they'd have sold her to Franklin. I broke my oath. I paid your recompense.'

She looks up at him.

'Thank you. She's tired, she needs to eat. Can't you see that? You'd better dismount.'

'The boy helped me get up. I rode her, all the way from City Square.'

She stands back and speaks as if repeating a lesson to a child.

'Feet out of the stirrups, lean forward, roll towards me.'

He flops onto her shoulder, an arm round Juno's neck. Pain shoots though his spine.

'Roll – and get your left foot up.'

He tumbles sideways and she catches him in both arms and the tension flows out of his body. He feels exhausted, like a wrestler at the end of a bout. She sets him on the ground and ducks out of his arm. He scrambles towards her, hauling himself up on Juno's stirrup. He longs to embrace her, to explain everything to her.

'I made sure she was looked after. I tried to explain Market World to you, but you….'

'Your world. You never asked what I wanted.'

'I groomed her in the stables. It was me plaited her mane. I wanted it to be a gift to you, a surprise.'

'You really don't get it, do you? You're from the City, Franklin's City.'

'I wanted to see you again.' Her eyes are cold, like water. He realises how wretched it sounds but he can't stop himself. 'Please. I broke my oath for you, I can't go back. I saved her for you.'

'I need to make sure Juno's OK. You'd better find yourself somewhere to stay.'

He swallows.

'Don't tell people I'm an Enforcer. I'm finished with that.'

'You've no idea of what it's like, living here. How can I trust you?'

'I broke my oath. I need to talk to you.'

She scans his face as if she's judging him.

'That's as maybe.'

Juno shifts her weight on her hind legs and she takes the bridle and leads her away. He stumbles after them, jolts of pain running through his thighs with every step. The children follow behind in a mass, the girl with the football at their head. They chatter, a tumult of sound like seagulls squabbling, and he knows they are talking about him. He rests against the timbers that support the top floor of a white-plastered house and stares after her. The children wash past. The girl with the football pauses and looks back at him, then hurries to catch up with the others.

He can walk no further. He feels like a traveller from a far country who comes at last to the house where the candle burns in the window, just for him, and the door stands open – and he reaches it and they slam it in his face.

When he wakes he's lying on a straw-filled mattress that pricks the back of his neck. The ceiling slopes in from both sides to a ridge above him and bright sun-light slants through a small window in the end wall. He stands, bumps his head on the ceiling and takes a pace forward, his neck bent. His legs ache. He kneels at the window and looks out on a landscape that is new to him and lingers there, taking in the richness of it all.

Pitched roofs, set at every angle, some with skylights in them, some with dormer windows, chimney pots poking up everywhere, like a patchwork of red and brown, spread before him. Beyond, open countryside reaches away to distant hills. A smudge of birds trails behind a plough. Thick hedges with trees at intervals run between the fields, and the sun glints on a dew-pond in the middle distance.

He draws in a deep breath and catches a whiff of fresh-mown hay over the smell of wood-smoke. The sound of voices rises up the stairs. He crawls back to the mattress and stretches his limbs and thinks about what he's seen, how different it is from the grey and black and navy blue and white of the City. Then he's ready.

The staircase comes out in a room running the full length of the house. The air is hot and close. Dark wooden timbers half embedded in white plaster walls support the roof beams. The floor is made of wooden planks, almost black, polished smooth by use. An iron range, the fire glowing red in the grate, stands at one end. He smells porridge, like damp earth, and his mouth waters.

A small girl with dark eyes and a solemn face looks up at him. She wears a dark dress sprigged with tiny yellow flowers, a red and green patterned apron tied over it, and clutches a rag doll with a shock of red wool hair to her chest.

He smiles at her and leans on a chair next to a scrubbed wood table:

'Good morning! What's your name?'

A large grey-haired woman in a dress and apron that match the little girl's swings round from the stove and pokes a wooden spoon at him. She peers through metal-rimmed spectacles.

'I know your name, Mr City-man Ashwood. You've never been to a village. Best you get back to your own people.'

'I want to help. I'd love to stay here for a bit if I may.'

'No-one wants you. I took you in because it was curfew and the mayor told me to.'

'Thank you. But where's Sarah? She has a glorious black mare with a plaited mane, Juno. I rode that horse. I want to be a friend to people.'

As he says the word 'friend' he understands. This is his task, between the Town and the City, he will help people, he will build trust.

The woman compresses her lips.

'You're not welcome.'

'I'm hungry. I plaited Juno's mane.'

She says nothing. The girl snatches up her rag-doll and hurries to her mother.

'I can pay you.'

The woman shakes her head.

'What with? Give your credits to Franklin, they're no use here.'

'I'd do things. Help out.'

She picks up a metal ladle and brandishes it at him, like a club.

'I asked you politely, go. You're not welcome. Get back to your City.'

The girl peeps at him from behind her skirts. He turns and tugs at the door-handle and he's outside.

All round him are similar, different houses, all half-timbered and plastered, the windows divided into squares. All of them lean one way or the other, each rests on its fellow so that the whole row depends on all its members together. He knows he is in the Old Town, beyond the Pit, where the Enforcers don't go and Franklin runs security, an area he's heard of but never seen. People here live lives closer to those of the villagers. The street is cobbled with patches of rough stone and beaten earth. An open gutter runs down the middle.

He hears the clamour of people to his right and walks down a short alley onto a cobbled street. His first impression is of movement and noise and colour so vivid he finds it hard to take it all in. Everywhere the people of the town pass by. They saunter and dawdle and greet each other, and shake hands and chat and smile. Each of them dresses in their own style, differently from the others. Some lead children by the hand, some push barrows and hand-carts, some carry parcels and bags, or have dogs at their heels or on leashes.

He stands at the mouth of the alley. A girl goes by, in yellow jeans and a green T-shirt, followed by an older man with a toddler, both in pink denim dungarees. The townspeople wear shorts, tights in many different colours, striped and spiral, in trousers or dungarees and jerkins and jackets and vests and jumpers and head-scarfs and berets and peaked hats and bonnets in scarlet and green and orange, and paisley silk and cross-stitch and Arran knit. It almost hurts his eyes and he feels uneasy, as if something he doesn't grasp skulks behind it all in ambush.

In front of him a grey-bearded older man in a red felt jacket and green shorts cradles a baby wrapped in a lace-work shawl in his arms and whispers into her ear. A six year old in a padded romper suit tugs at his hand. Behind him a young woman with curly hair greets an older woman in dungarees and a pink fedora and laughs at something she says. A Jack Russell stares up at him, as if bursting to ask him about why his clothes are so dull but too polite to do so.

He steps forward and allows the throng of people to sweep him along, talking, exclaiming, shouting, laughing around him and after a while he feels part of it. His heart lifts. He passes a shop window with clothes displayed on models, then another with pies and the fragrant smell almost overwhelms him. The shop bell clangs and a young woman in a black dress and pink apron smiles at him.

'A nice steak pie, please.'

He rubs his hands together without thinking. He feels hollow. Her forehead wrinkles.

''I'm afraid we don't have any of those, sir. No call for them.'

'Ah… bacon roll?'

'No-one's ever asked for one. What is it?'

'OK.' He scans the dishes on the counter. 'A cheese roll, two, three cheese rolls and a date loaf.'

'Certainly.'

He licks back the saliva in his gullet and considers which order he'll eat them in as she fetches them.

'That will be six thirty-seven.'

He pulls back his cuff. She frowns.

'Coins or notes?'

'I'm sorry?'

He offers his wrist. She curls a hand round the paper bags on the counter.

'I think you'd better go. I don't know what you think you're doing, but we don't use those here. Sir.'

He stares at her. He doesn't understand.

'I didn't mean to cause trouble. I have so much to learn.'

He feels tears heavy behind his eyes. He can't force himself away from the food. The young woman trembles. He looks up at her and the hunger grips him. She's laughing with her hand over her mouth.

'Oh take them. It's your face.'

'Thank you, I'm really grateful, it's the first time I've taken something like this.'

He coughs, a full cheese roll crammed into his mouth. Hot shame washes through him. She comes round the end of the counter and beats a fist on his back. He sits down and she brings water and he drinks.

'Listen. You're in the Old Town. We have our own ways here. No offence, but we don't like the City. All you've ever sent us is trouble and the Pit and Franklin's men and the curfew.'

'I feel terrible taking that food. I want to make things better.'

She shakes her head.

'You'd better go. Don't make me sorry I helped you. You need to go North. And don't go near the mills.'

'The mills?'

She clasps her arms round herself.

'Franklin's place. The factories. Don't go near them.'

She folds her arms again and watches him as he pulls at the door. He looks back at her, wipes his hand across his eyes and sets out into the hubbub of the street. Somehow it feels different since he entered the shop. Now there's always a little space around him. Everyone alters their course so they don't come near him. They glance at him, but then look away and chat or find something among the crowd to busy them.

In the City people stood back from him in respect. He was an Enforcer, one of the few, an oath-bearer, one who took on himself the burden of the One Law. Here it is somehow different, almost he feels that they don't like him, that he should be ashamed of himself, for being different, for wearing boring clothes, for being from the City.

He addresses a middle aged man whose costume resembles a business suit with red and white and yellow pinstripes, and a cream silk turban on his head.

'Excuse me.'

The man narrows his eyes. Two vertical lines appear in his brow above his nose.

'How can I help you?'

'I'm looking for Sarah. Tall, always laughing. She knows about horses.'

The man frowns.

'No idea.'

'Please, is there anyone I could ask?'

'Go North. Just go North.'

He swings away and is lost in the crowd. David continues north as far as he can judge by the sun. People continue to press pass him, mostly going the other way. His legs ache. He asks other passers-by, men and women, older and younger people. No-one helps him. Always the same message: go North, don't go near the mills. Panic blooms within him. He offers an older woman some credits if she'll help him. She glares at him:

'I don't want your money. All those bands ever bring is trouble.'

A younger man in a white T-shirt with a picture of a galloping bay mare on his chest, his face set, bustles through the crowd towards him.

David tries to smile.

'I wonder if you could help me.'

'Leave this good woman alone. She's my aunt.'

A crowd gathers round them. Someone shouts out:

'You tell him. He's one of Franklin's spies.'

David feels he could burst into tears. Somewhere in his head a voice is whispering: *But it's not fair.*

'No, you've got it all wrong. I want to help, to be a friend. Please. Find Sarah.'

The young man points north:

'That way. Back to your own people.'

Someone pushes him, but when he swings round, no-one's there. He shuffles away. He wants to be angry with them, but he can't. The emptiness fills him, as if he has offered them everything he has, and nobody wants it, and he has nothing more to give.

After a few hundred yards the crowds thin out and there are more children on the street in mobs and groups. Some of them follow him. He tries to ask them about Sarah and Juno, but they giggle and dance away from him.

Football

The first thing he notices as he moves north is the air. His skin itches for no obvious reason. He finds himself stopping from time to time to draw breath. The houses grow meaner and smaller and grubbier, some of them standing empty, some with the plasterwork crumbling as if no-one cared for them. He sees few shops and almost nobody on the streets. Ahead of him a great chimney, wide as a house, rises up, high above the roof-tops. Fumes and smoke burst from it in a roiling mass and drag to the side.

The street slopes away in front of him. He must be getting near the Pit. The chimney is in fact three chimneys braced together. Their foundations are set many metres below him, within another township within the Old Town, a domain of vast grey metal sheds, enclosed within a metal rampart. A continual rattling of corrugated sheets in the wind is carried towards him.

Dark clouds gather overhead. He looks for the great rubbish heap where the street people scavenge but can see no sign of it in the gloom before him. Tiredness grips him. He pauses and leans against a building. Opposite, a poster covers the side of a house:

'Franklin Cares for YOU. You Can Be Part of the New

Market World. A Fair Day's Work for a Fair Day's Pay. Full Training Offered at Cost.'

The text is set in huge black script, above it a giant image of Franklin's face, a younger Franklin than the one on yesterday's newscasts, thick blond hair swept back, the wolf's grin a welcoming smile, the dark eyes focused on you. Below a young man and woman, glowing with health, stride through the gates of a sunlit compound with a three-storey redbrick building, picture-windows along the side, before them, and a sky of blue above. They join a throng of other women and men, just like themselves, flooding in.

This is Franklin's double factory, more a town within a town. He had no idea it was so huge. Something sinister breeds within it. His duty is to investigate, for Ferris and Adam and the City. But he tricked them and they will know that. He broke his oath to pay Sarah's recompense and thwart the One Law.

He must find a way back to Sarah. He needs her to understand that he's on her side, that he saved Juno for her. But how will he find her if he presses on north?

He glances around him. He needs a decent sit-down meal. He'd settle for a sausage. With chips and gravy. His mouth waters. He doesn't know how long it is since he last ate. Something thuds into a wall behind him, with a sound like Juno buffeting her stall. It slams into his back between his shoulder-blades and he staggers forward, his hand grasping the corner of the building.

He coughs, sucks in breath and turns.

Someone shouts out:

'Sorry, mister!'

A girl, about ten years old, runs towards him. She's bare-footed and dressed in the blue and white strip of a team he doesn't know, but hers are drab through much washing and her shirt needs patching at the elbows. She's the older girl with the children he met yesterday, when everything went wrong.

She bends and scoops up the football, slips on a cobble and drops it. It trickles towards David who, without thinking, flips it up with his left foot and punts it to her at chest height so she can catch it. He likes football. Only thing he was good at in the Academy.

The girl grins, her teeth white in a dirt-smudged face, and ducks and knocks it back with a nod of her head. David opens his arms and it flies into them. The other children dash up and fan out behind her.

'Over here, mister'

'No here!'

'On me nut.'

A taller figure comes forward. His hair is brown and shoulder-length, a tangle of curls and waves. He's not smiling but there's something merry about his face. He's long-bodied, with wiry limbs and an agility that belies his proportions. He wears a blue and white T-shirt with the number 6 on it and jeans, frayed at the knees.

He holds out a hand:

'Please can we have our ball back?'

He bursts out laughing and a ripple of laughter fans out among the children round him.

'Why ever not, since you ask so nicely?'

David flips the ball and kicks it upwards, as hard as he can, so it sails above them all, roof-height, higher, hesitates, and plunges back to smack into the cobbles and bound up again. The young man plucks it out of the air.

'My name's Luke. How about a game? You get first pick.'

The first person to smile at him in the Old Town. Strength surges back into him.

'Pleased to meet you. I'm David. I want her,' (the girl he met first) 'and that one and him and her.'

He picks a brown-skinned boy with the legs of a gazelle, a girl who could be the ten year old's sister and a smaller boy who has so much energy in him he can't keep still.

'Oh no! You've got Susie and she's the champion, and all the best ones. No matter. We offered you first pick and you're a good judge.'

There follows the most disordered and good-spirited and successful game of football David has ever played. Football was the only item in the Enforcers' physical training routine he enjoyed. No-one else took it seriously. (Apart from cycling, which no-one took seriously either.) He hated boxing and wrestling and rope-climbing and assault courses and half-marathons and route marches and distance swimming and all the rest of it. He knew he couldn't run fast but he could glance round and flick out the ball where no-one expected it and he knew for certain which way to go to pick it up on the back-pass.

Susie has exactly the same knowledge, but she can run like a race-horse down the wing, then change direction in an instant. The others know what they're doing, especially the youngest boy, who's all arms and legs but can flip the ball out in a flurry of limbs exactly where you need it.

David chuckles, and glee bubbles up inside him. I'm worn out – why am I doing this? Who on earth cares?

Luke has some ideas about tactics, that's obvious. He keeps nodding to his team, signalling them to gallop to the other end of the field where he thinks he can lob a pass directly in front of them before anyone else realises what's going on. Trouble is he'd need his accuracy to match his dreams and they'd need to be champion sprinters to get there in time. He's an optimist.

Both teams are exhausted within a quarter of an hour. The tainted air rasps in David's throat. The kids collapse against each other at the foot of a rough brick wall and pant like greyhounds after a race. Luke bends forward, his hands on his knees, and gasps at the air, a grin across his face.

'That was good. Another five minutes and we would have had you. What shall we do now?'

'You're asking me? One thing. You could tell me about Franklin's Factories down there in the Pit.'

He indicates the poster behind them. The children start away from him, pressing closer together. Luke stares at him.

'Are you crazy? That's the mill.'

'Yes, the factory. I've seen posters.'

'You don't want to go in there. Don't talk about it.'

'What's wrong with it?'

'Yeah. Don't you understand? It's why we don't like the City, why we keep off the streets after curfew. Franklin's men. They take you in there and we don't see you again. You need looking after.'

He sees Susie nodding like she means it.

'Don't let him go.'

She takes his hand and he is surrounded by children holding onto his hands, his clothes, his shirt, reaching out to him.

'Don't let him, Luke. Let's take him back.'

David wants to put his arms round all of them.

'That's so kind…'

'Shhh…'

Luke stands stock still listening. The children shrink back.

'It's late. Let's go. You'd better come with us, it's curfew.'

'But…' David can't hear anything. He stares down. It's already dark towards the Pit. Then he catches it, a throbbing, like the pulse of a dragon, far away.

Luke glances down the street and beckons. They bundle themselves into a side alley. Luke lopes along then takes a right turn and almost immediately a left. The throbbing swells. David can hear wheels grinding on the cobbles, getting closer. There are no lights and the alleys show like dark clefts between rock walls. He trips on loose paving and recovers and skids on something slimy. They seem to be heading up-hill.

Light gleams ahead. The alley comes out on a street some ten metres in front of them. The throbbing swells to a roar and a search-light swings across the entrance to the alley.

'Greenjackets,' murmurs Susie and cringes. He seizes her hand. The roar cuts off. He smells hot oil and hears the slam of an iron hatch and the tramp of booted feet.

Luke motions them back.

'No noise.'

The children flatten themselves against the wall of the alley. Susie's hand quivers in his.

A figure appears at the end of the alley, the body dressed like an Enforcer, but the uniform is green leather. A helmet covers the whole head and has no face, just double optics, faceted, like the eyes of a wasp. Leather-gloved hands grasp the stock of a whip as if it were a truncheon. The head pivots round and seems to stare directly at him. He stares at it. The golden balance, insignia of the City is clearly emblazoned on it, above the eye-pieces. The creature swings away. He hears the rasp of its breathing.

It raises its hand and walks away. They hear the vehicle start its engine with a snarl and move off.

Luke exhales.

'Franklin's men. This way.'

'But the insignia, they're nothing to do with the City...'

'Shhh!'

Luke leads them back, then down a cross alley and up another, which seems endless. The children press on, not talking. The moon is down and the alleys are dark as tunnels. David runs his hand along the brickwork beside him. He knows he must not fall behind.

'Nearly there,' someone whispers.

They turn into another alley.

Luke halts beside a gate of rough planks, his hand raised. David comes to a stop against him. Silence. The vehicle pulses somewhere, like the purr of a giant cat. Luke knocks on the gate and then forces his shoulder against it. A shaft of light falls on them from an upstairs window.

Luke pushes the gate open and the children stream through. He shoves it back and jams a baulk of timber against it.

'In here,' he mutters, and they pass through a second door. Something scratches, a match flares and a lantern lights up, showing the faces all round lit like ghosts against the shadows. David breathes in. The air tastes purer in here than outside.

'Thanks, it's really good of you to take me in.'

'Sit yourself down, I'll get some tea. Couldn't leave you out there in the curfew.'

David feels a rough wood table with chairs, and sits and looks round. A kettle whistles and a couple of the children slip out of the room and come back in a minute with Luke, each carrying a tray.

'Not bad,' he says. 'I got a few slices of bread. One each.'

David waits until Luke's seated at the head of the table before biting into the bread. It's rich and rough with seeds in it. He fills his mouth and chews at it.

After a while he asks:

'Something else. I'm looking for Sarah. The Horse-Woman.'

Luke stops chewing. No-one speaks.

'You do ask questions, don't you? Someone should tell you. Leave Sarah alone.'

'But... it's me brought her horse back, the black mare, Juno.'

'You don't come from a village do you? Take my advice. She's not for you.' He looks down. 'I'll see if there's any chance of food.'

He opens a door behind him and the children watch him as he walks away from them, along a corridor and pushes open another door at the far end. Light and the uproar of many people talking and shouting and making music together floods through. The children stare at each other and chatter and glance up at him. He catches the word 'feast.'

Luke talks to a brown-skinned older man dressed in black and purple who looks back at them, his lips compressed, and at last nods. Luke gives them all a thumbs up and the children press forward. David follows. The older man has an arm out directing them:

'Over there. Try to make yourself useful for once. And don't get in the way.'

A Feast

Oil lamps dangle from chains and light up the hall. He sits next to Luke, with the children on both sides. They're on a wooden bench set against the wall with a rough wooden table in front of them. Stone columns reach up into the dimness above him where cross-braced wooden beams hold up the roof. The windows opposite curve up to pointed arches. Paintings of burghers and townspeople in gowns and headscarves and cloaks glow from the glass in soft rich colours. They tell a story of a long journey on horseback. Plates and cutlery are piled at the end of the table and the smell of rich food hangs in the air. David feels the tension flow from his body. There's a good feeling in the room.

Tables run along the other side of the hall and fill the area in the middle. The benches alongside them are packed with the brightly-clothed children, women and men he saw this morning in the Old Town. They remind him of the people in the window-pictures. All of them are busy. They gossip with their neighbours, spring to their feet to greet a friend, call out and wave to others further away, glance round at each other. Four generations of a family meet up, shake hands, embrace, admire grandchildren, help a great-grandfather who walks with two sticks to a seat and fit themselves round an entire table. They each dress differently but you'd know they were related, the slight roll to the gait as they walk, a plumpness in the cheeks, a way of smiling and talking all at once, without seeming to listen. A couple of hounds, lithe, with grey and white bodies and slender snouts, follow close to one of the girls.

A band sits on a platform at the right-hand end, led by a tall well-built woman with the pouch of a set of bagpipes clamped under her elbow. She pauses and drinks deep at a flagon of something brown, and wipes the foam from her lips. She passes it to the thin young man next to her with a guitar in his lap. Behind them sit a trumpeter and a drummer. Give it to them last, he thinks. I know drummers, they'll drain the lot.

David licks his lips.

'We used to have feasts – when we finished at the Academy, that was famous!'

Luke glances up at him.

'You were at an academy?'

'Yes…a while back. They sent me there, it wasn't my idea.'

He colours and Susie plucks at his sleeve.

'What's an academy?'

'It doesn't matter…' He feels Luke's eyes on him. 'Tell you later.'

The trumpet blares and everyone looks round, away from the band. He cranes his neck to see past the end pillar to where a table is set cross-ways with a row of people behind it. An older man with long grey hair in a dark velvet robe with a silver chain round his neck stands in the middle to address the throng, his knuckles resting on the table. One of the figures shifts into view and he stares. Sarah, now wearing a white satin jacket and with a thin band of silver in her hair, is at the far end, her face turned to gaze up at the speaker.

'Shhh,' says Luke. 'It's O'Connor. He's the mayor.'

Mistrust and admiration mingle in his expression.

The older man beams round at them.

'So good to see all of you!'

'And you!' roar the throng.

'Another week goes by, and we have another shipment from our brothers and sisters in the villages. We will feast!'

Cheers and applause resound round the hall. Someone calls out:

'All thanks to O'Connor!'

The patriarch raises a hand in acknowledgement. The bagpipes bellow and the drummer pounds out a roll. O'Connor sits and a double line of aproned cooks parade forth through doors at the back of the hall. They carry trays, laden with bowls and tureens, with the savour of hot pepper and garlic and fennel and mint issuing from them.

Luke nudges him and starts passing the plates round.

'See why we're happy? They've been cooking all afternoon.'

'What will we get? I'm really hungry. It was a roast ox at the academy barbecue.' David closes his eyes at the memory.

'You won't get that here. Here it's spiced potatoes with currants and hazelnuts and walnuts and garlic.' He ladles a mass of potato slices, mint-scented, with the nuts and currants dotted among them, onto a plate and pushes it towards David. 'Then there's bean stew, three kinds of bean, broad beans, dwarf beans, runner beans and beetroot and beef tomatoes, and the salad will be out in a minute. Oh and garlic cabbage and swede and leeks in cream sauce and bread and butter pudding and seven different cheeses. Enjoy yourself!'

'But…'

David lifts the spoon, touches it against his lips and takes a small amount, then the whole mouthful, then another. Susie gives a squeal of laughter next to him.

'You should see your face!'

'That is amazing. What is it?'

A tumult of flavours surge and tumble inside his mouth. His tongue feels as if the whole length of it is coated in squabbling tastes, sharp as lemon, the texture of mushroom, salt, a bitter tang, like chocolate, and the zest of sweetness, like grace notes. He takes a pull at the beaker of liquid and the full buttery flavour of the beer rushes into his throat. He blinks and smiles round at them.

'It's just a bean stew we eat in the villages. You should drop by sometime.'

'Gosh.'

He takes another mouthful and another. All round him the football team are munching away, as if they might not get a decent meal tomorrow. Someone finds a platter of flapjack, which disappears inside a minute, and another appears. David eats his way through a salad of celery, red pepper and miniature tomatoes that burst sweetly on his tongue and slices of apple and even dark grapes. He glances over towards Sarah as he chews the apple but he can't see her through the throng. O'Connor surveys the hall, his face shrewd as a chess-player.

The band strikes up, a lively tune in two/four time. Someone sings a harvest-song in a full baritone, and everyone takes up the chorus about the hay-wagon. The children clap in time. David finds another beaker of beer in his hand and sips it for the rich alluring savour and finds he's drained the lot and he wants another one.

A scraping noise cuts across the music as people push back the tables. Luke bounces to his feet and motions the team and they bound forward, in among the adults. They dance, everyone dances, round and round, the older ones guiding the smaller, the littlest being picked up and spun and tossed to the skirl and rhythm and clamour of the band. David is there among them, whirled along, his feet trip and leap and caper under him, his body pitches and lurches and totters and the grin beams from his face as if it is pasted on.

Later on, when some of the older people have left, he finds himself dancing with a dark-haired girl. She has eyes like a roe deer and shoulders like a stone-mason. Her name is Tania and she turns him and swings him and catches him as if he weighs no more that Susie. Benches and pillars and faces fly past like a fairground glimpsed from a carousel. The bandleader's red in the face, her cheeks puff out and the music is a maelstrom hurling him round and on.

Next, he is sitting on a bench leaning back against the rough stone of the wall. Someone gives him a cup of water. He rubs at his aching thighs. He remembers Luke's face close to his, asking him if he's OK. He definitely needs to sleep. He hears people talking next to him, something about the apple-harvest, and he turns to join in. A woman swings round. It's Sarah. Her white jacket is folded over the chair-back and her hair flops forward over her face.

Words crowd into his head.

'Sarah! It's so good to see you. I've been searching for you everywhere, I couldn't find you. How are you? How's Juno?'

She pushes the hair back from her forehead and holds it.

'Juno's fine.'

'You… maybe we could…'

'I'm a bit busy. We have to sort out what I'm going to tell them in the villages.'

'But…I've been looking for you. And Juno.' He stumbles to silence. His heart weighs in his breast. He puts his hand on hers and gazes at her, he knows he's a fool but he can't stop himself gazing at her.

She frowns.

'I like you, but you don't understand. I've learnt a lot about what's going on.' She purses her lips. 'It's a war. We're in Franklin's way. He wants to destroy us and your lot in the City will let him. His security patrols kidnap our people. How can we trust you? I'm sorry.'

She picks up his hand with her other hand and holds it and then sets it down in his lap.

'You're on the wrong side.'

David feels his heart shudder. He says nothing.

Someone grasps him by the shoulder.

'C'mon. You need to sleep.'

'Can't I just stay here a bit?'

Luke has more strength in his thin body than David realises. He hoists David to his feet and gets an arm round him.

'Listen. You're worn out. You need to sleep. They've got things to discuss.'

He half-walks half-marches David towards the door they came in by. Sarah watches him, the hair framing her face. She turns away and Luke guides him through the door.

The Hall of Monsters

His neck aches as if he's slept in a ditch and his head is vast and full of seaweed. He opens his eyes and closes them against the glare of sunlight. He hears someone chuckle and he knows they're laughing at him.

'Wakey-wakey!'

Luke holds out a cup to him. He's trying to make his face sympathetic but he keeps breaking into a grin.

'Fancy a game of football before you set off? The team's waiting.'

David gathers himself into a sitting position and pours the hot liquid into his mouth. He remembers Sarah, her face veiled by hair, looking away.

'That was … bad.'

Luke hands him a second cup.

'You seemed to be enjoying yourself. Maybe it's time to get going.'

He shakes his head.

'What?'

'I had a talk with Sarah. I know which academy you went to. I like you but you're better off back with your own people.' He looks down. 'Others might not be friendly.'

'I've left them. I can't be part of them. I'm on your side now.'

'Yeah. You're not the first to tell us that. Better you leave quietly. There's no choice. You have to go back.'

It's as if he's punched David in the face.

'Don't push me out.'

Luke takes the cup.

'Sorry.' He bites his lip. 'Come on. We'll come some of the way with you. Safer.'

David's been here before. Franklin sneers at him from the torn poster on the corner. The triple chimney reaches up and vomits its fumes over the town. The air tastes colder, sharper and harsher this morning and the clouds have the dull sheen of weathered lead.

Luke pats his arm.

'Just keep on. That's the Pit, where Franklin's mills are. Don't go all the way down, just circle round and up the other side. You'll be OK.'

'Right.' He sets his shoulders square. 'Maybe I need a job. The New Market World.'

'Don't be an idiot. Franklin hates us. You've seen his Greenjackets. People go in there, they don't come out.'

'You couldn't get a message to Sarah, could you?'

Luke shakes his head.

'See you again.'

'One day.'

David sets off. When he looks back a hundred metres later, Luke is still at the corner. He feels empty. He raises a hand and Luke waves, and he turns away and walks on.

After an hour he nears the mill. A throbbing, like the pulse of a sleeping giant pervades the area, first as a trembling behind every sound, them as a tremor in the cobbles under his feet. He leans against a wall and feels the vibration run through it, through everything, always there, just on the edge of feeling. He comes out in a small square with a drooping birch tree surrounded by a metal railing in the centre. Beyond is the mill.

He taps on the metal counter of a wooden stall crammed in against the wall of a house. An old man with milky blue eyes straightens up from behind the counter, like a child's toy. He wears a faded red and white jacket that reminds David of Sarah.

'Miracle bar, two Miracle bars, please.'

'Ain't got 'em. Got these.'

He drops a couple of chocolate sticks wrapped in gaudy foil labelled "Exercise Bar" on the counter.

'OK. You do wristbands?'

'Seen everything, do anything.'

He shrugs and flips back his cuff. The old man clicks bands with him.

'Have a good day.'

He bobs down.

The factory wall is a metal rampart twice as tall as David. A corrugated iron gate, the size of a house door, is set in it. No one about, he guesses they're inside. A screech, like the shriek of a sea-bird on a rock islet beyond the circling sea, echoes and dies and the throbbing fills the air. He touches his fingers to the letter in his pocket and hammers on the gate with his fist.

Something stirs inside, then silence. He pounds his fist again on cold metal and an opening half the size of a letter slot grates open. Sharp black eyes and bushy eye-brows are framed in it.

'What do you want?'

'I've come for a job. I want to be part of the New Market World. Like it says.'

'You're a fool. Wait there.'

The grating slams shut.

He steps back and braces himself. The door creaks, a belch of sour air engulfs him, they click wristbands and he steps inside.

He leans against the wall, his eyes watering and his throat constricted.

'Here.'

The door-keeper thrusts a yellow helmet towards him. He finds goggles in it and gets them over his eyes, and a face-mask which he puts on. He screws up his eyes and opens them and coughs the ashy air out of his windpipe.

He's at one end of a vast hall, the air obscured by fumes, orange lights glaring down, and the roof braced by metal girders far above him. He gasps again and cranes his neck. A colossal creature, yellow as a giant hornet, confronts him. Cold eyes like polished stones stare at him from each side of a giant ridged brow. The clangour of metal hammering on metal, people shouting and a horn braying batters at him from within the building. He sucks in air through the mask.

'Impressive isn't she? Come and have a look. She won't hurt you.'

A woman in spotless white overalls, a yellow helmet and a mask, a row of pens in her breast pocket and a steel clipboard in her hand, stands next to him. She holds out her wrist and they click. He follows her, keeping away from the creature. Where the legs should be, folded under it, are yellow wheels, taller than he is, with great black tyres. The woman climbs up rungs set in the side of it and swings open a hatch to reveal a cabin with a metal seat and levers.

He gapes.

'A man can ride this beast?'

She laughs.

'Well, women mainly. But we sometimes let men in.'

She has fair hair under her helmet and azure eyes. She slams the door shut.

'Some people call it a monster. This is the hall of monsters and this one is my personal monster.'

She pats the jowl of the beast. The sound of the factory lulls for a moment so that only the throbbing continues. She descends.

'I call her Number One. She's actually a very, very large truck but people call her a road-beast. Mr Franklin has some on the road already, we're phasing them in as we expand the operation. This one sleeps. Don't wake her.' She gestures. 'And here's the track.'

He looks beyond Number One. A roadway with metal shapes on it and machines ranged along both sides stretches away from him. More wheels rest on it, he can't count how many, double wheels on huge axles and a flat platform above them. Behind them is a metal desert with structures set out in ranks across it. He stares, his mouth open, and makes out other shapes, similar to Number One but smaller, on it. The horn blares again and the shapes jerk towards him. He flinches and it all halts.

The woman spreads her arms, her gesture taking in the road-beasts, the desert, the whole of the mill.

'This is the future, for all of us. Who'd live in a village when they've seen this?'

'But what are they all for?'

She grins.

'That would be telling. Come on.'

Other devices and shapes are scattered about the hall. He sees movement. Figures in yellow helmets and grubby overalls fidget and lumber among it all.

'You need some overalls, then we'll get you started. I'm Marion, Control Manager, I like to meet all new staff. You'll get used to it. Don't ever forget, you're part of something big, we're building the future.'

She takes him across the factory, down an alley between great mills that growl and bellow on either side, workers in yellow helmets bent over them, some perched high up. No-one looks at him. A gust of hot air blows into his face, pungent, caustic. His eyes water and he rubs at them.

'Keep your goggles on.'

The throbbing grows louder, more general, there's no way to escape from it. Light flares up, followed by a gale of air like the breath of Goliath and he bends double.

They emerge from the file of machinery and in front of him he sees a second monster, a huge pot belly of black iron, four times the height of a man, tiered and bulging, with the great crest of a chimney reaching up and back above it. Men heave at an iron wagon, twice the size of a farm-cart, inching it forward towards the behemoth on metal rails. Someone shouts out and Marion tugs at him and pulls him down. They crouch beside one of the smaller devices.

She turns to him, her eyes dancing:

'Recharge – the best bit. You're just in time.'

The workers ahead of him haul at a rope tied to a great lever, which grinds and clashes and angles down. A red slit grins open in the monster's belly and a blast of heat hits David. He throws up a hand and peers over it. The maw of the monster cracks open, a fiery tongue licks up and out of it and he sees into its very gorge and hears the thunder of its howl. The fury of its breath gusts over him. He shrinks back.

The workers shelter behind the wagon and shove with their shoulders, backs and arms against it, their necks straining. It tips forward, slack coal glints and tumbles and rumbles into the maw of the beast and the steel jaw slams shut. The steady pulse of its great belly resumes and the floor under him shakes.

Marion grins at him.

'Feeding time. I'm due elsewhere. You help out here for now.'

One of the figures from the wagon team comes over. He walks with a rolling gait. He's a head taller than David, with a chest like a beer-barrel and shoulders to match. His fellows sit back behind the cart, passing a bottle between them and glancing over as if David's a specimen up for appraisal.

A huge hand encloses David's, scarred flesh where the forefinger should be.

'Hi, good to meet you. I'm Damon. You start with the clean-up team, work your way up. See you in a bit.'

They click wristbands and he waves at a bank of silent machines and saunters away. A slight figure in grease-stained overalls slumps against the nearest machine.

David crosses over to him.

'Hi, I'm new.'

The figure hauls himself to his feet, moving as if underwater.

'You looking for the Number Two gang? You found it.'

'They said the clean-up team.'

'Nice. They're being polite. They call me Rabbie for some reason. I need a break.'

He yawns. His teeth are crammed together in his jaw and stained black as if he cleaned them with soot. David offers his wrist-band and the other nods and clicks.

He reels, straightens and stumbles forward, waving with his right hand. David takes a pace, leans on the machine to cough, and follows him. The throbbing beats out all round him.

Rabbie turns to him and shouts above the noise.

'We scrub up after they charge the furnace. Then we lie low. Got it? Here, you need a face-shield. Those plastic hats are just for decoration.'

He hands David a steel helmet with a visor riveted to it. David stands upright to use both hands to fit it over his goggles. The pulsations thrash at him, like a heavy sea, and he stumbles and jams the helmet on. His ears hurt.

He grunts:

'A dollar a day, eh?'

'Something like that. Here, you get the long-handled brush and the gloves.'

David pulls on gauntlets. The dizziness has gone now. He grasps the broom in both hands. It's twice the normal length. Scorch marks bite into one side. He takes four steps forward, up a metal ramp. Heat pours out of the black iron body of the furnace, pummelling at him. He knows he cannot bear this for more than a minute. He must endure. He will tell Sarah of this place. He squares his shoulders and shoves the broom forward into the pile of cinders directly below the fire-door.

The bristles smoulder and wisps of grey smoke coil upwards. He drags the broom back. The clinker slides towards him and as it rolls the red of smouldering embers fades to pewter and to ash-grey. Rabbie slides the shovel forward from behind him. Together they load the cinders into a metal hand-cart.

He works away and the pile of ashes shrinks. Later Damon comes over and gives them a bottle of beer and some bread and dripping to share. They click.

'You want yours toasted? You'd better get your heads down. Time to re-charge the beast.'

The wagon the re-charge team push forward is taller than David. Once the grate of the furnace is open, the team can only force it forward at the pace of water trickling. The heat hammers at them and they crouch behind it. The worst bit is the ramp itself, just before the grate. The wagon jolts and jams. They can't shift it.

Damon glances over to them. Rabbie looks away and crouches lower. David gets to his feet and lumbers towards the wagon, bent double, gauntlets crossed in front of his face. He throws himself down and the breath chokes in his throat.

Damon gives him a nod and waves his wrist.

'Shove!'

Everyone strains, thighs, shoulders, backs. David pushes against the leather jacket of the worker in front of him. The wagon jerks forward, then halts slightly sideways. They stop pushing and slump down. He lies flat and looks along the wagon and sees a cinder jammed in the track, ahead of the wheels. He turns back, blinded for a second.

Damon slaps his shoulder.

'Left Rabbie behind did you?'

He grins at David. David feels a gust of comradeship. You do these things, you don't know why, you do them for your mates.

'Get ready.'

He rolls out from behind the wagon and crawls, head down, the heat tearing at him. Just two metres, one, and he forces his arm forward against the inferno and flicks the cinder jammed in the track to one side. Scalding pain bursts through his finger tips and he collapses prone. The pounding of the mill throbs through his face, his chest, his body. Axles creak beside him, the truck rumbles past and starts to tip. Someone seizes him by both ankles and drags him backwards.

Someone tilts a water-bottle against his lips. He gulps and swallows and chokes and the hurt in his hand jerks at him. The gauntlets and helmet have gone and he sits on a wooden floor against a plywood wall, his legs stretched out in front of him. A linen bandage, already grimy and secured with a metal pin, encases his hand and forearm in an untidy bundle. The furnace glowers some way away outside the window opposite him, far above it the roof of the mill. The throbbing murmurs, more distant now.

'Don't do that again, you had me worried.'

He recognises the voice. Luke, his face serious, squats next to him.

'What? What are you doing here?'

'Someone has to look after you. I saw where you went, straight downhill, so I followed. I signed up like you did. Besides I got my own business with Franklin.'

Luke's face looks young again.

'Damon's pleased with you. You're the only one ever burnt through a gauntlet on your first day. Soon as that hand's healed you're on the recharge team and I'm on clean-up.'

'But you, it was you got me out of there wasn't it? The others were at the wagon. Thank you. I owe you.'

Luke drops a hand on his shoulder.

'Don't think about it. You're off until the hand's healed. I'm looking after you. And I've got a plan.'

David closes his eyes. Ideas swirl in his brain. He's found things out about Franklin and his factories but why are Ferris and Adam so interested? And why don't the people in the Old Town trust the City? And Sarah, with her hair forward over her face. *You're on the wrong side.* He can't think about Sarah.

And Juno. He'd like to see Juno again.

Luke comes back with a bowl of something in each hand.

'Bean stew. I got them to take the sausages out. Do you good.'

'I'd tell you to go and put them back if I wasn't so hungry!'

No flavour, no spices, the beans just taste of beans and sugar. He wolfs them down, belches, puts his good hand on a chair-back and pulls himself to his feet. They're in an office, abandoned by the look of it, with one rusty metal filing cabinet and a dirty window looking out over the factory floor. The furnace glows dull red away to the left and the yellow road-beast is on a level with them to the right. The yellow helmets of the workers bob as they fidget around the machines as if grooming them.

He flexes his fingers inside the bandage and the pain doesn't grow worse.

'What's your plan?'

'I've been looking around. This mill is huge, much bigger than any hall or barn I've ever been in, but there's more to it, I know there is. See the far wall? You have to put your face against the glass, the air is so bad.'

David squints. The wall the other side of the factory floor stretches left to right, grey and rusting.

'See?'

'What? It's a wall.'

'Yeah. A wall. No doors, no windows, no way through. You see that anywhere else? That's Franklin's other mill beyond it, the one no-one ever goes in, he doesn't want us to know about it. You put your hand against that wall, you feel the rumble of machinery and you can hear shouting. I've been over there.'

He pauses.

'Another thing. I heard a horse neigh, loud, on the other side. I heard a crack, like a whip. I swear it.'

'Let's get out of here, tell people what we've seen. Tell Sarah.'

'Alright. We'll do that later. Franklin's men take the people they kidnap down here, I'm sure of it, but they're not in this hall. We've got to find them.'

He squats and moves closer.

'People like to have fun in the Old Town. They don't like worrying about things. I look after the Football Team. You know what everyone's scared of, what they won't talk about? Being out on the streets after dark. We took you in pretty sharpish, didn't we? They blame your City for that.'

David sits himself on the chair and scratches at his cheek.

'Franklin's men. They patrol the streets. They catch you, you're not seen again. That's what the street people think. They don't come near here anymore. No-one goes to the Pit.'

He looks down.

'I've known people I don't see any more – my mate Sam. We used to hang out together, play football. Now he ain't around.'

He fiddles with a scrap of paper.

'That chancer, O'Connor. People like him. He does deals, deals with the villages, people say he's done a deal with Franklin. He's the one tells us not to trust you lot. Franklin, he's from the City, that's what people think.'

'I just want to help, to make things better. I hate Franklin.'

'Maybe.' Luke looks him in the eyes. 'Sam. O'Connor's his uncle, you know that? Sam was different. I used to work for O'Connor, Sam was my mate. I was very close to him.'

The Hall of Beasts

Luke pauses and looks back. David leans against the wall to gather his strength.

'Just give me a minute.'

They've worked their way right round the edge of the factory. Luke has a torn cardboard file from the office with sheets of blank paper in it under his arm and no-one shows any interest in them. The wall vibrates to the rhythm of machinery. They find a crack where a rivet has rusted through but they can't prise the metal sheets apart.

David puts his nose to it. He smells the factory odour of grease and soot and oil and over it something else, a whiff of horses and polished leather that takes him straight to the stables and Juno, back to a different life. He shakes his head but the smell's still there.

Luke squats down, elbows on knees:

'No way through.'

'Yup.'

'You can't see over the wall outside and besides there are guards. That's his other mill. What's he so keen to keep quiet?'

'Maybe we could give up?'

Luke sits back and stares upwards at the gantries above them.

'I'm not giving up. Sam's here somewhere, I know it. Besides, you need looking after. How do you think they get on the roof?'

David spots the metal ladders, three-quarters of the way round, close to where the chimney slants across the end wall and out at the corner of the roof. They're painted red and bolted to the side of the building, with metal safety-hoops round them. He stares upwards, trying to count the rungs, and gives up.

'After you.'

Luke steps back. He sounds like he's enjoying himself.

'You go first – you slip, you'll land on me. There's a platform half-way.'

David reaches up, grips the ladder and snatches his hand back as the pain jolts down his arm.

'Let's leave it. I'll be OK tomorrow.'

'We'll be on shift. You wait here, I'll go by myself.'

For answer, David hauls himself onto the ladder with his left arm and wraps his right behind it. He raises his foot and climbs up one rung and then another. He hesitates and raises his foot again and clambers upwards and halts again and looks out. The road-beast at the end of the rails with the lesser beasts behind it is directly opposite him, like a line of elephants following each other across a desert.

He looks down, his head whirls and he reels back against a hoop. Miniature workers, like white ants, scurrying about their business. City Square would look like that to a crow's eye, except the ants would be grey.

'Hold on!' yells Luke and shoves him back towards the rungs. He sucks air into his lungs and hauls himself onward. When they get to the platform he sits and rests, away from the edge. The air is hotter and heavier with fumes. He coughs again and gasps air into his lungs. Luke places a hand on the ladder.

'You could hang on here.'

'Not far, now. I'll come with you.'

He puts his good hand on the ladder and pulls himself to his feet, waits a moment for his head to clear, and raises his foot to the first rung. Higher up they transfer to another ladder, without hoops. He clings on, the pain in his hand forgotten, his eyes focused on the oblong of wall between the rungs in front of him. He steps sideways onto a small platform built in at the angle between the roof gantry and the wall, grips the knob of a metal door and shoves hard.

Chill air rushes past him and he breathes deep. He opens his eyes. To his left the chimney of the first mill trails its wake of vapour across the shifting cloud-banks. A second chimney emerges from the mill in front of him and a third beyond it, twice the girth of the other two. All three cluster together, like the devil's organ pipes.

Luke squeezes past him and onto a red-painted gantry which runs across to a metal door set in the roof opposite. He crosses and tugs the door open. David follows, holding on with one hand and stares past him, down, past red-painted gantries, into another vast metal hall.

Two-thirds of the floor of the mill, stretching away to their right, is green, the abundant green of well-watered grasslands. Hedges run across, with a coppice of fair-sized trees in the centre. Below the platform on which they are standing are pastures and paddocks and, at the near end, feeding troughs, with the sanded surface of a riding school to one side. A hooped ladder leads downwards.

Brown, black, grey and dappled shapes move about or stand in groups. Full-grown horses, and foals among them. Franklin breeds horses. He hears a shout. Tiny figures in white overalls bend and carry bundles or push barrows near the sheds. Some of them have rakes or shovels. The horses start moving, converging on them. One of them neighs and others take it up. They line up by the stables. Feeding time.

Bright light beams down from giant sunray lamps bolted to the girders just below them. The light sparkles on water in a pool at the corner of the meadow. The air is warm and clean, sweet-scented with grass and hay. He breathes in again and touches Luke's arm.

'Hey, I could like it here. It's a world made for horses.'

'Look over there: Greenjackets.'

A squad in the green uniforms of Franklin's security enter the nearest paddock. Horses, saddled and bridled, are led in and assigned one to each of them. A command rings out and they mount, heaving themselves up with difficulty. One of them slides back down. David's sure he hears laughter. A figure in white comes over and makes a stirrup with linked hands and the dunce is finally in the saddle. *Embarrassing for the horse.* The troop sets off at a walk, following the track worn in the grass round the edge of the field. The riders sway from side to side. Some of them can hardly keep a straight back in the saddle. *Your legs are going to ache tonight.*

'Franklin's teaching his men to ride. He can't be all bad.'

Luke doesn't say anything. He points to the left.

The final section of the mill floor, the other side of the platform, is bare, dirty yellow and covered in gravel. In the corner stands a larger shed, the height of a three-storey house, with double-doors tall enough to take a hay-wagon. A metal pipe snakes out of it and twists against the wall to climb up and out through the roof. David frowns. He doesn't understand. Some way along from the shed, another pipe, much larger, emerges from the floor with nothing near it. Heat shimmers from it. It rises vertically to where the first pipe ducts through the roof. The third chimney.

Almost directly beneath the platform, a section is fenced off. More figures in green uniforms are drawn up in rows. Opposite them, a line of black horses. A single figure stands in front of them. He gestures towards the horses and makes a sharp movement with his right arm as if flicking a whip.

Luke puts a hand on the ladder.

'We've got to get lower down, hear what's going on. I'll go. You stay here.'

He eases himself over the edge of the platform onto the ladder. David licks his lips and watches as he clambers down. After a minute, he crawls across and lowers himself onto the first rung and follows, his bad hand wrapped round behind the rungs. He moves down, rung to rung, feeling with his feet, not looking. He smells the rich raw scent of horses again, gusting up to him. He wonders who does the grooming. Luke steadies him as he steps onto the half-way platform.

'Keep your head down. They don't look up much.'

Closer, they see that the Greenjackets' uniforms are made of serge not leather. They wear peaked caps and carry whips, coiled at their belts. The squad are all male, and all carry themselves in the way of men who invite fights after the pub and don't lose.

A black mare with a white blaze along her nose whinnies and stamps her hooves. Someone shouts. A guard comes forward, a whip in his hand. Two others grip onto traces, one each side of the horse's bridle and drag down so she can't move. The guard flicks the whip up and cracks it with a sound like a pistol-shot. He lashes it down across the horse's face, just under the eyes. The mare neighs shrill and trembles and tries to rear up, teeth bared. The guards heave on the traces and she falls back. He brings the whip down again and she screams louder than David knew a horse could scream. He whips her again and again, across the nose, the mouth, the eyes and the cheeks, until she doesn't try to rear up, and lowers her head, twisting her neck from side to side. Red streaks criss-cross the white blaze.

One of the guards seizes the bridle at one side and says something. The other laughs. The guards jerk the horse forward and lead her, head down, towards the end shed.

The hairs on the back of David's neck bristle. Luke grips his arm and grunts:

'They break them in by beating them, that's how Franklin treats his horses. Look at the others.'

The beasts cower back, packed together into the corner of the paddock. Other guards stride towards them, whips ready. David holds onto the ladder with his good hand and peers down.

'What does Franklin want with horses? He has a hall-full of road-monsters next door.'

'Who knows? You use horses to travel between villages, where there are no roads.'

'We've got to get back. Tell everyone.'

'There's more.'

Luke leans out over the left-hand side of the platform. David stares past him. In the bare area alongside the huge shed stands a row of machines, like a miniature version of the other mill. Figures in white overalls bend over them and spotlights shine on their work. No furnace, no track, no grinding and grating of metal, and no monstrous machine, just the shed with its pipework. He cranes out as far as he dares. The figures are working with metal, fiddling with steel poles and rods and cylinders.

'Let's get out of here.'

Luke ignores him.

'I have to find Sam.'

'They'll see us if we stay here.'

A clangour, like the sound of hammer-blows on sheet iron, bursts out from the three-storey shed followed by a bellow that's half a whinny, half a roar. The guards look round, someone shouts an order and the whole squad moves forward, their whips gripped in their hands. The double doors swing open, pushed from inside, and light, brighter than day, floods out. The noise ceases and the guards tense themselves, the light glinting on their whips. The beasts in the paddock fall silent, and cram themselves tighter into their corner.

David arches over the edge of the platform and stares directly into the shed. The light half-blinds him. He makes out the mouth of a tunnel reaching down away from him, brilliantly lit. Something dark moves within it, lumbering upward, towards him. A chill runs along his veins. A great horse, a stallion, black as Juno, but giant, half as big again, heaves itself forward. A shiver runs through it. It stamps and shakes its mane and neighs, louder and louder, and the neigh turns into a bellow that echoes off the metal walls around it.

The guards run forward and seize on the chains that hang down from its bridle. It shakes its head again, swinging the guard nearest David off his feet. Another seizes the chain with him and they lurch sideways, their heels scoring a curve in the ground.

Luke whispers: 'Look!'

A framework of yellow metal struts surrounds the flanks and hindquarters and rear legs of the beast. The rods and hinges reach down, along its legs, to gleaming steel hooves. Cylinders are bolted to them and pipes run to some device, like trombone tubes clustered together, hanging close under the belly. David hears a hiss, like many geese, as it moves. Luke clutches at his arm.

Other guards crowd forward, some holding out padded shields in front of them, some with helmets and visors. They swarm round the chains and drag on the beast. It shakes its head and glares upwards and stares straight at David and Luke, its eyes wide and terror-struck, and bellows again. It stamps and rears up and kicks out with steel-shod hooves. Someone shouts an order and a guard in a helmet and padded suit ducks under the hooves and thrusts up with a rod like a lance. Electricity crackles, the bellow turns shrill and the beast plunges down on all four hooves and tosses its head.

The guard throws himself sideways and rolls out of danger. His fellows haul the creature round and drag it back into the shed. The metal rods slide into the cylinders as it moves. The light dims as it is forced into the tunnel-mouth and snaps out and the doors clamp shut, like a trap.

David and Luke lie silent on the platform, staring at each other. David shivers.

'I'd give anything for a Miracle bar.'

Luke looks down. His fingers press into David's forearm. He releases his hold.

'I'm not leaving without Sam.'

The Road-Beast

David grasps the ladder.

'We have to go back.'

Luke won't look at him. He hauls himself to his feet.

'That beast. No one can stand against that. They have to know, in the Old Town, in the villages.'

'There's a tunnel under that shed and another chimney, bigger than the other two, coming up. They've got some monstrous furnace down there, underground. Franklin's third mill. I'm sure of it.'

'We'll come back, bring more people. Very soon.'

David grips the ladder with his good hand and tugs himself up a rung. He pauses, his bandaged arm wrapped round behind it. His forehead rests on a rung and he sucks in air. He climbs another rung.

Luke slaps the metal of the platform.

'You'll never make it by yourself.'

He starts upward behind David, holding him onto the ladder and swings round and shouts out into the mill:

'I'll come back for you! I swear it!'

The cry echoes from the iron wall. Silence from below; white faces look up. The two of them freeze on the ladder. David feels the blood pulsing through his body. After a long time, a whip cracks below them. The noise of horses and of men giving orders returns and strengthens. David breathes out slowly and takes another step upwards.

The fumes from the Hall of Monsters catch David's throat as he slides through the door onto the platform above the red ladder. His skin itches. He coughs and stuffs his sleeve into his mouth. Luke glares at him, as if he's angry and pushes past him to the ladder. David stifles the cough and puts his foot on the first rung and they descend slowly into the uproar.

His hand pulses with pain and his legs ache. Luke keeps below him, holding him onto the ladder, not speaking. Then they are inside the hoops and he half climbs, half slides down into the din below. They slump against the wall in the shadow of a dead machine, like marionettes with the strings cut.

After a long time a horn sounds out, a long wailing blast. Luke helps David to his feet.

'Sounds like end of shift.'

Across the mill they see workers straighten their backs and stretch and start to climb down from the machines. The lights at the far end blink out and everyone makes for the exit. Behind it all the mill throbs, like the snore of a sleeping titan. Luke moves forward. David follows him along the wall to join the crowd pushing their way through the metal doors.

A hand claps David on the back and he staggers.

'See you tomorrow.'

It's Damon.

'Sure. Bit slower with the hand, but I can do most things. Been round the factory a bit today.'

'Great. You're part of the team. And your mate, if he wants.'

'Yeah. Now if there's a works football team, I'd have a go.' Damon chuckles.

'I'll put a couple of beers on ice for you.'

The mob of workers crowding through the exit door swallows him up, Luke tags on after them. David, his hand cradled against his chest, follows. He could have a life here, part of the team, another worker in Franklin's mill. Then he remembers the horses.

The workers stream out of the gates and turn to the left, north. It's dark in the little square. David and Luke hold back and stand in the shadow of one of the houses. Everyone else tramps past them and turns up the hill past the run-down residence blocks David remembers riding through. He sees them peeling off, entering the buildings. That's where Franklin's workers live, in the ill-lit streets below the city, one step away from the Pit.

As the crowd clears they see a figure, his arm out directing them. Light from a streetlamp falls on him. He wears the green serge uniform of Franklin's security and the golden balance on his breast pocket glints in the lamplight. They wait there, in the dark. The guard follows the last worker, north, up the hill.

When everyone's gone, they set off the other way, towards the Old Town. Luke ignores him, but after a long time he says, not looking at him,

'Sam was my mate.'

'I know. I'll come back with you.'

He puts a hand on Luke's shoulder. He doesn't know what to say.

Luke looks up at him. His eyes blaze.

'You going to tell me Franklin's not from your City? You saw where they went, all the people who work in that place.'

'They're poor, they have to work.'

'Sure.'

Luke turns and walks fast, past houses and the occasional shop, towards the Old Town where the light of day still gleams through between broken clouds. David tries to keep up but the breath rasps in his throat and he falls behind. His hand aches inside the bandage. They pass the occasional walker, all in their bright-coloured clothes but dulled as the shadows lengthen. People greet Luke, but he says nothing. They ignore David.

After a while Luke goes through a door, without looking back, and it slams shut behind him. David pauses on the threshold, then knocks. Nothing happens and he knocks again. The door is pulled open from inside. Sarah stands across the door-way, her arms folded.

'You.'

'It's good to see you. I've been in Franklin's mill.'

'I know. I'm sorry. I've seen you in your black uniform. How can we trust you?'

Her face is sad. He feels a tightness in his chest. He needs her to listen to him.

'I went to the mill. To find out. You have to tell everyone. Franklin makes animals into machines. I saw it.'

She sighs.

'Go round the back. You can sleep there.'

She pulls the door shut.

He finds his way along an alley and pushes open a rough plank door and shuts it behind him. He hears the familiar rustle of a horse shifting its weight from one leg to another, and smells the sweet smell of straw. A lantern on a stool lights up the stables.

'Hello Juno. Bet no-one's given you a good brush down for a while.'

She whinnies and bumps against the stall, with a noise like a boxer smacking a punch-bag. He finds brushes and combs set out on a shelf at the far end and edges his way into the stall and squeezes his belly past the bulk of Juno's hind-quarters. She stretches her head round and regards him with large liquid eyes. He leans against the soft, warm coat on her neck for a long time, thinking, not thinking, his arm reaching up to her mane.

The brush fits squat in his hand. He starts with the long downward strokes, pushing with both hands and she whinnies again. He moves onto the circular strokes, working along the barrel of her chest and her flanks and onto her hind-quarters. She shifts over and he brushes along her other side and her neck. He fetches the softest brush and the cloth and rubs down her face, carefully round her eyes, her cheeks and her nose and very gently across her lips and round her mouth. She stands very still for him, a tremor running along her body from time to time.

'I'll never let Franklin have you. I swear it.'

He checks with the lantern. She still has hay and oats in the trough in front of her, and water in the wooden bucket. He crawls past it and eases himself into the space between the trough and the wall, blows out the lantern and burrows into the straw. Juno makes a sound like a human yawn and bumps the side of the stall again. He's too hungry to sleep.

When he wakes, he's ravenous. He finds hay and a pump at the end of the stable and he feeds and waters Juno and strokes her face with his hand. He undoes the bandage on his other hand and examines the scabs on fore-finger and thumb. The ache is duller and doesn't hurt when he flexes his fingers.

Later, the door opens and Sarah enters with the sunshine behind her.

'Thank you for letting me sleep here.'

She edges into the stall and talks to Juno and rests her head against the rough coat of her neck and strokes her face. He leans against the end. She watches him as if she's trying to make a decision.

'You know how to groom a horse properly.'

'It was me plaited her mane before.'

'You?'

He shrugs.

'I like plaiting.'

'Yeah, well. Luke's asleep now.'

She puts a hand on his forearm and she sobs. He moves to comfort her and she shakes her head and wipes her eyes on the back of her hand.

'Sorry. He told me about Sam. I knew him too. It was after that Luke went a bit wild.'

'I'm very sorry. Maybe I should go.'

She makes a flat farewell gesture and as he turns to go seizes him by the shoulders, presses her lips roughly against his and thrusts him away from her. He stands, desolate, and she looks down, her hair forward over her face, and he slips out round the edge of the gate.

He'll find his way back to the Enforcers and tell Ferris about the mills, about Franklin. He trusts the Commander, there's something about the way he looks at you, you know he takes what you say seriously.

When he passes the poster at the corner above the mill, Susie calls out to him from the side-street. The other kids are pressed together behind her. They fidget and stare at him, open-mouthed.

'Where's Luke?'

She speaks like she's accusing him of something.

'He's busy. Give him a couple of days.'

'I'm not a kid any more.'

'He's unhappy. One of his friends is in trouble and he can't help him – someone he loves.'

'Where is he? We should go to him.'

'Sometimes people need a little space.'

Someone pipes up:

'Let's ask Sarah.'

They stream past him and he watches them go.

An hour later he's near the mill. Three old men with full beards and thick green and pink jackets sit on a bench next to the stall, chatting and clutching cups of hot liquid. He nods to them and they fall silent and stare at him. The beat of the factory pulses through his feet, and another sound overlays it, a swelling mechanical roar, a howling, snarling, grating within it. When he looks round, the old men have gone. He follows an alley round the wall of the factory and comes out on a roadway next to a giant metal gate, topped with spikes.

The roar grows louder and he shrinks back. A broad straight road, new-laid tarmac, runs along the valley floor, cut through the residence blocks, reaching through the suburbs and the fields. He glimpses the green of the forest far away. A tumbling cloud of dust and smoke rolls towards him, two yellow eyes blazing out of it. Behind him the gate starts to grind open. He flattens himself against the wall and three road-monsters, with blank flat sides as high as the blocks, like moving fortresses, lumber past him and into the mill. The gate crashes shut. He watches the dust cloud settle and the air clear, and stills his panicked breath. The throbbing pounds all round him.

Someone touches his shoulder.

'Road-Monsters in action.'

He whirls round and Luke's there, grinning at him. Joy fizzes inside him and he throws his arms around Luke's shoulders and feels ribs thin as knife-handles.

'Luke! Thought no-one wanted me here, best I could do was go back to the City'

Susie and the kids spread round and cling onto them both.

'Susie said you were down here. Told you – you need looking after.'

David swallows. 'I'm truly sorry about Sam. Those guards, they're not my people, they're Franklin's.'

'We discussed you, Sarah and me. She said I had to look after you.'

The smile blooms, right across David's face.

'I don't know how to prove it to you. I want people to get on with each other, I want to make peace. I hate Franklin.'

A shudder runs through the children and they pull at him and Luke. He hears a rumbling, like distant thunder. It grows to a growling, then a roar.

The children scramble round the corner. Luke pushes at him:

'Get back – they're coming.'

The first road-monster is slowing now. Thoughts jumble in his head then clear, pure as ice. The gate clatters and starts to grind open behind him. He slips his arm away from Luke and walks out, his arms spread wide and faces the dazzle of its eyes. It howls, a moaning blast of sound, then howls again. He crosses both arms in front of his face and braces himself. The monster shrieks and slows and he feels the heat of its fury. It taps against him and comes to rest, grunting. He topples forwards onto hot metal and down onto the road. The stink of burning iron is all round him.

The children shout out and someone screams. He pulls himself to his knees, leaning against the monster. It starts to edge forward at him, its hideous voice blaring out again. The children are all round him. They pull at him, and Luke's with them, shouting at him. He staggers sideways and leans on the monster's flank, then stumbles back along it. It bellows and moves and he slams his hand against it and something answers him from deep inside it. He pounds again and a horse neighs within it, and another, more loudly. He hears hooves skid and trample and a heavy body thud against the carapace from within the belly of the beast.

More children pour down the hill, adults among them, their clothes bright against the dull cobbles. They yell, bang saucepans, bin-lids and ladles, and hammer and beat and batter on the creature. It creeps forward. More children pack in front of it, and it halts and howls at them, as if maddened.

He's behind it now and there's a metal gate, with a hatch the size of a house-door set in it. He wrenches it open and throws himself through. It bangs shut and he's in complete darkness, the sweet raw scent of horses all round him. Their rough shoulders and bellies and hindquarters press against him. Everywhere horses neigh and whinny and stamp their hooves. Panic surges in his breast. Something rough and powerful shoves against his face and forces him sideways. He feels a forehead nudge against his back to hold him upright. "Thank you," he mutters. He squeezes himself between two of the horses and finds himself jammed into a corner.

Outside, he hears someone shout. He's sure it's Luke. A whistle screeches out and there's an instant's silence and a whip cracks, like the sound of a slap. A child shrieks at the top of her voice. The road-beast sways and shifts forward.

He slaps the flank in front of him and heaves at it with all his strength and then smacks at the hindquarters of the creature next to him and dodges sideways. The neighing brays out louder and the horses press away from him and he shoves again, harder. They all move as one to the left, then crowd back and he feels everything lurch and twist to the right and tip over. The monster wails and stops dead and horses stumble and recover all round him. The gate at the back crashes open. He plunges to the side and horses flood past him like water racing round a rock.

One of Franklin's guards confronts them, his arms spread wide. He throws up his whip and the horses brush him aside. Another guard jabs at them with a metal pole and disappears in the cascade of horses. More of them surge round the side of the beast, black, bay, piebald, sorrel. He crouches back into the crevice at the hind end of the monster's belly. His body is bruised from head to toe and all he wants to do is laugh.

He follows the horses down the ramp and rests against the wall and looks back. The monster lies tilted in the mill-yard gateway. Its hide is torn and peeled back where the stone-work of the gate pillar has gashed it. No blood flows and the flesh is hard and jagged round the wound. The beast wheezes and its breathing labours. The gate at the back hangs open and the cavity inside is dark and empty but for a bale of dirty straw. The horses are gone. He hears the clatter of hooves and the rush of the stampede behind him.

A whip lies on the ground and a green-uniformed guard slouches back against the wall, bare-headed and cradling his arm. Another lies prone, his leg at a strange angle, moaning. His eyes fix on David's and he stretches out an arm, offering his wristband. The trample of booted feet, stamping towards him, echoes from the mill.

Someone shouts:

'Move!' an arm grabs him and whirls him round and he stumbles up the hill and into an alley and Sarah holds him close to her.

'What did you do that for? You could have been killed.'

His head clears.

'What else could I do?'

'Come on.'

'Sarah, wait.'

She stares at him.

'I did it so you'd trust me. Franklin's taking all the horses. What he does is brutal, monstrous.'

'Come on, we have to go.'

She tugs at him and they scramble onwards through alleyways, across small squares and up the street he strode down earlier, to come out at the corner with the poster. The whole road is packed with children and adults from the Old Town. David recognises the woman from the band, taller than almost everybody, O'Connor, the silver-bearded man in the velvet robe, one of the cooks whom he remembered because he enjoyed his food so much and the drummer, grinning and lifting up a tankard of ale to toast him.

Luke throws an arm round his shoulders.

'You made it! That's so good what you did.'

The velvet-gowned man forces his way through the press of people. He holds out his hand and grips David's. His hands are large and rough, as if he's a carpenter or a woodsman.

'Thank you very much indeed. We're proud of you. We confer on you honorary citizenship of the Old Town.'

He stands to one side and holds up David's arm. The whole crowd starts to cheer and clap. Someone tries to organise "Three cheers for David", but the shouts are engulfed in a tempest of yelling and hooting and whistling and applause. David bursts out laughing and waves both hands. Juno's there, with Sarah holding the reins, and he buries his face in the warm coat of her neck and his heart calms.

O'Connor gestures to them.

'You must go. Now. The Greenjackets will be after you.'

His eyes are suddenly those of a businessman making a deal.

Luke embraces him again. Sarah swings herself up on Juno's back and reaches down to him and he hauls himself half onto the hindquarters and slides forwards. Luke shoves at him and he wriggles sideways and Sarah pulls at his arm and he sits behind her and grins round at everyone. He feels Sarah shake the reins and nudge Juno with her knees. The crowd parts and they walk forward. People reach up to touch him and Sarah.

Luke runs behind shouting farewell.

'See you soon!' he shouts and waves and prays it is so. The crowd starts to thin out. People scatter and soon only Luke is left, waving both arms to him. A siren howls from the Pit and Luke turns and runs to one side. David's last sight of the Old Town is Franklin staring at him from the poster, torn across just under the eyes, as high as a child could reach.

Sarah's Journey

Sarah rises in the stirrups and urges Juno forwards. David grips the back of the saddle, the wind in his face, and thinks of Luke and the children and the battle with the beast. They gallop out of the Old Town and thunder through a district of wooden sheds and barns and ramshackle huts. People come out and stare up at them with white hungry faces.

Other horses, black, grey, brown and sorrel, the horses from inside the road-monster, stand by the road or straggle along behind. People dash after them with ropes or leather straps and try to catch them. A young bare-foot woman in a long ragged skirt of green and red pitches a home-made lasso at a bay mare and claps her hands as it catches on one ear. The mare shakes her head, the noose slips off and she turns and bares her teeth at the woman who shrinks back from her.

The roadway becomes rougher, in places no more than rutted mud between the paved areas. Gaps open between the buildings with grass or market gardens or rows of vegetables in them. The horses are everywhere. They crop at the vegetables, shoulder over the canes for the bean plants and trample everything. An older woman hurls a three-legged stool at a small spotted horse with a bedraggled white mane. It shies away and canters onto the road and neighs and falls in behind Juno.

None of the horses are the size of Juno and they look up and whicker in greeting and start to walk and trot towards her. Juno shakes her head and neighs and sometimes whinnies back. A troop forms round her, forcing the people back towards the barns and sheds and the garden fences. Behind them more horses stream in. He looks back as the dust-cloud behind them grows larger and larger.

Sarah shouts over her shoulder:

'The horses from the road-monster – they're coming with us.'

The smile is back on her lips and his heart lightens. Fields of yellow squash and potato plants and, once, red roses stretch out on each side. Tall poles with young vines twisting round them mark out a hop field. Their way now runs along a dirt track. No more houses stand beside it and they press onwards. The last building he sees is a swaybacked barn, with one end fallen sideways. A small child, naked, stands at the door with her hand to her mouth and stares up at him.

They ride on, into the countryside, between larger fields, most of them plough land. They're now on a by-way and the horses from the road-beast follow on behind, in single file, occasionally stopping to crop at the grass. The sun breaks through the clouds. In some places the winter wheat is in, yellowing. In the distance a team of horses with well-muscled shoulders and hindquarters like Juno but not so large, pull at a plough. The ploughman rides on the tail of the share to hold it down and white birds cluster noisily behind it.

The hedge-rows are thick with brambles. Sarah reins Juno in and reaches down and picks a handful of blackberries and passes sweet, globed fruit back to him. They chew at it with purple-stained lips. A ragged scratch runs across the back of her hand. He takes it and binds a handkerchief round it although she doesn't really need it. Her eyes are on his. She withdraws her hand and he feels Juno shift restlessly beneath them and they press on.

Later, when the sun is overhead, they pass down a grassy bank into a wooded cleft with a stream rolling over rocks at the bottom. He hears birdsong and a charm of small brightly-coloured finches flies up and lodges in one of the trees. Sarah slips one leg over Juno's back and dismounts. He copies her, his leg won't go high enough and he topples sideways. She catches him and sets him on his feet and giggles.

'We'll let the horses eat. Poor Juno. She's tired and we've a way to go.'

He doesn't ask where they are going. The air's chill under the trees and his thighs ache, and his back, and his neck.

The crisp sound of horses busy cropping grass encircles them. She hands him a cup and he moves to the stream and finds a place where he can dip it, lying prone to stretch out his thighs. Horses drink thirstily on both sides of him. He brings her some water and then gets some for himself. She tears a small sourdough loaf in half.

'Didn't have time to get much.'

He rolls the mouthful of bread round against his teeth and swallows.

'Tastes wonderful. Did you bake it?'

'Nope.'

She sits with her back against a tree with golden leaves and white blotches on the bark. He squats down beside her.

'You know, I want to explain, in the City, we aren't all on Franklin's side. I just wanted to make things fair, to help people.'

'There's more to life than trade and bargains and willing buyer and willing seller. Let's talk later. I'm tired.'

She is almost instantly asleep. He can't sleep for the soreness in his body. He gets to his feet and walks stiff-legged over to Juno and leans into her neck and reaches up and grasps her mane. He feels easier, as if a burden is taken from him.

'Things I don't understand, Juno. But I'm learning. And I want to be here.'

She tears at the grass by his feet.

Something tickles his cheek and he swats at it. It's back at his ear and he opens his eyes. Sarah laughs at him. She's teasing him with a blade of grass.

'First person I've met who can sleep standing up, like a horse. Sun's well past midday. We need to get going. It's another couple of hours.'

She swings herself up onto Juno's back, and hauls him up behind her. He's beginning to get the idea, but still lurches over to the far side and has to slip an arm round her waist. They ride up a path the other side of the stream, with the other horses following in single file. The track leads them to the edge of the grasslands and into pine forest. It's darker and colder among the trees as if night comes early here. They cross a wider track with wheel-ruts in it. He recognises it.

'I've been here before.'

'Yes. Just up there is where you lot tried to ambush me.'

'Not my idea.'

'Sure.'

'This was as far as we came on patrols. It was for training. To toughen us up.'

'Did it work?'

He regards the bank and the dark trees beyond it. There are no birds. Once he wanted to be an Enforcer. It doesn't matter.

'Where are we going?'

'My village. Coneystone, nearest village to the City. It's safe there. They like horses.'

The track turns a corner and runs down a slope. Horses flow down on both sides and suddenly he feels proud of what he's done. They turn another corner and he sees the first hut. It's solidly built of undressed tree-trucks, laid horizontal, with a rough boarded roof. Other huts, set at angles to the track, are spaced out beyond it. The trees have been cut back all round the village and there's an open area in the middle with a roof supported on undressed tree trunks, and a brick hearth and chimney at one end. He guesses all the people in the village could meet there and maybe cook themselves a feast together. Over to the side is a long shed with a high doorway, a stable block.

Nobody comes out to meet them. The horses spread out on both sides and start cropping at grass again. The cottager in the first cabin has fenced off an area behind her dwelling and planted a garden – beans, leeks, onions and gooseberry bushes and a cherry tree at the end. A large bay leans over the fence and tears at a cabbage and others press in behind it.

'Are they hiding?' he asks.

'Not from us. I don't like it.'

She slides down and stands by Juno holding the bridle. He slips off and lands on both feet, jarring his knees. The only sounds are the chewing of the horses and Juno's breathing and the wind among the pine trees. He smells the resinous odour.

A sharp rap sounds out from behind a cabin on their right. They crouch and move towards it. He puts up a hand and inches along the wall. The cabin backs onto the forest. He ducks his head out to look and straightens and strolls round the end of the building. A branch slaps against the corner of the roof with a sound like a door-knocker. Sarah reaches up and twists the tip and breaks it off.

'They've gone.'

She strides past the cottages, pushing at doors to peer inside. She finishes in the middle and shouts out:

'Anybody home?'

'They didn't lock up?'

'We don't do that. My father's house is over there.'

The hut is smaller than the others and set away from them beyond the stables and at an angle so that it faces the forest, not the open area in the middle. It has a small veranda, with steps up to it and three bentwood chairs. She pushes open the door. Inside there are four rooms. Everything is clean and the embroidered coverlet is pulled back to air the bedding. He stands in the kitchen by the table while she pulls open cupboard doors and sniffs at the stove. Containers of food are stacked at the side and there's a basket of eggs and a bucket of water by the sink. She dips her finger in and tastes it.

'Fresh. They haven't been gone long.'

'Juno's tired. Let's stay here. Sort things out in the morning.'

'We'll bolt the shutters and wedge the door.'

Sarah opens the stables and scares a family of picnicking rats away. They feed the horses with hay from the racks. He finds some dried oats and they share those out and haul up buckets of water from the well. Later he brushes Juno down and she watches him as he wipes her face with a flannel cloth. The mare lowers her head and he puts his face against hers.

By the time they're finished it's dark. He looks up at stars, impossibly distant and dusted across a cloudless sky with no moon. They cook eggs and potatoes and fresh mushrooms, and a kind of swede she finds that tastes of carrots. His whole body aches and his belly is sated and he wonders what he saw in bacon rolls.

She hands him an apple.

'See? You'd recognise this taste anywhere. You can't blame me for losing my temper.'

She holds him close against her and he swallows the mouthful of apple and bends down his head and she presses her face into his shoulder then releases him.

'I'll take the bed. I'll get you some blankets and a mattress here on the floor.'

He wakes in the night and eases the door open. A full

moon shines out over the clearing, silvering the pines and the cabin roofs and the grass. He listens for a long time and hears an owl hoot in the forest and another answer. That's what woke him.

The Moot

The sun is a great yellow ball, too bright to look at, floating just above the tree-tops. Shadows fill the clearing in front of the hut. David hears a rustling, the sound someone might make if they were trying to creep silently through long grass. He is fully awake. Nothing moves in front of the window but outside wood raps on wood. He pushes the door half-open so he can peer through the gap.

A man wearing a tall felt hat leans against the post at the top of the veranda steps. He wears a brown cloak, but David can't make out his face in the shadow. A girl, nine or ten years old, in a bright blue cloak stands beside him. He rests a hand on her shoulder. He nods, leans and swings himself forward, taking his weight on a long oak staff. David shoves the door fully open.

'Good morning.'

The man halts, balanced on his staff.

'What are you doing in my house?'

'You'd better take a seat.'

The girl stares at David, then glances over his shoulder. A smile lights up her face and her cheeks dimple and he knows who she is.

Sarah bursts past him, with a striped red and white blanket wrapped round her shoulders and her hair loose.

'Dad – and Annie! Wow! Wonderful to see you!'

She flings an arm round the girl and pulls her tight against her breast and rests her other arm along the man's shoulders, folding them both inside the blanket. The girl speaks in a light musical voice, addressing Sarah:

'Daddy was worried about you. That's why we came back.'

The man slides a hand round her and pats her.

'Sal! Good to see you back home, girl.'

Sarah glances over her shoulder:

'David meet my family: my father, Jeb Cordell, and my sister Annie. I was only supposed to be away overnight. You are not allowed to call me Sal.'

David bows.

'Very pleased to meet you, Mr Cordell, and you, Ms Annie Cordell.'

He sees the likeness between Sarah and her father, but where she is light and merry, her mouth hardly ever still, her feelings obvious in her face, he is dark and sober, with grim lips and serious eyes.

She sits them at the table, but Annie springs up and helps her, making a kind of porridge with herbs he doesn't recognise and with berries in it. She places mugs of a warm drink, like coffee but not coffee, on the table. He tries to join in but he doesn't know where anything is and she tells him to sit down.

'She was always the brave one,' says Jeb. 'That's why she wanted to take the produce in, though they said she shouldn't. And then we were called to the Meeting, but I had to come back, just to see if she'd turned up.'

He smiles at her.

'Yes,' says Annie, 'and there are men in green suits and a big fat man with funny hair who talks all the time and keeps giving out sweets but he's not nice. He wanted to pat my head, but I wouldn't let him.'

David smiles at her.

'You're as clever as your sister.'

Sarah leans on the dresser and looks at her father.

'What's going on?'

Jeb pulls at his ear.

'I'm not sure. He says he wants to help. Build roads, a school, a hospital, give us jobs. Make us all richer. He's a good talker.'

'Do you trust him?'

'I don't know.'

Annie ladles porridge into pottery bowls glazed a lustrous blue. David puts them on the table and licks spillage from his finger. He chips in:

'I know who he is. He's a good talker alright but Annie's right. He gives out sweets, but he's not a nice man.'

'He says his name's Franklin. There's a moot about it over at Pettiford.'

Sarah sniffs. Her father continues:

'The moots are always at Pettiford. Just cos they're nearest the Old Road and the market's there, they think they own the other villages. That road. It's a curse.'

Sarah hands round spoons.

'Eat up. We ought to go. I wouldn't trust Franklin if he promised Juno fresh oats every day for life.'

David feels a chill seep into him.

'Don't ever trust him. Don't ever work for him. You've never seen the inside of one of his mills.'

They leave the horses to rest and follow a narrow path between trees with scaly trunks. Overhead the leaves form a canopy through which sunshine filters to dapple the ground ahead of them. The air is heavy with the scent of pine. Sarah and Annie walk behind and chatter, both of them talking at once. David helps Jeb along when he can, but most of the time the old man won't have it.

He slaps his staff into the ground. 'You from the City? That's where I got this. Horse stepped on my foot. They said it was my fault.

'Yes, Daddy used to take the crops into the Old Town,' calls Sarah from behind.'

'More fool me. So my girl took 'em this year. Told her to leave it, but she never listens to me – do you?'

'We need to keep friends with the Old Town.'

'Yeah, what have they ever done for us? She's a good girl, but headstrong.' Jeb flashes a glance at David. 'Anyway, that Franklin came with his green-coats making all sorts of promises – and here we are.'

The path opens out into a larger clearing, already packed with villagers, women, men, children, older people, one or two on crutches, babies in slings. More stream in from every side. Everyone wears their best clothes, the bright colours that people wear in the Old Town, like the plumage of birds in spring.

The huts are larger than those in Sarah's village, some of them with two storeys, one with an outside staircase, and are grouped on the other side of the clearing. A trackway runs along the nearer edge and a conveyance of a kind David has never seen before stands on it. It's a light two-wheeled cart, dark in colour and glossy, but it has a striped green and white canopy to shade the passengers, and seats like armchairs with padded cushions. The slender shafts tilt down and rest on the grass. A groom, dressed in green and wearing a green jockey cap, fusses with a dappled mare beside it.

Annie points:

'Down there you get to the Road. We don't go there.'

Sarah frowns:

'Franklin's world.'

The meeting has already started. They join the crowd at the back and people nod and make room for them. An older woman in a brown knitted shawl says something to Sarah and smiles at Annie. Others look round. Their faces light up when they see Sarah. They murmur greetings, shake hands or touch her arm.

A voice booms out.

'My friends. I'm here to help you, but I won't pretend to help you for nothing. We will go forward hand in hand.'

Franklin stands on a makeshift platform of wooden tables dragged together. He is dressed in a chequered red and black and orange jacket, and a round red hat with a feather in it. He's done his homework, David thinks, and he's brought his own PA system.

He whispers:

'He looks like a giant turkey-cock.'

'Game-cock more like. He struts.'

'Shhh!'

More people press in behind them. He feels stifled.

Somewhere in front of him the voice goes on:

'... The tractor will be yours to keep. I want you to learn how much easier your lives will be if you help me. A simple deal: sell me your land and you will have more money than you have ever had in your lives. I'll give you a fair price. Ask anyone. I always pay a fair price.'

'Yeah. Trust him and you'll trust anyone,' mutters David.

The older woman frowns at him.

'Shhh! I want to listen.'

Franklin smiles, showing his teeth and holds up a roll of paper.

'Here's the contract: one side of paper, that can't hurt you. Do a deal with me, you'll all be able to buy tractors, two tractors each. Would any of you like to ask a question?'

People swarm in on all sides. For a moment David feels the panic that gripped him among the horses in the belly of the road-beast. He hears Sarah's voice and forces himself to listen.

'I've been to the Old Town. I know what they think about Franklin there. Please don't trust him – he'll trick you. He makes machines out of horses.'

Someone else is talking though the microphone. People hush Sarah.

A young man in a cream drape jacket turns:

'Shut up, that's Caleb. He's our Chief Elder in case you don't know.'

Jeb pokes him with his staff.

'That's my daughter you're talking to.'

Others turn and glare at him and Sarah. She meets their gaze.

'I can look after myself. You can't trust Franklin.'

Caleb talks slowly with a wheeze. It's sometimes hard to make out what he says:

'My friends. We are simple villagers. We are not used

to doing business with people from the city. We need to think this over.'

'Yes.' Sarah waves her arms. 'Listen to me! I know Franklin. He'll take your land and you'll have no choice. You'll work on his farms and you'll have nothing but what he pays you and what will that be worth?'

The older man on the platform turns away from her.

'Mr Franklin, please excuse our country ways. Young women can be very excitable.'

A woman with a baby in a sling shouts:

'Yeah and old men can be stupid and forget they're left the microphone on.'

People titter. Franklin holds up his hands.

'Never let it be said I don't argue my case. You disagree with me? Come up here and state your views. Let her through. Let's hear you properly.'

Caleb starts to protest, but Franklin makes a calming gesture and beckons Sarah forward.

'Let her though.'

People edge to one side and a gap opens in the crowd. David follows behind. Near the platform a group of children in yellow and mauve and pink dungarees wave and call out to her and the men and women with them smile. A woman with a baby in a sling leans forward to pat Sarah's arm.

'Good luck!'

That's the voice that called out, thinks David. Optimism glows within him, like a candle-flame.

Franklin bends and offers a hand to pull her onto the platform, but she shakes her head and scrambles up. David is at the front of the crowd. He turns and looks back at the upturned faces, like a field of cauliflowers.

'Thank you.'

Sarah's voice, louder than ever he's heard it, comes from behind him.

'You all know me. Sarah Cordell. I'm from Coneystone. You know I speak the truth. You know I've been to the City.'

People start cheering and applauding. Someone among the women with the children starts a chant:

'Sarah! Sarah!'

Sarah spreads her arms and quiets them. She is a good head taller than Franklin, a falcon beside a game-cock.

'Mr Franklin is a very rich man and he didn't get rich by being generous. He wants your land. He says he'll pay you for it. He'll even give you his machine. What's he going to get out of it? You can't trust him'

She pauses and looks round at them all and continues:

'He owns most of the City, now he wants to own the forest. He wants to own our villages. He wants to own the woods and the fields and everything in them. He wants to own the whole world, and he will if we let him. Don't sell anything to him. You'll turn round and you'll find you have nothing left but the money and you can't eat that. Then he'll own you.'

David thumps his hands together and others take up the applause. Franklin steps forward smiling.

'Ms Cordell. You have many hard things to say about me. I don't hold them against you.'

He looks down, then back at his audience.

'But where is your evidence? I believe in trade. I love a good bargain. Who doesn't? I'll bet you do.'

He grins his wolf's grin and a cheer comes up from a group of men in work clothes over to the side of the clearing. A bulky figure in a brown leather jacket with a fleece collar stands at the centre of the group and claps, smacking his palms hard together. He has untidy black hair and a full sailor's beard. Sarah stares directly at him.

Franklin spreads his hands palms out.

'But all this about wanting to own everything. Honestly, I've never thought about it. About owning people?' He surveys them, as if trying to look each of them in the eye. 'Really? Have you any evidence?'

'Yes of course I do. You run the police force in the Old Town, you can't deny it. We call them Greenjackets. They beat people. Everybody knows your police kidnap anyone out after dark. You make them into slaves in your mills and we never see them again.'

'Ah. Something everybody knows. But I don't.'

He sweeps his arm out over the audience and lowers his voice.

'Do you know?'

A moment's silence and he continues before anyone answers:

'Policing a city is not easy. My officers keep order in the Old Town, they protect citizens. There are criminals in this world, you know that, there are bad people. We arrest them and train them in our re-education academy. All according to the Law. What is wrong with that? Perhaps your informants had fallen foul of the police. You should be careful about the company you keep.'

Someone laughs and Sarah glares at the group of men.

'You kidnap them and we never see them again. My

friend, Luke Ibsen, has seen your men take them, at night in the Old Town.'

Franklin claps his hands, like the crack of a whip.

'Young lady, I must interrupt. I am sure you believe what you say. But …slavery? Your friend has seen it? Really? Am I expected to answer this? It is ridiculous. Have any of you met this Luke Ibsen? Do you know him? This is hearsay.'

Someone shouts: 'No!' then 'Luke who? What sort of a name is that?'

The knot of men applaud. They clap and cheer and whistle. People shout at them to quieten down but they don't stop. They push their way nearer to the platform.

David waves his arms.

'Listen to me! Sarah's right. Don't trust him.'

Someone shoves into him and he stumbles away from the platform, only held up by the people round him. The women in front of him gather their children close to them.

Sarah raises her voice.

'You make horses into machines. David Ashwood here has seen that with his own eyes. You turn normal horses into monsters – beasts with iron legs and metal hooves.'

She keeps on talking, repeating herself, but now the laughter of the pack drowns out her words. Franklin's grin broadens into a chuckle. He takes the microphone from her.

'More ridiculous lies! I try to breed better horses. Don't we all? But monsters, half-horse, half-machine? What on earth is that? I have no idea what you are talking about.'

Sarah stares round and frowns as if she is being tricked but can't see how.

Franklin smiles his wolf's smile and offers to shake her

hand. She ignores him. He turns to the audience and rubs his hands together.

'Enough of this nonsense. Let's move on. Believe me, I want to do the right thing. I want to help you. I will discuss the details with the Council of Elders. Meanwhile I invite you to my demonstration. My tractor will show what it can do for you to make your lives better.'

He pauses and looks round at them.

'Remember, now is your chance. You'll regret it for the rest of your lives if you turn me down today.'

He throws an arm round Caleb's shoulders. The older man flinches and grimaces.

The men surge forward to the platform. They grasp the edge and start to rock it. Sarah staggers, regains her footing and pitches forward. David reaches out and catches her in his arms. He sets her on her feet and hugs her. Tears mark her cheeks. She dashes them away:

'I hate that man.'

David releases her and she shouts to anyone who'll listen:

'Don't trust him. If you sell your land he'll make you his workers and then his slaves. You'll have nothing.'

People turn their backs and the crowd streams past them onto the track that leads away from the Great Road. The woman with the baby in the sling finds her way through and clasps Sarah's hand again, then slips her arms round her and hugs her.

'You did good. At least someone speaks out for us. Caleb is a waste of space.'

Something roars out, then slackens to a growl, a sound like the whelp of the beast that swallowed David outside the mill howling for its mother. A tremor runs through the crowd.

Annie pushes past him.

'Are you OK?'

She slips off her cloak and swirls it round Sarah. It comes to her waist. She smiles.

'Annie. I do love you.'

Someone pokes him from the side. Jeb's too close to him. He smells garlic on the older man's breath.

'What you been doing to look after her, eh? Sounds like you made a fool of yourself in that Old Town. Never trusted City folk.'

Sarah turns to him.

'I told you I don't need looking after. Come on, we need to see this.'

She takes Annie's hand and leads her after the villagers. David picks up a child's shoe lying in the mud, white with a single strap, and wipes it. He thinks of the baby in the sling and hangs it on a hawthorn bush.

Jeb calls out:

'Who's going to give me a hand, then?'

He goes back for the older man and puts his arm out for the other to grasp, and they totter after the others. He glances back and he sees a figure in a jockey cap standing on the track some way back, hands on hips, watching them.

He nudges Jeb.

'That's Franklin's groom. Why's he staring at us?'

'Who cares? He don't know much about horses – see the way he's put the harness on that nag? He's got the girths too tight. Keep that up, she'll have sores on her belly and you'll get no carriage work out of her.'

David glances back but the figure has gone.

The Yellow Beast

Franklin's tractor is a yellow beast with huge rear wheels
and tiny front ones. The great chest throbs with life but
it has no belly, like a greyhound. Blue smoke issues
from a pipe in its side in a thin stream and it stinks of
hot oil and burning charcoal. The creature judders, as if
chafing at a tether. Heat pours out of it. Harnessed with
a leather strap to the hook behind it is a wagon loaded
with straw.

Jeb spits and remarks: 'No-one's putting a monster like
that in my barn', to anyone near enough to hear.

One of Franklin's men, clad in white overalls and
yellow gloves, sits perched up high on the beast, holding
twisted metal reins. Another, bearded as if he didn't know
what a razor was, stands in front of it. He broadcasts a grin
to them all, the grin of a stock-breeder who is proud of the
beast he brings to the show.

'I'm Tom. Gather round. It's perfectly safe. We have
absolute control. We call it a tractor. It's a machine, we
made it in our workshop... our smithy. We have many
other machines.'

'What breed of beast is that?' shouts a broad-chested
young man in checked tweeds and matching flat cap, with
polished leather gaiters on his calves.

'It's not exactly a breed, it's a contrivance, a device, made of metal by artificers, more like a plough or a clock. It'll make your life easier.'

Tom thinks for a moment.

'You must have seen the wagons that go by themselves on the Road over there? They're Franklin's.'

A tremor runs through the crowd and they edge back as one. Someone hisses 'Road-monsters.'

A young woman with long dark hair in a moss green cloak calls out: 'Crippled Jo and Terry's little boy three month's back. Smashed him. Didn't stop. No-one'll go there these days.'

'Except my Sal,' mutters Jeb.

'There's absolutely nothing to be frightened of.' Tom lays a hand on the wheel beside him, which stands as high as his head. 'OK Derek. Let's go.'

The beast roars again and throws itself forward. Everyone flinches away from it. The young man in tweeds slips and sprawls. A woman in a long blue skirt and blouse and a straw hat next to him laughs and says something and helps him to his feet.

Tom waves his hands. 'Enough! Easy! Just edge it forward a bit.'

The creature sighs and lets out a rumble, as if it's hungry, and moves forward, at the pace of a heavy horse walking. The villagers follow at a distance.

Tom raises his voice:

'You see? Perfectly well schooled. Does just what we say. Now would anyone like a ride in my hay-cart?'

Jeb spits again:

'That's straw. You try feeding your nag on that.'

Tom laughs:

'Sorry. But you'll only need horses for show when you've got these. Come on, roll up! It's perfectly safe, I'll show you.'

He hauls himself up on the back of the moving cart, edges forward and gets to his feet, swaying from side to side with the motion. The crowd follows behind. Tom waves and pitches forward and disappears into the straw. His head pokes up a second later with yellow strands stuck in his hair. He blows the straw out of his mouth and grins.

'You see, perfectly safe. Stop so they can climb on, Derek. Who's first?'

The beast judders to a halt and growls. Tom reaches out to the woman in the straw hat and she shrugs and seizes his hand and clambers up. The young man in tweeds follows her and soon the cart is cram-full of women, men and children, shouting and waving to those still on the track, as if they're setting off on a Saturday afternoon jaunt.

Sarah watches, her face stern.

'Franklin. He's as cunning as a weasel. That beast stinks!'

The beast jerks forward and they follow on behind.

The track turns a corner and in front of them it narrows and drops down to the river-crossing. The children squeal and scramble for hand-holds as the wagon lurches onto the slope. It reaches the bottom and starts forward, the water reaching half-way up the huge wheels. A little black haired boy in a blue felt jacket cranes out over the tail-board, staring into the turbulence behind.

David rushes forward and splashes into the water.

'Hold on!'

He's already half way across when the wagon bumps into the far bank, sways and tilts up over it. The child tumbles headfirst into the water and bobs up a second later some way downstream. David throws himself forward, grabs at an ankle and hauls him out. The boy stares open-mouthed at David as the water drips from him.

David gasps and lifts him up to his mum who clasps him close. The child wriggles against her, opens his mouth even wider and wails as if Christmas had been cancelled. David stands with the river up to his thighs and brushes water from his sleeves as the wagon lurches away from him and the yellow beast roars louder as it heaves itself up the slope. One of the villagers starts a song about horses and the others take it up. David makes his way back to Sarah, and Jeb and Annie on the far bank.

Later the beast drags the wagon back through the ford. Tom sits at the front of it, a mug of beer in his hand. The others are singing away and there seem to be even more villagers packed in and a barrel of beer from somewhere balanced on the tail-board. A voice rings out as it reaches the foot of the slope up to the track, the voice of someone who knows he's right before he's told you what he's got to say.

'Listen everyone.'

The bearded man in the leather jacket stands at the top of the slope, hands on hips.

'Let's celebrate. Feast in the marketplace, courtesy of Mr Franklin.'

A cheer goes up from a group of villagers standing on the bank. David looks round at them. He hadn't realised how many they were. People start to climb back up the slope.

The bearded man beams down at them.

'We're all going to be rich and buy tractors! The Council of Elders have signed the deal with Mr Franklin. Come on. Celebration!'

'But you can't do that!' yells Sarah. 'Caleb never asked us what we thought.'

The man shrugs.

'You should have been there. We've done it.'

He turns his back. The beast gives tongue, a long baying sound, and roars past them. The little boy waves at David from inside his mother's shawl. Sarah watches them as they move away from her.

'It's not over.'

She starts forward and stumbles on a loose stone. Annie draws closer to her and helps her up the path.

Someone's strung bunting, red, yellow and green pennants and green and yellow banners from the trees round the clearing. The tables are spread with food – great cauldrons of bean stew, a giant marrow, stuffed with onion and tomatoes and rice, a pyramid of chickpea fritters, dishes of swedes, cabbages, beetroot, and potato chips, and bowls of hazelnuts and roast chestnuts. The rich and varied aroma of garlic compounded with fennel and pepper rises up over it all.

At one end Franklin sits with Caleb and other women and men in purple, orange and yellow robes, older people, most of them portly, their eyes on the food. The Council, thinks David.

Villagers pass round plates piled high with food and flagons of beer. A baritone starts to sing a song about harvest home and the others take it up.

The young man in the drape jacket gestures to them with a beer mug.

'Don't stand there like you've lost your favourite chicken. Come and enjoy yourselves!'

Sarah ignores him. Jeb grunts. 'I'm tired. I've no stomach for this. It's getting dark.'

She yawns. 'Me too.'

'You did good, girl. I'm proud of you. They were just too many for you. Let's get back.'

Little Mikey

David looks back across the clearing. Something moves in among the trees on the far side, where the track runs towards the Road. Franklin's conveyance is still where it was but there's no sign of the groom. The mare is hobbled and munches at her feed in a canvas nosebag. She edges sideways to keep her back in the last rays of sunshine and whisks her tail. That's not what caught his eye.

The sun is now behind the trees and shadows stretch out across the track. Within the forest it's already black night but he has the impression of something shifting among the trees, the shuffle a restless horse, compelled to keep still and silent, might make. He stares into the gloom. Shadows lengthen. He sees nothing more.

He touches Sarah's arm.

'Franklin's up to something. We need to get back to the City, tell the Enforcers. The yellow beast, all that food – any gift is a breach of the One Law. They'll listen to us now.'

She shakes her head.

'We need to get Dad home. We'll talk later.'

Night has now fallen in the forest. He has the sensation of walking into an unlit cavern as they follow the track between the trees. He lags back to help Jeb but the old man twists away from him and stumps on at his own pace. David trails behind. A thought smoulders within him: *You wanted to be the one who brought the City and the Old Town and the villages together, you wanted to be the one who built trust, who was respected. You've just seen a real deal-maker in action.*

The trees reach up and in places join overhead. Sarah and Annie are some way ahead. A night-bird hoots, a dull, base note, repeated. Another answers, just to the side of him. He looks back, into blackness. He hears a creature rustle through the leaves, loud in the silence, and he thinks of Franklin's beast, only tiny and become something that slithers and pounces. He shivers and takes the old man's arm.

'Let's get back.'

Jeb doesn't answer, but he doesn't shake him off. When they reach Coneystone a yellow half-moon has risen. Nothing moves. He hears the horses shifting in the stables but the forest is still.

He takes buckets of water and bundles of hay across to them. It's warm among them and the closeness of the beasts and the rhythm of their breathing eases him. *One thing I like about you, you don't judge me,* he thinks. He lingers a while talking to Juno, telling her about the moot and Sarah and the yellow beast, talking out loud.

'You'd have been proud of her.'

She watches him with intelligent eyes.

'I'll come early tomorrow. We've got a journey to go, you and I. Fresh grass. I won't let you down. Goodnight.'

For some reason he makes sure the stable-door is fastened and props a baulk of timber across it and checks it. He inspects the earth on the tracks into the clearing for hoof-prints but doesn't find anything.

When he gets back to the cottage, they're all at table, bean and hazel-nut fritters and grilled tomatoes, and stewed apple with currants and slivers of almond in it. He clears his plate and leans back in his chair.

'That was good. I must cook sometime.'

'Hooray!' says Annie.

'I'm starting back for the City tomorrow.'

'But you won't have a chance to cook. Don't go.'

Jeb scowls:

'What good has that lot ever done us?'

Sarah takes his empty plate.

'Don't you remember, in that café? I said maybe I'd show you my village. Don't go.'

Her dad sniffs.

'So he should stay here. You can do some real work. Harden your hands up a bit.'

She turns to the sink.

'We'll talk in the morning. Annie, bed-time. David, washing up.'

He squirms in the narrow bed and the covers scratch at his skin. In the night, a cool wind rises and blows the shutters open. He gets up to close them and watches. The trees sway and toss their branches like men and women crowded together and uncertain what to do, but nothing moves in the clearing.

Later he falls into troubled sleep. He hears Sarah cry out to him from far away. The sound blurs and echoes in his dream as if she's trapped underground. He lies on wet grass, unable to rise. A mob surrounds him and glares and snarls: "City-man! Charlatan! Trickster! Fraud!" Ferris, his head inclined, pushes through them and smiles down at him: 'We know we can rely on you.' Greenjackets in insect helmets paw him and pinion his arms in a mesh of rods and cylinders. They weld a helmet to his head and he squints out through eye-slits.

Franklin sneers at him: 'Everybody trusts me! Me! Me!' and looms over him, closer and closer. All he can see is the mouth, snarling and then bellowing with laughter. A shutter slams down and traps him in darkness with the guffaws, and he is laughing too, and the whole world giggles, chuckles, chortles and bays with mockery. The noise pounds and batters him and he's imprisoned in the helmet and cannot fight back.

He wakes and the wind has gone and he closes his eyes and tumbles into sleep once more.

Something plucks at the edge of his consciousness. He twists in the bed, in a tangle of sheets and covers, then is instantly awake. The air in the house is different, there's a hollowness to it. He hears the sound again, a rap, the sound a billiard ball makes when it strikes another.

He slides out of bed and pads to the door, pulls it ajar and peers through the slit between door and jamb and shivers. The outer door hangs open. Light streams in from a full moon above the tree-tops. Something black lies across the threshold. The hair rises on his scalp. The thing becomes a person, a woman. She grunts and heaves herself up and raps at the door once and sighs and falls back and sobs.

He kneels in the doorway and holds her in his arms. She's bundled in a ragged cloak. She stares up at him with dull eyes and licks her lips and gasps:

'Help him. Please. Help Michael.'

The cloak slips open and he sees the baby held against her and the red blotches, the size of florins, on her hands and face.

Sarah is next to him. She lifts the woman and he takes the child. She carries the woman through and lays her on her own bed. The baby gazes at him with blue eyes as if he is the only thing in the world and scrabbles at him with starfish hands. He feels love for the child well up deep within him. The child starts to weep, a tiny grizzling noise. He settles down on the floor next to the bed with the baby clasped to his breast and whispers to him:

'Your mummy loves you very, very much.'

Annie comes through with warm milk in a pan. She tests it with her elbow and offers the baby a teaspoonful. He stops crying for a few seconds and splutters and coughs and cries louder. The woman next to him on the bed stirs and murmurs something and falls back into deep sleep. He wipes his forefinger and dips it in the milk and places it between the baby's lips and feels the tongue trap it against the roof of the mouth and the tiny body suck at it. He gives him another finger-load and another and another, and the baby grows calmer in his arms. Annie holds the spoon delicately against his lips and he turns his head and sips. They feed him more and more and he takes the food as if it was nectar.

Much later, dawn gleams far to the east and birds call out in the forest around them. The baby sleeps. Annie offers to take him but he hugs the baby tighter against him, as if he could warm him with his body. He feels a calm, like sunrise over a great ocean, wash within him.

Much later he wakes from a light sleep. The baby stirs in his arms. Sarah smiles at him.

'You do look sweet, but I think it's change time after all that milk. Maybe I should take him. The mother's deep asleep and I haven't the heart to wake her.'

He shakes his head. 'I can groom a horse, I can change a nappy.'

She has a mat and a bowl of water on the floor. Annie warms towels in front of the stove.

He rises from the bed and slides into a sitting position next to the bowl and starts to unwrap the cloths from round the body in his lap. Sarah helps him. The baby gazes up and for the first time looks round the room and then back at him. A tiny hand bats against his and the fingers fasten tight around his forefinger. He pulls the last layer of cloth gently away from the chest and the rounded tummy.

Sarah sits beside him.

'His mother is very poorly. I tried to feed her, but she won't take anything. She's barely awake.'

He strokes his hand over the tummy. His fingers are so coarse.

'Look. He's smiling at me.'

'Wind.'

He lifts the tiny figure up from the stained cloth and lowers him gently towards the water. The baby starts to grizzle and turn his head and his foot brushes the water. He stops crying and his face wrinkles. David thinks of a puzzled old man. He lowers the baby a little further. Sarah splashes water onto him and together they smooth it over his body, stroking him, easing their fingers through the crevices and folds in his skin.

He sings:

'In the bleak mid-winter, frosty wind made moan,

Earth stood hard as iron, water like a stone...'

'I've never heard that before.'

'It's an old song. It came into my head. I remember someone used to sing it to me, long ago. There was always singing. I don't know any more of it.'

The baby makes a cooing noise. Annie holds out a towel and he lifts him up, his hands each side of his body, under the armpits. They wrap him like something precious in the towel and gently pat him dry. Sarah shows him how to fold the softer cloth of the nappy round the swelling tummy, warm as new-baked bread, and fasten it without hurting him. He watches carefully and tries hard to learn.

'Used to do this for you Annie,' she says.

'Did you? After...'

'Yes, bad times. But we made it.'

Annie slips her arms round Sarah's neck and squeezes her. David thinks of the family's story, the history that he is not part of.

They dress Mikey in a jersey many sizes too large and wrap a patchwork quilt round him and fit a lace cap ('Mother made those, for me and you, Annie') on his naked head. Annie comes forward with warm milk again, this time with tiny fragments of bread softened in it.

'You think he's ready for those?' she asks Sarah.

Sarah nods.

After they've fed him, he sleeps. Sarah smiles at David. 'You need to let him rest.'

She takes the baby from him and lays him in a drawer from the kitchen, emptied and lined with blankets.

'There. He'll sleep well in that.' She folds a quilt over him. 'What will we call him?'

'His mother called him Michael.'

'Yes, I like that. Little Mikey.'

He strokes Mikey's cheek and the baby wriggles against his fingertips and yawns and snores.

They sit round the kitchen table, and drink some of the soup he made from the vegetables and some flour and garlic and dried mint he found. Annie takes a cautious mouthful. Sarah nudges her and they drink it down and smile at him.

Jeb doesn't touch his.

'That woman. She came out the forest. Like your mother.'

He pulls on boots and a hat and goes outside. They hear the thwack of an axe.

'He needs to do that sometimes,' Sarah says. 'I'll take some soup to the woman and check on little Mikey.'

He heats some water for washing up. This is a good life, he thinks. Something crashes onto the floor in Sarah's bedroom. He whirls round. Annie springs to her feet and by the time he's crossed the room she's next to Sarah with her arms round her. The bowl lies smashed in the doorway and the soup spreads in brown rivulets across the floor.

Annie stretches out her arm.

'She's so cold.' Her voice is faint and vague and without hope, like an echo.

Jeb slams the axe into the round of wood and splits it neatly in half. His breath comes harsh. He doesn't look at David.

'Put the half-round on the block.'

He raises the axe and sunlight flashes from the blade. David stands back, arms folded.

'Will you put that axe down and listen to me?'

The older man slams the axe into the block. It bites and jumps and skids sideways and falls on the ground.

'Don't disturb a man when he's working with an axe. Don't you know that?'

'Jeb, listen to me. The woman's dead.'

Jeb grunts. He leans forward, one arm on the block, and twists his body and sits on it. David kicks the axe to one side.

'You know where she came from don't you?'

'Who knows where they come from? They come out the forest. She was starving, that's why she died. Nothing more to it.'

He wants to shake him. He bends forward and rests his hand on the old man's shoulder. Jeb looks up at him. Tears track down the grizzled face into the beard.

'Tell me. Where do they come from?'

'They're from the valley beyond the forest. The Secret Valley. Something bad happened, people don't like to talk about it. The people wander in the forest. Sometimes they come here and they die. They say there are armed men, like devils, that come in the night.'

'Does Sarah know about this?'

Jeb feels for the axe-haft. He can't find it. He gets to his feet.

'Give me my axe.'

'You need to eat something. Does Sarah know? Why didn't anyone say anything yesterday?'

'I told you, half of them don't believe it and no-one'll talk about it, they're too scared. They think Franklin will save them.'

'Don't you?'

'Trust that jackanapes? I been around a long time. Bring the axe.'

The old man stumps off towards the cabin.

'Wait.'

David takes something wrapped in a piece of cloth out from under his arm.

'The woman – she had this with her.'

It's an empty flask, made of a tough, transparent, slightly flexible material he hasn't seen before. The top is red and screws on and the label reads 'Top quality milk for babies, from Franklin's dairy.' The image shows a cow with impossible udders.

The old man grunts and shakes his head. David clutches his arm.

'You have seen it before, haven't you? It's what kept the baby alive.'

'What if I have? They just come. Most of them die in the forest, the others say things that don't make sense.'

He wrenches his arm away and stumps off towards the hut. David picks up the axe, checks that the blade is turned away from him, and follows.

Sarah holds the baby in the crook of her arm in front of the stove. Annie kneels next to her. He looks down at the body on the bed. The woman is half-starved, hollows under her eyes, her cheeks caved in, her wrists thin as candles. He's never seen red blotches like those on her skin before. He wraps her in the sheet and heaves her over his shoulder. She hardly weighs anything.

'Where are you going?'

'Back soon. You need to wash things.'

Mikey stares up at him.

'See you soon, little fellow.'

The blue eyes follow him and his burden as he steps out, into the light of common day.

He takes her a long way into the forest and finds a clearing and goes back for the axe and a flint and wood. He passes two of the villagers straggling back from the feast, an older women and a boy in a corduroy shorts and a check jacket. The woman ignores him and strides on, but the boy looks back, until she seizes his arm and pulls him after her.

It takes him most of the afternoon to build the pyre. He looks up. Two yellow eyes, low down, watch him from between the trees. A wolf pads out and bares its teeth at him. He stands his ground and grips the axe-haft in both hands. The wolf sniffs once at the woman and swings round and lopes silently away.

He lifts her and lays her in her shroud on the pyre. He takes the flint and scratches a spark out of the axe-blade with it and the kindling catches and he shields it with his hands to nurture the tiny flame. It glows warm on his palms and smoke curls up. He steps back as the fire take hold.

The flames whirl up and he smells the odour of pinewood ablaze and under it flesh baking. He stands back and speaks out.

'You did the best anyone could for your son. May you find peace.'

When he gets back to the cabin, Mikey sleeps in the makeshift cradle. Jeb fusses round it with pieces of wood shaped like rockers. Sarah and Annie have just finished scrubbing the floor. They wear fresh outfits in green and blue and red. Everything gleams with cleanliness and the smell of soap.

Sarah looks up.

'Get your clothes off.'

'I can wash my own clothes.'

'Now. All of them. You can borrow Dad's. She didn't die of hunger.'

'I know.'

Later, after they've fed and changed Mikey, David shows her the milk bottle.

'Something terrible, in the valley beyond the forest. Everyone knows it, they just won't talk about it. I'm sure it's Franklin's work. We have to find out, tell them back in the City. We have to.'

'You'll make trouble,' says Jeb. He spits into the fire.

'Everything's changed. Now Franklin's taking over he'll bring his world here.'

Jeb shrugs and doesn't meet his eye. David knows with absolute certainty what he will do.

'We have to stop this. Commander Ferris asked me for a report. He's the only one with enough power to face

Franklin down. I'm going into the forest, to the Secret Valley, to find out exactly what Franklin's doing. And I'll report back. You won't stop me.'

Sarah moves closer to him.

'I'll come with you. You'll just get lost. Besides, what else is there to do?'

Annie watches them wide-eyed.

'What about Mikey? You haven't thought of him.'

'We thought maybe you…'

'I want to come.'

'No!' It's the first time David's heard such emptiness in Jeb's voice. At first he doesn't realise who's speaking. 'No. Not like your mother. One of you must stay.'

Annie sighs.

'OK. But I'm nearly ten and I'm coming on the next adventure.'

Into the Forest

They tramp across the clearing, Sarah in the lead. The trees are closer together on this side, ancient, smooth-barked and immensely tall, as if the forest set a margin to the village. She casts about for a few moments and finds the entrance to a narrow pathway between two trunks and sets off. He squeezes in behind her, the pack on his back catching on one of them.

He is struck by how much colder it is among the trees, how much darker, as if he has entered a different, undersea, world.

Sarah is already some way ahead.

'Hey. Wait for me!'

She doesn't answer right away. He pauses. A spider hangs motionless on a web beside him, a hand's-breadth away. Something glides towards him under the myriad tri-folate leaves of the bush to his right and the urge to run consumes him. Then he hears Sarah call out among the trees some way ahead. He presses on, forcing his way through the underbrush.

He bursts out into a small clearing, bright after the half-light under the trees. Sarah stands there.

'Do try to keep up. I was getting worried about you.' Her voice changes. 'You've scratched yourself.'

She touches his cheek with her finger-tips, then swings away, between smooth trunks and onwards.

The woods are brighter here, the trees more evenly spaced, with smooth grey trunks and sunlight finding its way down between them and flickering on the forest floor. He plucks a leaf from one of the saplings and crushes it. The scent is sharp, almost minty. The air grows warmer and he senses new growth all round him. A woodpigeon calls up ahead, immediately answered, and the flowing tune of a small black bird with a yellow beak follows him for some way. It keeps its distance, flitting from bush to bush and watches him with bright black eyes.

Sarah strides on ahead, glancing from side to side. He notices her hair has grown since she taught him to load apples, she no longer needs to flick it out of her eyes.

'Have you been up this way before?'

'No. Village people don't come up here.'

'Who made the path?'

'Forest people used to live here. These woods are a maze of paths. It's easy to get lost, there are places you get stuck in thickets, there's even a swamp. The trees go on for miles.'

He wants to keep talking. He likes her voice.

'What do you think we'll find?'

'No idea. Dad doesn't like talking about it.'

'Why not? Your mother used to come up here, didn't she?'

'You've got a lot of questions. Save your breath for walking.'

The yellow-billed bird whistles twice and clatters up into the leaves at the crest of the tree high above him. He thinks of it bursting through the canopy into a clear blue sky and flying up, higher and higher. It scans an ocean of trees in every direction. In the distance, just at the margin of its vision, it glimpses something different, something new, the object of their journeys, and it flies onward, towards it.

He trudges on. The forest seems limitless. The path rises but they can see nothing when they reach the top of the slope. The trees press in closer on all sides.

Sarah halts.

'Time for a break.'

She offers him her water bottle.

'Not too much. We don't know what the water's like out here.'

He twists out of the straps and drops the pack and sits. The leaves crumple under his hand. He brushes them aside and discovers a different world. A beetle scuttles out from under the leaf-mould, pauses, looks up and waves two branched feelers at him, then dives head down into the humus and immediately disappears. A parade of ants treks across one side of the space he's cleared. He watches, fascinated.

'I'll take the pack for a bit.' Sarah lays a hand on it.

'No.'

'My turn.'

'It's OK.' He is surprised by how much he wants to be the bearer. He swings it onto his back.

'Ready.'

She sets off down the slope. He catches up with her where the path levels out.

They tramp on through the forest. The afternoon sunlight slants through the trees and the air grows cooler.

A solitary dove somewhere high above him still coos, and the sound echoes about them.

Later she says:

'Afternoon break.'

She flops down and he joins her. His stride has become a tramp has become a trudge. They rest, their heads on the pack, close together. He seeks out her hand and takes it. She returns the pressure.

They lie there for a long time.

'You know,' he says, 'it seems so long ago I was in the Enforcers. I was a bit of an idiot then.'

She says nothing. He lifts himself on one elbow. Her face is turned away. She bites her lip.

He continues

'I believed what people told me. You do when you're young.'

'Yup.'

'Then you find things out. You learn you have to stand up for yourself.'

'Yup.'

'People make a difference.' He pokes at a leaf. 'I'm so glad I met you.'

She rolls towards him and looks up. Her eyes rove over his face, as if she is learning it, every detail, by heart. He bends towards her and tenderly, so tenderly, kisses her. Her hands clasp behind the nape of his neck. She kisses him back and gently pulls away.

Shadows deepen among the trees. She sighs.

'We'll get a few more miles behind us before we sleep.'

He squeezes her hand and releases it.

She swings the pack onto her back and they set off

between the trees, together. Much later when it's almost completely dark and the forest is still, they set up camp at the foot of a slope which reaches up into the shadows in front of them, so far they cannot see how high it is. Sarah finds a spot sheltered by bushes just off the path where the ground is soft. They lay out an oblong of canvas and set their blankets at either side of it.

'Shhh.'

She holds up a finger.

He hears it, the rush and tinkle of a stream. He takes the flask and works his way along the foot of the slope until he finds it. He fills the flask at a waterfall where the water splashes cold as ice on his hand and glances round. A bird calls out with a hollow sonorous call, twice repeated. Something swoops past on silent wings, a white ghost, and he starts and nearly drops the water.

Flames flicker among the trees to guide him back. Sarah crouches over a fire.

'You can see that for miles,' he says.

She nods and banks earth round it. He hands her the flask. She sniffs the water and sets it to boil in a pan. They poke twigs and dry moss under it to keep the fire alive. Later they eat beans and tomatoes and drink black tea.

She reaches into the pack.

'Treat time.'

She has something hidden in each hand. She unfolds her fingers to make twin platters, and on each she presents an apple. He grins and feels a rush of warmth for her. He takes his first bite and says:

'Juno would think an apple was a treat. Wonder how she's getting on now.'

'Summer holiday for her, lots of company, idyllic setting, Dad will look after her, he's better with horses than babies.'

'Wait a moment, I just want to sort out the fire.'

She sits close to him.

'That's when I realised you had something to you. When I saw how you'd groomed Juno, in the stable in the Old Town, when things hadn't gone well for you.'

She leans against him and he slips an arm round her and answers:

'I knew you had more to you, the first time I saw you, when you were surrounded by Enforcers and you laughed at them. That was cool. You have a lovely laugh.'

'I'm serious now.'

She turns her face to his and kisses him, pressing him back onto the blankets.

The Broken Land

When the sunlight filters through the trees and wakes him next morning she is still curled against him, her head on his shoulder. He brushes his lips against her forehead, and eases out the arm on which she rests her head. She sighs and nestles down and arches her neck and turns away from him. Pins and needles prickle down his arm. He swings it and clenches and unclenches his fist. His finger-tips tingle and he feels the arm come alive. He folds the blanket over her and she burrows down and is fast asleep.

He stands and listens. The stream gossips some way away, but he hears nothing else, no birdsong, no creature on its errand through the leaves, nothing. He pulls back the earth from the fire and feeds dry grass then twigs into it and smells wood burning. A wisp of smoke rises and he blows on the ashes. His eyes water and a flame flickers, dies back and takes hold. He places larger twigs and then a dry branch on it and sets the pan of water on top.

By the time the tea brews, Sarah is awake. She sits up and sips at a mugful. He finds the half-eaten loaf wrapped in a square of chequered cloth.

'Sleepy head.'

She smiles and nuzzles him.

'It was a good sleep.'

'More tea?'

He reaches for the pan and continues:

'Have you noticed how still everything is?'

She sits upright, alert, and listens for a moment, then jumps to her feet, slopping tea-leaves out of her cup. She scrapes more earth together and banks it over the fire and checks to make sure no air can enter.

'We need to move.'

She stuffs the blankets into the backpack. He takes it from her, pulls her towards him and clasps her in his arms. She pushes her face into the angle of his shoulder and he feels her breath warm on his neck.

She kisses him on the cheek.

'Come on.'

She sets off up the slope. He glances behind. Grey-green trunks rise up above the russet-brown forest floor. A leaf spirals down close to him and he looks up. No movement in the canopy of leaves. He shivers and takes a long stride after her and soon he has closed the gap.

The slope grows steeper as they climb up. The straps of the pack cut into his shoulders, and he slides them further apart to ease the pain. Smaller trees with slender white trunks surround them. The bark flakes off in his hand, showing dark moist wood underneath. Outcrops of rock poke through the turf, layered, mossy and often slippery.

Sarah keeps ahead of him. She uses both her hands to haul herself between two boulders and onto the next ledge. Further on they cross a stream bed. Water soaks through the earth and tumbles out over a lip of rock to cascade over moss-covered rocks. Everything is damp and smells of decay.

She slips and clutches a root. He guides her foot onto a ledge.

'Thanks,' she grunts.

'The ledge widens out up there. Let's rest.'

They sit, backs against rock, to catch their breath and look out over the foliage of the forest below. He hadn't realise how high up they had climbed.

He hands her the flask. She points:

'That clearing must be Coneystone. Wonder how they are getting on.'

'Yes and there's Pettiford. And beyond it, that cleft in the trees, that's Franklin's Road.'

'First time you've called it that. Usually it's the Great Road or the Old Road.'

'First time I realised what it is.'

He glances behind and up.

'Not far now.'

A breeze blows chill over the top of the ridge and the dark mouth of a cave opens onto the ledge a bit further along. He licks his lips and crawls along on all fours and peers into blackness. The air grows colder as he clambers into the opening. The cave narrows but a slim human could slide in backwards and lie there in the dark, unseen, watching him. As his eyes grow used to the gloom, he makes out a pattern on a smooth area of the cave wall, just in front of his face. He takes his weight on his elbow and reaches up and fits his hand to it. Someone had rubbed red ochre on their palm once and pressed it against that wall. He edges backwards. Some of the ochre has rubbed off, as if they had pressed their palm against his, in greeting.

'Look.' He holds out his hand. 'Palm-prints. Someone visited that cave once and it meant something to them.'

They pull themselves to their feet. She finds a hand-hold among tree roots on the next ledge and scrambles up. She twists herself sideways and stretches down to take the back-pack and then help him up.

'It's on my hand too, now.'

She kisses him and strokes his cheek and leaves an orange smudge.

The slope diminishes and they walk over coarse grass, towards the crest of the ridge, the wind in their faces. A white four-petalled flower with a crimson heart that nestles in a hollow among the grass bends towards him. He smells something in the wind that catches in his throat, like the fumes from Franklin's road-monster, far away. He reaches out to take Sarah's hand. The wind gusts and her grip tightens.

'Down!'

They lie side by side just below the crest. She puts her finger to her lips. A squall of wind rushes over them and, quite clearly, he hears voices in it. He can't make out the words.

They lie there, clutching onto the grass with the wind gusting over them. He slips out of the straps of the back-pack and slides it sideways. He catches the snap of an order followed by the click of metal on metal.

'Where's it come from?' he whispers.

She raises herself a few inches and peers along the ridge.

'Greenjackets!' she hisses and presses herself into the grass. She turns to him, her face pale, and he longs to hold her in her arms.

They twist round and edge backwards using their toes and fingers to drag themselves, then crawling once they are below the line of the ridge. His heart beats against the earth.

She puts her lips against his ear and whispers:

'There's a blockhouse, built into the hillside, just below the crest a bit along. Two of them came out, looked round and set off down the hillside the way we came. If we'd been ten metres further over, they couldn't have missed us.'

'Guards – are there more of them?'

'Can't see. There's a darkness in the air.'

The wind gusts over them and he tastes the smell of rotting timber in it. She moves ahead of him in a crouching run along the cliff top and away from the guard-post. He grabs the back-pack and follows her. They creep up over the ridge and down into a narrow defile among stunted trees. A decaying trunk with yellow spotted dinner-plate fungus sprouting out of it lies across the track.

The trees thin out and she crouches down. The breeze is raw on their faces. He sits beside her, her body warming his. He shades his eyes to gaze out over the valley in front of them.

The air is heavier here, almost a fog which grows thicker and darker lower down, so they look out through haze over a floor of cloud. The sky clears to the left and he glimpses the yellow of one of Franklin's road-monsters lumbering forwards far away, noiseless with the distance, its eyes stabbing yellow beams into the gloom in front of it. His eyes ache with the strain of peering through the mist after it.

Sarah moves beside him.

'The Secret Valley. It was never like this before. Look – there.'

Something flickers in the cloud far in the distance and disappears. He squints. A tower rises through the fog, metallic and as grey as the mist. Dark vapour floods up through it and spills out and sinks to thicken the murk on all sides. It would be hard to pick out, except that the flame licks out of it from time to time, lighting up the cloud. The light fades and he can't see it any more.

'That's Franklin's work.'

'OK. It's a day's march, whatever it is.'

They set off down the slope, treading carefully round outcrops of rock. The trees on this side of the ridge are misshapen, squat, with mottled bark and growths where branches should be. They crack and collapse if you lean on them. David and Sarah force their way through the underbrush and clamber over fallen trunks.

Lower down the woods are thicker and a kind of thorny bramble clogs the way. They lose the path and have to fight their way through. The air grows darker as they descend into the haze, although it's not long after mid-day. He feels as if he is choking on the foulness of it. Sarah takes his hand and leads him onwards.

She freezes and touches his cheek. They crouch down. A few yards ahead of them he makes out the figure of a Greenjacket leaning on a tree. He has a rubber mask on his face bound to a metal bottle in a harness on his back by a thick pipe. After a minute the guard grunts and slinks off to the side. They stay there for a long time, not moving. She exhales and shakes her head and creeps to the side and he follows her in an arc round the place. Later they hear the sound of booted feet, somewhere to their right and cringe down and listen as it fades into the silence of the dead forest.

The thickness of the air in this other forest is almost palpable, a quality like a watery paste that clogs his nostrils. There are no real smells, rather a heavy desolation pervades everything that surrounds them, a world of fumes and vapours. He forces himself on.

Time passes. The forest thins and they look out over a desert land, a heath of dying trees and crumpled peaty ground. To the side stretches a marsh of foul water. A solitary bird croaks once, a rasping sound that chills him. They clasp each other's hands without knowing they have done so. His eyes water and he blinks.

Tiny insects swarm up from the marsh and surround them, and bite like red-hot cinders against the flesh. Sarah slaps at her arms and waves her hands in front of her face.

'We have to keep moving.'

They stumble on, where the ground seems firmest. His leg sinks into a sticky mud that grips onto him. He uses his hands to drag his foot out and blunders after her. They wrap cloths around their faces against the midges and totter up a claggy slope where their feet slip. He finds wooden stumps set in a row beside him with a rotten plank nailed to one of them, slanting downwards, and another lying in the mud. He realises that they're following what was once a fence. Ahead of them he glimpses a shape, straight-edged, in the gloom. He tugs at Sarah's hand and they make for it. They reach an abandoned settlement, derelict cabins of wood and mud, and collapse onto a bench in front of the largest. The air is better here and they can breathe.

He swings the backpack down in front of them.

'Nice place, once.'

'A bit like Coneystone, huts grouped round a market ground. An inn. A community.'

She unlaces the bag and pulls out two apples, yellow as sunlight in the greyness.

'Let's eat.'

They rest. He rises and pushes open the door behind them.

The roof has rotted through at the back but most of the floor is dry. Mildewed planks on oak supports make a counter and there's a rust-eaten metal cabinet behind it. He kicks the door and tugs at it and the bottom hinge gives way.

'This place was a shop. Tinned beans.'

Sarah comes over. She reaches into the jumble of tins and picks out a container. The label is half-rotted. He makes out the cow from the bottle that baby Mikey's mother had and frowns:

'That woman, back in the village, she came from here.'

'People lived here. But why did they buy milk and beans from a shop? Hadn't they got cows and fields?'

He sets the tin of beans on the counter.

'It's nearly dark and there's food. We could stay here.'

'Less time we spend in this stinking valley the better. Leave the bag here, press on.'

The strength has left him.

'I need to rest.'

He trudges outside and slumps on the bench.

The wall behind him trembles and a roar comes at him out of the night. Two yellow eyes stab at him, almost blinding him. The monster bounds past and throws itself onward and diminishes into the night.

He gasps and tries to still his quaking breast. He slips his arm round her.

'You OK? I didn't know we were next to the road.'

She looks up at him, her eyes huge in her face.

'That's why the village was here. The store's Franklin's. All that stuff carries his labels, he was selling it to them. And there's something else, over there.'

She leads him to an area on the far side of the hut with a half-rotten picket-fence round it.

'I saw it in the head-lights.'

Mildewed wooden crosses, some of them with the cross-pieces missing, stand in rows, row after row reaching away into the fog. The smell of decay hangs heavy in the air. Behind each cross the earth mounds up.

'A burial ground.' He makes the sign of the cross, left shoulder, right shoulder, lips, navel.

'Why do you do that?'

'I don't know. Respect.'

They stand there for a while, thinking of the villagers. She grips his hand.

'Something very bad happened here.'

They move on, faster now, although their way lies uphill. They travel along the edge of the road, throwing themselves down into the mud when they hear monsters behind them. Once he slips and his arm sprawls out. He feels a blow to his middle finger as the beast hurls his hand aside. A tiny sliver of skin is missing at the tip and the flesh shows red. They trudge on, through darkness, guided by the white stripe that bounds the highway, Sarah in the lead. He thinks of the sky above, the same sky as he saw in Coneystone, dusted with glinting stars looking down at this petty adventure on one of myriad whirling worlds.

Ahead of them they see a glow flaring on the cloud-bank above as the tower spits out flame, then the faint gleam of metal ramparts.

'Franklin's castle.'

Another road-monster roars past and they press themselves into the mud of the ditch and stare up at it. It slows and shrieks with the wail of a seabird alone in the ocean. The castle wall groans and splits. Huge gates scrape open and the monster passes through. David raises himself to stare inside. He sees steel walls lit red and purple by the garish light of furnaces and metal sheds with larger sheds behind them. A framework of girders reaches up next to the tower and a gantry juts out with a great wheel, spinning slowly atop it. The monster rests against the structure and he hears bubbling and sighing as if it is feeding. The throbbing beats at him, like sea-waves in the air. A searchlight stabs out and he throws himself down and the gates clang shut.

'What on earth is that?' he says.

'We have to get inside.'

'The road-beasts enter.'

'We'll follow them.' She says, her face grim. 'We have to.'

Franklin's Castle

They crouch in the chill air at the foot of the ramparts and wind the cloths tighter round their faces against the stink of oil and hot iron and furnace fumes that comes at them. The air trembles round them. He presses his hand against the metal wall and feels it tremble.

Yellow eyes glare against the gate and a monster shrieks out. He looks up and sees the rider high within it, insect-faced, in goggles and a rubber mask that covers his nose and mouth. The figure takes one hand from the twisted reins and rubs it across his forehead. The gates creak and the monster creeps forward and its huge wheels turn slowly in front of him. He feels the gust of its breath hot across his face.

'Wait here. Anything happens, tell them in the City.'

He steals forward and follows the beast, its hindquarters towering over him, as close to it as he dares. Sarah watches him march into the lair shadowed from the furnace-glare by the beast itself.

The beast halts and he flings himself to one side and crouches down inside the wall. No Greenjackets, but there are slits glowing like cats' eyes in the metal ramparts on both sides of the gateway. In front of him the metal framework reaches across the castle's courtyard. Beyond he makes out giant sheds and other structures. Studded pipes snake out of the buildings, join up, swell and disappear through walls to reappear higher up. The tower rises up from within them and behind it further buildings reach away into the gloom. The great wheel turns and a gantry tilts itself up and out and spins out a cable with claws at the end of it which bite and snap. He presses his body against the wall.

The beast creeps forward and rests against the lattice of steel. Its eyes grow dim and it moans and bubbles. The throbbing rises to a pounding and the wheel spins faster. The framework vibrates and something stirs within it. Metal gates crash open high up. Slabs and beams and poles of iron tumble forth, into the belly of the road-beast. The cascade of rubble slows and ceases, the gates slam shut, the pounding slows to a throb and the beast sighs long, like a tiger glutted on buffalo.

Beyond it, from within the castle, light blazes out and flares against the fog-cloud above. Metal grinds on metal and a red slit opens across the wall of the largest shed and widens as a shutter grinds up. The light is so intense he can make nothing out. The heat beats on his face and he throws up his hand and peers between fingers. A giant pot-bellied furnace with pipes twisting into it from both sides, the grandsire of the one he fed in the mill, scowls at him against the glare. The furnace roars like a hungry wolf and liquid fire pours out and streams along a channel, flame dancing above it. He breathes scorching air. He forces his face down against the metal and the throbbing pounds through him.

He feels the heat on his back grow dull and braces himself and looks up. The fire within the castle dies down.

Helmeted figures, black against the flames push shields, mounted on wheels and taller than they are, forwards. All wear masks with tubes running to cylinders on their backs. Above them a gantry, like the arm of a metal giant, swings round and whines and spins out cable with a massive claw dangling from it. It scrabbles at something behind the screens and rises.

It squeals and reaches over towards him. His whole body shakes. The claw hesitates and the gantry moves nearer to him. He crams himself into the angle of the wall. He can go back no further. The claw travels forward and swings onward over him. Glowing coals tumble out of it and explode on the castle floor in showers of sparks. He can hardly breathe. The claw reaches beyond him, out and over the castle wall and releases its grip. Glowing embers, like the ash of a giant's fire, rain down. A hiss, like water poured on seething fat in the devil's cauldron, sounds out. Steam and fumes mingled together boil up above the rampart. The arm withdraws and the empty claw swings over him and the shutter croaks down.

He lies against the wall, in darkness, his eyes tight shut. A hand grips his and strokes it.

'Sarah!'

'I followed you.'

'But I wanted you to stay outside, in case...'

'Nope.'

Metal grates on metal and a door opens in the wall opposite them. A leather-clad figure steps through and glares round. The light shimmers on the helmeted head. It walks stiff-legged to the beast and climbs up a ladder bolted to its side. A door opens above it and David sees the rider, a stem like the tendril of some sea creature curling up to the face-mask, binding him to the beast. The figure passes something to the rider and descends, glares round once more and returns though the metal door.

The yellow eyes of the beast jab out spears of light. It waddles forward and wails once more and the crack shows at the centre of the gates.

'Quick.'

Sarah beckons and creeps after the beast and dodges between its wheels. He swallows, looks round and throws himself after her. The beast roars and makes a sound like metal clashing on metal and jerks forward. The black bulk of the wheel brushes against his shoulder and he cries out and the roar slackens and redoubles.

Sarah tugs at him. Her lips move, but he can't hear her words. The beast lurches forward and a metal plate scrapes over them and tears at his shirt. Then the shadow of it is gone from him. He's outside, flat on his face on smooth stone with Sarah beside him. The monster lumbers away from them and howls as if in victory and dwindles into darkness.

The search-light stabs out above him and wavers as if seeking some presence in the fog. He feels the tremor at the castle's heart and over it the rattle of the gates and the crash as they slam shut, and the beam snaps off.

He rolls onto his back and gasps and coughs foul air out of his lungs.

Sarah calls to him:

'Over here!'

He rolls sideways and they lie in the ditch beside the roadway and stare up. Cool water soaks into their clothes.

The fog-bank above parts for an instant and stars shine down, the same stars as he saw over Coneystone, and the murk rolls back.

He steels himself.

'We have to go back. That claw, it went outside the wall on the other side.'

She nods and gets to her feet and offers him her hand. They stumble forward following the steel wall away from the road, the cloths round their faces, hand in hand. The mud sucks at their feet. She halts.

A dark lake stretches in front of them, an oily sheen to it and the castle reflected dimly from it. Noisome fumes rise from the water. The air rasps at his throat.

'We can't stay.'

A gout of flame blazes from the tower above them and lights up the scene. The mound along the shore of the lake he had taken for reeds is made up of the corpses of water-birds, geese and ducks and, in front of him, a heron, its plumage dull and streaked with tar. Among them lie fish, rotten and decayed, stinking. The lake is dead, nothing moves on it apart from the mist.

'No wolves, no foxes, no snakes, no living thing,' he says after a while, 'Nothing feeds on them.'

'It's downhill to the village. The water flows there. It poisoned them…'

They move back to the road, silent, numbed by what they have seen. Behind them they hear the clatter as the giant arm reaches out and the wail of the claw and the monstrous hiss as the poison from the furnace rains down into the water.

They trudge on. The throb of the castle fades behind them and the air grows chill.

A road-monster roars out of the dark and the twin beams glare out at them. She wraps her arms round him and they plunge into the ditch and lie there, face down, as it sweeps by.

He hauls himself to his feet and turns to her. She is caked with mud, as black as tar from head to toe, her eyes white, like pebbles

'Look at you!'

'And you!'

They both burst out laughing and fling their arms round one another, and the eye-beams of the next monster sweep over them and they still can't stop laughing, their faces buried in each other's shoulders. Later they stagger onwards, their arms round each other's shoulders, like a couple who have spent too long in the ale-house. The shadow of the ruined village thickens to a deeper dark against the gloom.

He guesses it is the dead time of the night. Nothing moves on the road and he seems to be looking into nothing when he stares upwards. The air tastes acid on his tongue.

They sink down on the bench and gasp for breath. Sarah sits upright.

'We know one thing.'

'What?'

He knows you can pass through Franklin's Castle and live.

'The Road. Franklin's beasts don't just carry goods to the City. That's a lie. They don't just bring the horses to the mills. They bring the slabs of iron that are poured into them back there.'

'And that wheel. They drag the cage up from underground. They tear rubble from deep in the earth and burn it in the castle.'

They both know this. They have to talk about it, as if the words make it less abominable.

'They dump the furnace ash and poison the water.'

'The villagers. They never knew what was killing them. They just knew the only way to live was to buy the junk in Franklin's store.'

They cling to each other and sleep, huddled on the bench.

Return to the City

The furnace in Franklin's mill gapes at him. Flames burst out of its gorge. It grins and bares hideous teeth and shakes itself and groans, with a sound like the gates of the Castle, and waddles forward towards him. Giant iron wheels turn slowly on each side and he feels the fire burn at his face and the fumes sear his throat.

He moans and jerks awake. Sarah leans against his shoulder. She stirs and falls back into sleep. Far away the yellow glow of a road-beast lights up the haze. He touches her cheek. She reaches up and seizes his forefinger and pulls his hand away and snores. The beast rumbles as if hungry. He gets both arms round her and links hands across her chest and drags her back into the hut. The monster thunders past wailing as if it were the only one of its kind left in the world.

They lie together on the earth floor. Cold seeps into him. She sleeps.

After a while, he rests a hand on her shoulder. 'Wake up. We have to get going.'

She sighs and opens her eyes. 'I'm so thirsty, my mouth tastes of ashes.'

He passes her the flask and she sips a mouthful and hands it back and he takes one swallow and shoulders the backpack. At first they follow the course of the road as they did on the way out, stopping every few yards to suck in the foetid air. His throat burns and Sarah leans against him and coughs and rubs at her face. Every time a monster passes they crouch in the ditch and it is harder to rise.

After a while they turn away from the road, towards the ridge, hoping to find the path they came down. They are now some way from the hutment on a tract of waterlogged land with broken fences on each side. The fence-posts are black with mould and the wood crumbles to the touch as if it had been bathed in acid. A spinney looms out of the miasma ahead of them and dead trees lie across each other or lean against the dying. The fog grows thicker around them. Moisture coats the skin of his face and his eyes are so sore that he blinks continually.

Later they pass a thicket of bent white sticks beside the track next to a tainted pool. In the centre, from what he at first takes for a giant seashell, two empty eye-sockets stare at him and he recognises the horse's skull and then the rib-cage.

'The land is poisoned. The village died.'

She nods and they stumble on. He knows he won't make it up the ridge and lets the backpack tumble from his shoulders and slap into the mud behind him. He has the flask in his pocket.

The fog thins to the left. Sarah tugs at his arm. They splash through marsh-water. He trips on something that shifts under him and she wraps an arm round him and he does not fall. The slope of the ridge rises before them and they throw themselves onto it, between two white boulders. A beetle meanders across his fingers, pauses and salutes him with branched feelers.

'Have I met you before, in the forest?'

Sarah blinks.

'What did you say?'

He pulls himself to a crouching position and shows her. She bends towards the tiny creature.

'I'd stroke you, but you might not like it.'

She shakes the empty flask and drips one drop of their water on the back of his hand just in front of it and it scuttles forward and drinks. He sets it down and offers her his hand and they rise and start to clamber up.

When they emerge above the cloud bank, it's already night. A gibbous moon hangs above them, soft as candle-light, illuminating everything. The clouds below seem at rest, like a quiet sea. He wipes the dampness from his face and breathes. The soreness leaves his eyes. They pass a stream. He sniffs at the water and dips his forefinger into it and wets his lips and licks. Sarah lies next to him and they plunge their faces in and drink. Relief floods through him.

They sit and look out over the blighted land.

'The flare of the chimney. Looks like an oil-lamp in a cottage window, doesn't it?'

'The woman. Franklin poisoned her world. She saved little Mikey by giving him bottled milk. Who knows what it cost her?'

'Let's rest.'

They creep up to the crest of the ridge in the darkness before dawn. The moon is down and the cold bites into him. He shivers. A noise as of insects chittering comes from the guard post. They crawl over the skyline. The ocean of trees stretches dark and always in movement before him. On the far horizon colours glow like fire under ice. The City does not sleep.

Climbing down the ridge is harder than climbing up. They cling to the rocks, scrabbling for foot-holds. Once he looks down and sees tree-tops far below his feet and sways, gripped by vertigo, and does not look down again. Sometimes he helps Sarah find foot-holds, sometimes she guides him. Halfway down she recognises the berries on a thorn-bush, purple and over-sweet.

'They taste awful, but you can eat them.'

She offers him a handful. They rest on a shelf of rock, and cram the fruit into their mouths until they feel sick and swig down draughts of water. He feels light-headed but the strength returns to his limbs.

Once they reach the forest floor, among tall trees with smooth green-brown trunks, they move faster. The first birdsong, the trill of the blackbird amazes him and he is shocked and stands still. Twice they hear voices in the forest and lie silent among bushes, and once they see daylight flash on metal far to their right and crouch down. He crushes a leaf to take in the minty smell and his head feels clear, his senses sharpened. They walk fast.

Much later they reach the forest of dark-trunked scaly trees, where bushes grow half across the path and Sarah goes ahead to find the way.

They are among the smooth-trunked trees that crowd close and stretch far above them, and shed leaves in russet-brown banks on the forest-floor. At last they squeeze between the two straight trunks. He brushes the dust from his shoulders and follows Sarah across the clearing. An older woman in a shawl and headscarf sits outside the smallest cabin with a five-year-old child, dressed identically, on a foot-stool next to her. Both of them shell peas as if they are in a competition. The mother raises her hand and calls out a greeting to Sarah and the child mimics her.

Annie greets them at the door to the hut, with Mikey in her arms. Pans boil on the stove behind her and he smells the bread baking in the oven.

'Just in time,' she says and hands the baby to Sarah, who holds him against her breast. Mikey wriggles and starts to grizzle, and won't look at her. David puts out his arms and she hands him on. He takes him into the bedroom.

'Warm water, please,' he calls over his shoulder, and lays him on the bed and fiddles with the fastenings of his nappy. Once he has cleaned the baby's bottom and soothed it with a cream Annie hands him, Mikey lies there and looks up at him and he is clasped in that bond of mutual admiration, when each is the most wondrous thing to the other.

'Your mummy loved you so very much,' he says, 'so very, very much.'

He bows his head to the plump belly, a hand's breadth wide, and blows out through half-closed lips. Mikey chortles and grasps a handful of hair in each fist and wrenches his hands apart and David gasps aloud.

Annie mutters behind him.

'He needs food, not messing about.'

She sits on the bed with a bowl of bread and milk, tests it on her wrist and spoons the mixture into the tiny voracious mouth.

When they've all eaten and Mikey, replete, yawns and squirms on David's lap, Jeb stokes up the stove and sits back.

'Well?'

Sarah has changed into clean clothes. She did most of the cooking.

'We travelled two days' journey. We found where the road goes. It's bad up there.'

'And?' The old man leans forward in his chair. His eyes gleam. David butts in.

'You know what's in the valley the other side of the forest, don't you? Why didn't you warn us?'

'Who listens to an old fool? They think I'm mad in the village.'

Sarah touches his arm:

'Dad used to be a woodsman.'

'Aye, still a match for any of them with an axe.'

'Tell him. It was in the forest you met mother. She was from the village in the valley. Lucky for her she met Dad.'

'Lucky for me.' The old man stares into the fire. 'She was looking for honey, she followed the bees into the wood. They used to let me sleep on the inn floor.'

His eyes glisten but Sarah keeps on.

'Dad, we can't go on pretending that nothing's happened.'

'I know.'

'Franklin built an iron castle. His road-beasts thunder along the road. They carry ores that he tears from the earth.'

'I know.'

'He poisons the earth, the water, the sky. The bees are dead, the cattle are dead, the trees are dead and the people are dead. Michael's mother came from the village. Mikey is the last of them.'

'I know.'

'We must tell everyone, tomorrow, in Pettiford, then in the Old Town and the City.'

'You think they'll listen to you? No-one wants to hear bad news.'

Jeb sits back. He seems satisfied.

'Oh Dad. We can't just give up.'

'That's what your mother said. You know, you looked just like her when you said that.'

David stands up with Mikey asleep in his arms.

'No point in arguing with the Elders in Pettiford. We'll go to the City. This is beyond all of us. These crimes are monstrous, unspeakable. I'll talk to Commander Ferris and the Enforcers, they have to believe me. Franklin will be punished. Now we sleep.'

He stares out of the window across the huts to the forest. No light, no sounds, only the whisper of branches brushing against each other. He is so tired he could sleep standing up. He pulls the shutter to and falls onto the bed. Far away something raps twice, a sound like a door-knocker on a city door. He stirs and listens and there is nothing. He glides into a sleep without dreams.

Jeb wakes him before dawn and he pulls on his clothes. The older man watches him.

'You're going to sort this out, aren't you? And you're going to look after Sarah?'

He doesn't answer. Sarah's already stowing food into

a back-pack. He catches a whimper from little Mikey and goes in and lifts him out of the makeshift cradle and feeds him warm milk from a teaspoon the way Sarah showed him. Annie brings hot water and he changes the nappy and strokes his hand across the little tummy, full of milk and tight as a drum. Mikey stares up at him with blue eyes and he kisses him. Then Jeb's beside him, holding out his arms, his face open, unguarded, for the first time. David settles the baby in his arms and the older man rocks him and bends forward making a cooing sound.

Annie comes out with them to the stables and they work fast. He pours the feed into Juno's trough and they groom her and feed the other horses while she eats. Sarah helps him slip the bridle over Juno's head and shows him how to fit the bit in her mouth without hurting her. She ties a bag of oats behind the saddle and hooks on a leather water-bottle and leads Juno out. They mount, Sarah in the saddle and David behind her. Jeb watches them, one arm round Annie's shoulders, Mikey cradled in the other.

'Goodbye,' he calls to them. 'Don't forget what I said. And look after Juno.'

'Do my best.'

Annie waves and David shouts 'Hang on a minute.'

He slips off Juno's back and takes Mikey and holds the scrap of life tight and feels the tiny heart beat against him.

'Cheerio, little fellow. See you again.'

The blue eyes stare up at him. The tiny face puckers, the mouth gapes open and Mikey bawls out, so loud that Juno turns her head and David flinches. He pats Mikey and rocks him, but the child screams and won't stop.

'You're holding him too tight.'

Annie takes him but Mikey won't look at her or at David and sucks in breath and howls louder, as if he's lost something he knows will never return. David stands for a few seconds, then remounts.

'I just wanted to say goodbye.'

He twists round and stares back at the three of them, Jeb with his hands on Annie's shoulders, Annie with Mikey clasped against her, Mikey's cries sounding even louder. He waves until the trail turns into the forest but no-one responds. Tall pines overshadow the track. An army could hide between the trunks and you'd be none the wiser.

A slightly-built figure steps out of the darkness between the trees at a place where the forest slopes down to the track on either side. He holds up a hand.

Sarah slows to a walk. 'Good morning.'

The man wears a green jockey cap and a waistcoat over riding clothes. He rests his hand on the bridle. David recognises him – Franklin's groom from the meeting at Pettiford – and his throat tightens.

'I know you. What do you want?'

The groom glances back at the trees. He pats Juno. 'Nice horse. Well-looked after, anyone can see that.'

Sarah tugs at the rein.

'Take you hand off my horse.'

David looks up. He can't be sure but he thinks he sees movement among the trees.

'Ride on!'

He puts his foot against the groom's chest and kicks out, but the man hangs onto the bridle and Juno twists sideways.

Hooves sound behind them. Sarah smacks her fist down at the groom's arm and he lets go and falls. Helmeted Greenjackets mounted on huge black stallions, cylinders hissing under their bellies, gallop down the slope towards them. They ride in, one on each side, and seize Sarah by the arms, wrenching her hands from the bridle and twisting them behind her back. Their horses dwarf Juno.

David grabs at them. A Greenjacket punches him and he falls from Juno's back. He scrambles up, his head ringing, the blood pulsing in his body, and smashes his fist into the thigh of the nearest horseman. A great horse comes at him and he dodges sideways and sprawls backwards across the track. He looks up aghast at the red frames bolted into the stallion's thighs and the blood on the cylinders where the rods chafe against the flesh and prays that they never treat Juno like this.

He seizes a booted foot and wrenches at it. A hand like an iron claw grips him by the back of the neck and lifts him as if he weighed nothing.

A voice mutters, close by:

'Keep still or I'll break your neck.'

Sarah writhes in their grasp: 'Get off me, you insects.'

They twist her round and fix a leather gag across her mouth.

One of the Greenjackets, with an inverted V symbol on his helmet between the eyepieces, hisses and addresses the groom,

'You sure this is the one?'

He draws in breath with a whistle and the S sounds seethe and sputter in his voice. The groom nods. He won't look up. He's lost his cap and there's a bald patch on his scalp.

The Greenjacket hisses again. 'Say it.'

'Yes, Sir, this is Sarah Cordell.'

The groom raises his wrist and the band glints in the sunshine.

The Greenjacket laughs.

'You know something? You just lost your value.'

He rides his horse forward pushing the groom backwards until he staggers and falls, his arms spread wide. The great hooves stamp down on the man's chest and crush it. Blood spurts across the waistcoat and he gasps and shudders and is still. The horse whinnies and shakes its head and steps back. Blood stains the feathering of its hooves.

David screams 'You murderer!' and the Greenjacket tightens his grip and sets him on his feet.

They tie Sarah across the shoulders of one of the giant beasts and strap her hands behind her back. She stares at David. Her eyes are huge and flash with anger. The guard forces her head away from him.

The Greenjacket leader's head swivels to David. The helmet shifts as the eyes inspect him.

'Take the horse. Go back to your village. Tell them what happens to those who resist my master.' He turns to the others 'We ride!'

A hood is pulled over his head from behind. He flails out with his arms but they are pinioned behind his back and he feels himself lifted and tied over Juno's back. The hood smothers him, he can't breathe and panic rises within him. He hears the steel hooves of the great horses drum on the track and fade towards the City. Juno's muscles work under him as she makes her way back towards the village first at a trot, then a canter, then a gallop. He is thrown from side to side. The darkness whirls round him and surges in and swallows him.

David and Juno

'Wake up! Oh please wake up!'

He opens his eyes and the pain roars into his head. Annie tugs at his hand. Behind her Jeb stares down at him, holding out a glass with a dark liquid in it. He lies on the grass in front of the hut and Juno bends over him, nuzzling him with soft lips. He pats Juno's face and sits up.

Annie helps him to his feet. Jeb thrusts the glass into his hand.

'Drink this.'

The liquid burns a track down his gullet.

He coughs and they help him into the house. He splashes water on his face at the sink and his head clears enough to tell them what happened.

'I'm going after her.'

Jeb nods.

'Take any horse you like. Take Juno. She's not a racehorse but she'll outlast anything. Take the saddle, the bridle, feed, take anything.' He swallows. 'And tell them in the City. Tell them everything. Save her.'

Annie watches him with serious eyes. 'You will save her, won't you?'

He mounts Juno and she sets off at a canter before he has time to shake the reins. He turns in the saddle and looks back when he reaches the place where the track plunges into the forest, and waves to them and then he's alone with Juno. She canters on and lengthens her stride and soon they are moving at a full gallop.

Later, they reach the place where the track is rougher and she slows to a trot. He rests his hand on her withers and feels the roll of the muscles in her shoulders and trusts her. His neck, where they tied the bag, is as sore as if it had been scalded.

The prints of many horses going the same way as he is pock-mark the track. They're still sharp even where the mud is soft, and so large that Juno's prints would fit inside them.

When he reaches the place where the track narrows and leads down to the river he slips out of the saddle and walks in front of Juno, one hand on the bridle.

'Break time.'

She crops at the grass where it's greenest at the edge of the stream. He squats in the mud to inspect the hoof-prints, but he can't make anything out of them, there are too many, as of horses milling together. He thinks of the crowd of villagers at the moot.

'Maybe Sarah put up a bit of a fight here.'

He leads Juno into the water and she bends her head and drinks up great draughts. His boots fill with water. He doesn't care. On the other side he unstraps the nose bag and half fills it and hooks it over Juno's neck. He casts around and finds more prints, overlapping, as if the horses trampled against each other. One set makes away from them. Other tracks converge on it from the sides.

A flash of light, like a match-flare, catches his eye. He scoops at the mud and dredges up a fragment of clear plastic, faceted, like a lens, part of an eye-piece from one of their helmets. He can't be sure, but there's a smear across it, that might be blood. An image comes into his mind: a horse, her face wild, her teeth bared, rears up on its hind legs and lashes out with steel hooves. Good for you, Sarah!

He leads Juno up the slope at a run and swings himself onto her back. He twists and finds the stirrup with his foot at the second attempt. The reins are in his hands and he shakes them and realises that the mare has already started off at a canter.

They follow the same path they rode out from the City on, four days, it seems so long, ago. The sun beats down and he wishes he had a hat. In the far distance he makes out an irregularity in the horizon, black, like twigs poking up – the Towers of the City. He thinks of the office at the head of the spiral staircase and of Ferris and Adam with Franklin's tower looming over them from across the square. He thinks of Sarah and where she is now, and shivers. The mill. Re-education. Franklin's slaves. He shakes the reins.

The afternoon wears on. Ragged-feathered birds fly past him, black, their calls harsh. Others come in from both sides. They mass together ahead of him at a turn in the path. Juno slows her pace. He smells foulness on the air.

A shape lies beside the path. He shouts out and the birds fly up with a clatter of wings and shriek at him and circle overhead. Juno pulls away and halts. He shakes the reins and jams his knees into her. She moves forward a few paces and stops. He slides down and grips the rein and pulls at her and she walks after him. They keep to the side of the path and she won't look at the black mound.

As they draw next to the dead horse she gives a whinny, long-drawn out and desolate, like the call of a creature who knows there is no-one to answer it.

He shields his face from the rank sweet carrion smell and forces himself to inspect it. The eyes have gone and blood stains the sable coat around the mouth and the nostrils. The yellow metal struts have worn livid patches in the flesh of the flanks and hind quarters. The contrivance of trumpet-tubes, flecked with blood, hangs down below the barrel of the chest. The birds have savaged the belly and more blood soaks into the ground beneath. He remounts.

A tremor runs through Juno from nose to tail and she tosses her head. She trots forward and canters, then she is galloping away from that place. Clean wind blows into his face. The hedge-rows hurtle by and the thunder of Juno's hooves drowns out everything. He can think of nothing but clinging onto the reins and crouching forward, with his feet slotted into the stirrups. As they hurtle over the plain, he looks back. The dark birds circle and settle again onto their feast.

So he works his horses to death, too.

Later he sees more birds massing ahead of him and he slows Juno to a walk and takes her through a gate and along hedge-rows and back onto the path further on. He bows his head as they pass the place. The birds mass and shriek at him and fly back and Juno whinnies again, the long-drawn wail of respect for suffering.

The sky darkens. The towers are closer now and black against the evening sky. They pass the first farms at the edge of the Old Town. No-one else journeys in the night. The few people he sees wrap their cloaks more tightly round themselves or shrink back or disappear down side turnings.

Juno stumbles and slows even more, placing her right foreleg delicately, as if treading on marbles. He slides to the ground and halts her. Annie has put a flannel in the tack-bag. He strokes Juno's neck and takes the cloth and wipes down her face. He talks to her while he does this, not really aware of what he's saying.

'I'm so sorry, Juno, I didn't know about Franklin's horses. We'll find Sarah. It's very hard for you.'

There are apples in the lunch pack Jeb gave him. He holds one out to her. He's not hungry.

While she munches at it, he lifts her right foreleg and bends it and probes inside the hoof. He feels something hard and jagged wedged between the flesh of the sole and the hoof. He works his forefinger inside it. Juno whinnies and he tugs at it and feels a stab of pain and flicks it out. She whinnies again, more loudly. He sucks at the gash across the tip of his forefinger.

Juno presses against him. He hears the tramp of boots behind him and whirls round. Two figures in olive green cloaks come towards him, their faces masked. He gets a foot in the stirrup and swings himself up and Juno is off before he shakes the reins. He hangs, on fumbling for the other stirrup. The road he's on heads straight for the mills, and that's where they took Sarah.

When Juno slows he pulls at the reins and they trot down a side street and turn right onto another, then, some way along, a larger road under street-lights.

He navigates by the chimneys of Franklin's mills. His route follows the by-roads, and curves round the edge of the Old Town and keeps away from the Pit. He passes through an area of ill-paved streets and meagre lighting with the rough-cast concrete facades of the residence blocks on either side. Juno's hooves echo from the buildings. A poster of Franklin hangs on a street corner. He pauses and reaches up and tears it across and rides on. A chill breeze blows on his face. He meets almost no-one.

Sometimes curtains part in the windows and people peer out. He waves to a small boy in Enforcer pyjamas being held up by a young black woman to see him pass and the child claps his hands. Soon they come out on the broader streets nearer to City Square where there are more street-lights and more people out to enjoy the evening.

People look up at him and point him out to their companions. An older man with a grey beard waves and he smiles and nods. A crowd of children, some in ragged clothes, some of them better dressed in the drab denims and knitwear of the City, follow behind. *Why aren't you in bed?* He thinks. He sits taller.

He comes out on Eastern Boulevard just along from the square. A group of young women outside a bar, in sequinned dresses that glitter blue and mauve and green, cheer and whistle and raise their glasses to him. They wave wristbands too, despite the mud on his trousers and his filthy jacket.

He turns at the entrance to the square and Juno trots along the side of the Halls of Justice and everyone falls back. When he reaches the rear of the building, he calls out 'Martin!' He dismounts and hammers on the gates and bellows 'I'm back!'

The latch grates and for an instant the groan of the steel portal of Franklin's Castle fills his mind and his throat tightens.

Martin stares at him.

'Shh! Do you want everyone to know?'

'I don't care.'

He leads Juno through, the stink of the midden fills his nostrils, and she follows him into the stables.

'So you brought her back?' The stable lad pats Juno and strokes the side of her face. 'Reckon you're a horseman now. Maybe you need a wash and some clothes?'

'Later. Will you do something for me? Give her a good feed? I'll be back in a bit to rub her down.'

'I'll look after her. She's one of a kind, that mare.'

He flicks his sleeve back. David clicks wristbands and takes a deep breath and sets off, across the courtyard. The sky is clear, alive with bright stars. It's colder than it was earlier. He doesn't care.

The Halls of Justice are in darkness. He listens and there's no sound, apart from the soft bump that horses make when they shift in their stalls, like a troop of soldiers at ease after a route march. A yellow light clicks on in a window high above. Someone stands there, arms spread, leaning on the sill. The light clicks out and he's left staring up at darkness, as the silhouette fades on the back of his eye. He could swear it was Adam.

Truth to Power

Jan peers at him down the spiral case and her face lights up:

'You're back. Where have you been?' She frowns. 'Where's your uniform? You look terrible.'

He shakes his head and squeezes past her.

'Sorry, I really want to talk to you, but....'

He grasps both rails and heaves himself upward.

'David!' she shouts after him. Then louder, 'David!'

By the time he reaches the top floor he's gasping for breath. His heart hammers in his chest. He bends double and sucks air into his lungs. Someone grips his shoulder and hauls him upright.

'Ashwood! Stand up man!'

Adam pushes him two paces forward and knocks on the door marked "Commander".

David stumbles into the room and finds his voice and gasps out.

'Sir! You must send Enforcers now. The Old Town. Franklin has Sarah.'

Ferris touches the balance at the corner of his desk. He looks up at David, and his voice is as mild as if he were speaking to one of his family. David feels a calmness within him. The clutter of words in his head clears.

'David. I'm glad to see you back. Please tell me about your mission.'

Adam breaks in:

'Ashwood, your report. And stand to attention when you address on officer!'

Ferris raises a hand.

'Adam. Perhaps you could leave us for a few minutes.'

The door clicks shut. David swallows.

'There's no time. The Greenjackets took Sarah. She's in Franklin's mill in the Old Town. You have to save her.'

'Calm yourself. Start at the beginning and tell me who the Greenjackets are. Your mission was to find out what's happening in the mills. And take a seat. Do you want some water? You're wheezing.'

Ferris smiles. Suddenly David no longer trusts him.

'They're Franklin's guards. They're thugs. And they bear the symbol of the City, the golden balance, and everyone blames us.'

'That is unfortunate. Franklin has the contract to provide security in the Old Town. His operatives have the right to bear the insignia just as we do.'

'He has Sarah. He kidnapped her.'

Ferris raises an eyebrow. David feels as if he is walking into fog and there are no waymarks.

'You don't understand. I've seen hideous things, unspeakable things. Franklin is buying the forest, the villages, everything. He builds steel castles and he poisons the air. He makes great road-beasts that swallow people. He traps horses in metal and works them to death.'

He wants Ferris to answer him, to be shocked or angry or grim, as if this mattered to him. He finishes:

'You must save Sarah.'

'We must live by the Law. Take a deep breath and drink some water. Why does this Sarah matter so much? Tell me everything from the beginning.'

The liquid cools his throat. He tries to think when he last drank water. He remembers the golden taste when he plunged his face into the stream at the edge of the desolation, with Sarah beside him. He draws breath and tells his story from the beginning.

Ferris listens. He interrupts once:

'Tell me again about the beast they called the tractor, everything about it.'

David finishes and takes the jug from the side-table and refills his glass and drinks it down. He is exhausted. He could sleep in the upright chair. He hears Ferris cross the room. A few minutes later, the door opens and someone comes in behind him and speaks, a woman

'Mr Ashwood. I believe you have a report. For the City.'

He looks up at a woman in a navy-blue trouser suit, her mouth set as if she is used to authority, her hair lustrous, sculpted. Rachel West, Chair of the Council, President of the City. He grips the table and pulls himself to his feet.

'Madam. I'm sorry. Please, help Sarah.'

She perches herself on the table. There's a young woman with her, holding a notepad and a pen.

'Do sit down. We will do everything to save your friend. But there are larger issues. Please tell me your story. From the beginning.'

And he does. The words slip easily from his mouth. The Old Town, The Hall of Monsters, the Hall of Beasts, the third chimney, the battle with the road-beast and the wild ride, the village and Franklin's bargain, the journey through the forest, the poisoned valley, and at its heart the iron castle. He stumbles as he tells her about the Greenjackets and the slave-horses and Sarah.

'… and you must save her,' he finishes.

'Thank you. We have recorded your statement. Please sign here, the Commander can witness it. I will leave you now to consider the matter.'

'But aren't you…?'

She ignores him and turns to Ferris.

'This is a complex matter. There are a number of interests involved. I will circulate this report to the City Council. Make sure Mr Ashwood claims a consultancy fee for it.'

She steps out of the room followed by her assistant. He stares after them and feels emptiness within him.

Later, he rests in the chair, eyes closed, but he can't sleep. Adam is in the room, talking to Ferris, more than David's ever heard him talk.

'We must act, Sir. This may be our only chance. I could take an assault squad into the mills. We'd have her out before anyone knew what we were doing. We'd have evidence.'

Ferris responds in his measured reasonable voice.

'I'm sorry, Adam. You know I cannot authorise a sortie without the support of the Council.'

'Sir. I'm a soldier, not a politician. We must take action. Now. The troops will expect it.'

'And you know the rules. You may undertake training exercises. Nothing more. That is a direct order.'

Adam does not answer. His boots thud on the carpet as he marches to the door.

'Adam,' Ferris raises his voice. 'Do you understand? I cannot permit an unauthorised raid on a citizen's property.'

The door creaks as it opens.

David hears Adam grunt one word, 'Sir.' Then he mutters, 'Only training exercises.' The door slams behind him.

He sits at the corner of a long table in a high-ceilinged room with tall windows, the golden balance in front of him. It's still night outside and he's half-asleep. The President is at the far end, the Commander half-way down. Other people take their places along the sides of the room and sometimes pass notes to the two principals. No-one pays him any attention. Adam stands by the door.

Rachel West and Commander Ferris talk together, and ignore the others. He had no idea there were so many words in the world.

Ferris points to the folder.

'Madam, this is a serious matter. Franklin has exceeded his brief. He is buying up land, water, the villages and the forest, all he can get. He is mining, making new things and selling them. This creates pollution.'

The President slips something in her mouth, chews briefly, and taps the wine-coloured folder in front of her.

'None of that is beyond the One Law. Willing buyer, willing seller. The City is founded on trade and enterprise.'

'He is experimenting with nature.'

'He is a popular man. He develops new markets.'

'He is poisoning our world.'

'You exaggerate. Progress impacts on our environment and we deal with it. Look at the Pit. It is a price we pay. No doubt he will say that it is costed in.'

David dozes, his head on his hands. When he wakes, Ferris seems more confident.

'The tractor. That is clearly a gift, not a bargain between buyer and seller. We might do something with that. We have a witness.'

'But... it is trivial. He entertains people to fairground wagon-rides? He will buy the best lawyers in Market World.'

'The Law does not admit exceptions.'

David remembers the wagon and the child in the river. He thinks of Sarah at the ford, when he slept on his feet, leaning on Juno and she tickled his cheek. He is instantly alert. He shouts:

'You must save Sarah!'

The faces, wide-eyed in shock, turn to him. Only Adam, by the door, does not move. Ferris stretches out a hand.

'I'm sorry. Thank you for your report. Please... a week's home leave. Have a bath and get a meal and a new uniform.'

The President smiles as if she knew him.

'Please, you have done well and you need to relax. Leave these matters to your superiors.'

She continues but the words swoop at him, like crows on the dead horse. They dive and peck and swirl round him, mocking him with their shrieking. He throws out his hands and sweeps the balance from the desk and it tumbles to the floor in a tangle of wire and pans and rods.

'No! If you won't save her, I will.'

'Ashwood!' barks Ferris. 'You will say nothing of this to anyone, that's an order. It is a delicate matter.'

'I resign. I can no longer be an Enforcer. Good-day. Excuse me.'

'Ashwood, wait.'

As he pushes the door open, Adam drops a hand on his wrist. He flinches and looks up. Adam nods once at him, as if in approval, and smiles, the only time David has ever seen him smile, and releases him.

He makes for the spiral stairs, then swerves and hurries on to the main staircase. He takes it at a run, stumbles on the first landing, recovers, and rushes down, three steps at a time.

Curtis is on duty at the exit desk under the tall windows that look out onto the square. He licks his lips.

'Ashwood! Report.'

David strides past, then turns and walks back.

'Yes?'

Curtis is on his feet, his face red. His moustache quivers.

'Salute a superior. You're on a charge. Gross insolence.'

'Yup. How about very gross insolence?'

He'd never realised how short Curtis was. A tremor of enjoyment runs through him. 'Or very very gross insolence?'

'You...'

'Didn't they tell you? I've resigned.'

He places both hands against Curtis' chest and pushes. Curtis staggers backwards and collapses into the metal chair.

'Too many pies, Curtis. And click your own wristband.'

He carries on down the main steps and salutes the moon as it comes through the clouds over City Square.

Friends and Half-Friends

He crosses the Square, the same way he led Sarah ten days ago, to teach her the glory of Market World. His mind is full of that day, of the conceit that fizzed within him and how he lost what he most desired and rode Juno in pursuit and learned so much. He slows to a walk and wraps his arms round himself against the cold. He is older now.

Most of the stalls on Eastern Boulevard have been wheeled away. Some are folded and stowed in the angle between pavement and wall. Something rustles like a bird in the underbrush of the forest. A puff of breath shows white in the darkness and fades above one of the mounds of canvas and grimy blankets he'd taken for stall-holders' gear. He catches sight of a face, eyes glittering in the dark, like an animal, watching him.

'Hi, is this where you live?'

'Naw, just me place in town.'

Someone laughs. People shift, swathe blankets tighter round themselves, look up, and wait.

'I recognise you. I bought some fudge from you once.'

'I'm busy. Got some sleeping to do.' The fudge-seller smooths out the blanket but doesn't wrap it round him.

'I'll take your whole stock. How much you got?'

'You what?'

'I'm serious.'

The sweet taste, the joy of it, crowds into his brain. His mouth waters and he gulps. An arm stretches up and offers him a canvas bag. He reaches out and the bag is snatched back. The curly-headed man, his cap pulled down over his forehead, crouches forward, his wrist held out. David clicks and, takes the bag. The other touches the peak of his hat.

Figures move towards him.

'You need some veg with that? Onions?'

'How about a nice tea-cake?'

He clicks with a young woman bundled into a torn anorak far too large for her and backs away. More people come at him. He clicks with an older black woman in dungarees who doesn't seem to bother about the cold and a lad in a jersey with the sleeve ravelled, grabs at bags and parcels, bows his head and makes off.

Back in City Square he looks up at Franklin's Tower and remembers the saying: 'Franklin Never Sleeps'. Figures move past lighted windows in the upper storeys. His wits clear. The horsemen rode straight into the Old Town, they took Sarah to the mills. He runs along the side of the square and behind the Halls and bangs his fist against the rear gate.

'I need Juno! Now.'

After a minute the gate swings open and warm air laden with the rich odour of the stable gusts out. Martin rubs the sleep from his eyes and yawns.

'Ain't you going to have a wash?'

'Here, present for you.'

He shoves the bags at the stable boy, keeping hold of the fudge, and lifts the bridle off the pegs at the end.

'Onions, yeah and bread, cakes, lots of apples. Take some for Juno.'

He's busy with the saddle-girth. Juno shifts sideways and he shuffles along, past her shoulders.

'Sorry. Did I pinch you? I didn't think, I never think.' He strokes Juno's neck and remembers the flannel and wipes her face and folds it into his pocket. 'You should have an apple.'

Martin is waiting as he leads Juno out.

'Here, someone wants to meet you.'

He tugs at a leading-rein and a dark shape moves behind him. A grey face with large eyes and a pale oversized muzzle pokes over his shoulder. The ears are tall, delicate and mobile. The creature wrinkles thick lips, the mouth opens and a trumpet blast brays out. Juno backs away one pace, pauses, swings her head from side to side and comes forward.

The two beasts confront each other. The smaller creature stands his ground and looks up, his head cocked to one side, considering. Juno dips her head and whinnies.

The creature draws breath and Martin offers him an apple and hands David one, for Juno.

David sighs:

'I've got enough on. I can't.'

'No-one wants him, he'll go to Franklin.'

'It's not on.'

David checks he has the oats and the other gear.

'He's called Jupiter, like he's meant for you. He's a tough little beggar. No trouble.'

'I said "No".'

'Look at them.'

Juno's bows her head and Jupiter's tongue licks gently down her face. Juno snorts and lowers her head further.

Martin holds a feed bag out to him.

'Made for each other.'

He doesn't answer but swings himself up into the saddle. He's got the trick of it now. You have to jump up and get your foot in the stirrup and not think about whether you'll make it.

Martin attaches the leading rein to the side of the saddle.

'See you again, won't I?'

David waves to him.

At the gate he asks:

'Is his name really Jupiter?'

'Naw, made that bit up. Knew you'd like it. Good luck.'

He remembers nothing of his night-ride through the City, the clatter of Juno's hooves echoing off the buildings on both sides, Jupiter trotting along behind. He circles round the Pit and recognizes some of the buildings he passes, a residence block shored up with timbers, a corner shop with old bottles on the display stands in the window and later the lath and plaster buildings of the Old Town.

He knows he's near the stables where he rested that night with Juno. He stands in the stirrups and looks round. No-one to be seen, no lights in the windows. He listens and sniffs the air but can't smell the stables. Jupiter clicks a hoof, taking his weight on one hind leg to rest the other. He swings his leg up and slides down from Juno's back and takes an apple from his pocket and offers it to her. Jupiter snorts and breathes in and he strolls back and offers him one before he brays out.

'Juno,' he whispers. 'I need your help. Hay. Oats. Water. Can you smell it out?'

He slackens the rein. Juno takes one pace forwards and swings her head round and looks at him, then swings back and he hears her sniff at the air. She sniffs again and sets off, to the left, then right at the next side-street and out into a small moon-lit square and he knows he is very near the hall where the feast was held. He throws his arms round her.

'You're a genius! And you, Jupiter, your turn next.'

He calls out:

'Anyone there? Someone help me?'

A light gleams in an upstairs window. He turns towards it and it snuffs out and the shutter slams shut.

'Anyone else?'

Silence.

He takes the last apple from his pocket, polishes it and holds it up. It shines like lamplight and he offers it to Jupiter on the flat of his hand. The donkey wrinkles his lips and cranes forward, and he slips it back into his pocket.

The donkey's chest swells as he inhales. His mouth gapes and he brays, loud as a foghorn, echoing off cobbles and walls and buildings. He sucks in a huge draught of air and redoubles his braying.

David grins.

'You've done well and I've found another apple.'

As he hands them out the shutters bang open all round him.

'You idiot! You'll bring Greenjackets!'

A grey-bearded portly man in a pleated nightshirt stands in the doorway of the three-storey house behind him. He has a tasselled night cap on his head and velvet slippers on his feet. David recognises him.

'O'Connor! The man I want to see! Franklin's taken Sarah. You must help me.'

'Don't I know you?' The older man peers at him. 'You made all that trouble with Luke. Go back to your City, and take those...' he makes a shooing gesture, '...things with you.'

He retreats into his hall-way.

David feels the merriment inside him. No time for that.

'You've hurt his feelings. You want some more donkey-noise? He hasn't started yet.'

Jupiter strains against the leading rein and licks his lips.

O'Connor throws up both hands, palms out.

'Follow me.'

He leads the way to the stables, still in his slippers. David wipes Juno and Jupiter down and whispers his thanks to them. He takes oats and hay from the rack and pumps up fresh water for them. He makes sure they have clean straw and settles them for the night. For some reason he thinks of baby Mikey casketed in his drawer-cradle.

When he closes the stable door, he finds that O'Connor has slipped away. He's back in his house, dressed in a striped red and purple gown with a fur collar. The mayor spreads himself, his belly against a dark oak table, a mug of ale in his right hand, and he talks and makes chopping gestures with his left.

David refuses the ale. A plate of stew and another of salad are set beside him. He pays them no attention. The fire in the iron range at the end of the room warms him. His back aches and his eyelids droop.

He breaks into the older man's talk.

'Franklin's kidnapped Sarah. The Greenjackets took her in Coneystone, because she stood up against him. Don't you understand? Franklin's your enemy. He's got Sarah trapped in that mill, that prison, that slave-camp right now. We have to do something.'

O'Connor frowns as if he's not used to people interrupting him.

'Not easy dealing with Franklin. He owns the City, he owns the police – the Greenjackets – he owns most of our houses.' He holds up a hand as if David had tried to break in again. 'No one likes him, granted, but it's as if a serpent has chosen to burrow into your back-garden. If you feed it a sucking pig from time to time, it sleeps, it keeps the rats down. If you poke it with a stick it slithers forth and takes you for the sucking pig. I'm sorry to hear about Sarah, but...'

He spreads his hands. David slams his fist into the table and gravy slops from the plate. Energy flows through him like electricity.

'He has Sam too. You know Sam don't you?'

O'Connor tenses and fixes his eyes on David. His hands do not move on the table.

'Don't bring him into it.'

'Sam. You let him down, didn't you? What do his parents think about that?'

'Sarah is Sarah. I am truly sorry for her. I liked – I like her. But she made trouble, like Luke, like you do. Sam is different.' He finds the word, the correct diplomatic word, and relaxes. 'I regret Sam.'

David glares at him. He hates these talking people who build snares out of words to trap you.

'She's the only one who fights for you! You let Franklin grow stronger every day. You let him take Sam, you let him take Sarah. One day he'll come for you.'

'Young man! You watch your words in my house, I…'

'She's my friend. And so is Luke.'

He snatches the nightcap off the old man's head and hurls it into the fire and strides from the room.

Cloudbanks mass above him and a red band smoulders in the sky to the east. A pair of older women, bundled up in thick padded clothes with headscarves and dun cloaks wrapped round them sweep each side of the street with brooms. He steps back into the doorway and the woman on his side grunts but doesn't look up as she works her way past him.

Juno whinnies a greeting to him and Jupiter looks up. He stalled them together where the stables open out at the end. It's warm beside them with the hot sweet smell of hay and horse-flesh and feed and he grows calmer. He bridles them and straps on Juno's saddle and fixes Jupiter's leading rein and braces himself and leads them out.

He passes few citizens of the Old Town as he heads towards the Pit steering by the banner of smoke from the triple chimney. He ignores the shops, opening all round them. He doesn't have the cash they use anyway. He's hungry.

He recognizes the poster, Franklin's face torn in half, "The road-beast must die" scrawled across it in red ink that's dripped down, like blood. He slackens the reins and Juno halts and he slides down to the cobbles. Jupiter nuzzles against him and he strokes the pale, over-large nose and thinks.

Someone shouts:

'David! And Juno! And what…who on earth is that?'

'Luke! I forgot how good it is to see you.'

He hugs Luke to him. The bones of his shoulders are like kindling-sticks through the thin T-shirt. The children crowd round and Susie jumps up and down, clasping her brother's hand and shouting.

'He's back and Juno's back and he's brought a new friend!'

They cluster round Jupiter and reach out to pet him. He tells them about donkeys, about their delicate ears and the cross on their back.

Susie nods.

'You mustn't forget Juno.'

'You're right.'

Luke grins.

'Does he play football?'

'Yeah, four legs too. That's for later. Hate to say this but I'm trouble. Your mayor just told me I am.'

'Him. Finger in every pie, that one.'

'Well he thinks you're trouble too.'

Luke looks down. His shoulders slump. David bites his lip.

'I'm a fool. Sorry.'

'It's OK.' He pats David's arm, 'Long story. Fell out with him when I started with Sam. He blames me for everything.'

Luke falls silent. David continues:

'Franklin's taken Sarah. Greenjackets seized her in the

village cos she tried to stop his schemes. They've taken her to the mills.'

Luke slaps himself in the face, hard.

'That is horrible.' He's silent for a full half-minute. Then he looks up and says, as if they'd talked it over and agreed on it, 'We'll go back, won't we? Back to that place.'

David feels the tears prick behind his eyes. He tries to think what he should say, what would be right, but the only words that come are:

'You're a good friend to me.'

'No worries. Sam was good with horses. Used to work in the stables. You look a bit like him.'

He claps his hands,

'C'mon kids. No fun and games today. Sorry.'

The children groan as one. Jupiter brays. An idea strikes David so brilliant it must be obvious to everyone.

'Hey Susie, children. Will you do something for me? Do you know anything about horses? Will you look after Juno and Jupiter for me?'

They crowd forward, shouting out 'Yes!' and 'We'll take care of them!'

He explains about the tack strapped on behind the saddle and what horses and donkeys need and how to be kind to them. Then Luke talks to them with a serious expression on his face and they gather round him and listen and none of them fidgets.

'Remember. You're grown-ups today. Susie, you're in charge. It'll be OK. Some of them have kin who work in stables.'

He slaps David on the back.

'I've got a plan. No point in going til it's dark. You look like you need a decent meal and a bit of rest.'

David winces. Luke is tougher than you'd think, but he knew that already. For the first time since leaving Coneystone a glimmer of hope flickers within him.

Re-education

Raindrops like hailstones pelt down, drenching everything. Rivulets wash along the streets towards the mills, tumbling rubbish, vegetable peelings, wood shavings and crumpled paper along with them. Luke and David and the children wait it out in the stables. David shows them how to plait Jupiter's tail. First time any of them have ever done anything like that. They muck out and get the stall ready for Juno and Jupiter. They eat and David sleeps.

Luke peers out at the rain.

'Suits us. They don't come out so much when it's like this.'

He finds a piece of folded cardboard to hold like a penthouse roof over his head. David offers him one of the grey oilskin cloaks from the row of pegs by the door.

'You OK? You'll be soaked.'

'Used to it. It's slackening.'

They bid farewell to the horses, at peace in their stalls, and duck out of the warmth onto the street. Dark clouds hang heavy above them and the moist cobbles shine silver. Few people are out and those they meet wrap their cloaks tight round them and hurry past. David has a spare oilskin bundled up under his arm. In the end he persuades Luke to wear it 'for camouflage.'

'You have to stop punishing yourself.'

'Why?'

They make for the streets above the mill. Once they hear the tramp of booted feet and the harsh whistle of the Greenjackets and shrink back into a dead-end alley. They find the place Luke marked out earlier, the mouth of a lane with a dead-end side-alley off it not two yards from the entrance. It's choked with scraps and rubbish from the eating house next door and reeks of decaying cabbages. David forces his way in first. Nausea swells in his throat as Luke scrapes the rotting mass to the side with his foot and squeezes into the shadows of the side-alley His face is grim, like Adam's on parade. David hasn't seen him like this.

He grips David's hand.

'Sam's in there too. I know it. This is going to work.'

He steps back, into darkness. They wait.

The rain stops, the sky clears and David shivers and wraps his arms round himself. He watches the shadow cast by the moon shift slowly across the end of the lane. Something scuttles past. A rat sniffs at his ankle and stands erect on hind legs to inspect him.

'Hello,' he whispers. 'You know your way round the alleys. Do you think it'll work?'

The rat flicks its tail and disappears into the rubbish. Nothing happens.

Metal scrapes on the cobbles, then a whistle wails twice. They ready themselves. A figure appears at the end of the lane, its head grotesque in the outsize helmet. Light glitters on the faceted insect-eye lenses. It swings its head from side to side as it stalks past and makes no noise.

225

David lets out a breath. Luke touches the back of his hand and presses himself further back into the gloom.

'Now! Quick.'

David moves forward and cries out:

'Help me!'

He screams and smacks a stick of wood against the wall beside him.

Silence.

He shouts louder with all the breath in his lungs:

'Help me – please...'

His voice chokes.

The creature halts at the mouth of the lane, not two metres from him. It tilts its head sideways and hisses. A leathery arm stretches towards him, the whip haft thrust out like a wasp-sting. It gives a short whistle.

He steps backward, away from it, stumbles, flails out with one hand against the wall, and falls backwards. It takes a pace towards him, then another, tilting its head from side to side. The body is slim, leather-clad under the helmet. It pauses and in the same instant smashes its whip down and hisses again. The rat squirms on the paving stones, its back broken. The Greenjacket stamps down on it and grunts. David raises his hand, bloody from where he's grazed the skin, and lets it flop and moans.

The creature takes another step into the lane and prods at him with the butt of the whip. He seizes it with his other hand. A bolt that crackles scalds his palm and he screams again. The Greenjacket hisses and shoves the whip at him. Luke steps out from the shadows behind it and slips something David doesn't see over the helmet and jerks the figure backwards. The whip falls from its hand and David grabs it.

'Stand back.'

He stabs it at the creature's throat, finds a button on the side and presses it and smells the odour of lightning. The Greenjacket writhes, its head bent back, and lies still. He is struck by how slight the body is. Luke fumbles with the helmet and lifts it up. A mane of dark hair tumbles out. The head slumps back and he sees the face of a young white woman, pale as paper, eyes closed. He slaps her. She doesn't respond. His hand trembles.

Luke looks up and meets his eye:

'They've got Sarah. And Sam. It was her or us.'

They pull at the gloves and boots. The woman stirs and David sees the glint of the pupil under her eye-lid. He snatches the whip away from her, rams it into her palm but doesn't press the button and cuffs her with his free hand instead. She falls back. He crouches and listens.

'She's breathing.'

He hands Luke the boots.

'You get the outfit. I'm too fat.'

They tie and gag the woman, bundle her up in the capes and stash her under the vegetables. Luke slides the helmet over his head.

'There's all sorts in here.'

His voice echoes as if he were shouting through a funnel. The helmet whistles.

'Sorry!'

'No, go ahead. And get someone fatter.'

They stand at the end of the alley. Luke whistles twice, hard, and they hear boots on cobblestones a street away.

David slips back into the shadows. He swallows. If he reaches out he'll touch the unconscious Greenjacket. Why on earth did she become one of them? A whistle wails from further down the street, towards the mill.

'Ready,' whispers Luke. 'They're coming.'

He moves out into the road and David creeps back to the mouth of the lane. Light flashes on a helmet fifty yards distant.

'Only one of them. Easy.'

David ducks back. A voice crackles as through a microphone:

'Where's your whip? Report.'

Luke takes a pace back and the Greenjacket follows him past the mouth of the lane.

David grips the whip tight and hisses:

'Behind you!'

He leaps onto the Greenjacket's back and jams the whip under the helmet, into the nape of its neck.

A whip cracks down on the back of his hand and he gasps and tumbles face-first onto the cobble-stones. He hears running feet and someone kicks him hard in the ribs. The blow shoves him sideways and onto his back. Three Greenjackets peer down at him through their goggle-eyed helmets. They came down the street from the other direction, behind Luke, and ambushed him. The one in the centre hisses and slams its whip against his lips. His face scalds in agony and everything splinters into shards of light.

David retches but can't vomit. He rolls across the floor of a metal cell that jerks from side to side as if shaken in a giant's fist. His lips ache as if they had been ironed. Something shrieks outside and the motion stops. The throb of Franklin's mills surrounds him and the metal floor quivers in time with it.

The hollowed-out voices of helmeted Greenjackets sound outside. The end wall of his cell cracks along the side and becomes a door and the throbbing deepens.

'Out!'

He finds a handhold on the doorway and drags himself out. His mouth scalds and he can't feel his tongue. Everything round him smells of burnt oil. Lamps like yellow streetlights glare down from a rough stone roof twice a man's height above him. A smaller cousin of the road-beast crouches at rest behind him, the tailgate open. Behind it a long concrete ramp, half the length of the wall, reaches up into darkness.

Luke's next to him, in T-shirt and shorts.

'David, are you OK? I…'

'Silence.'

A Greenjacket steps forward and pokes a metal pole, spiked like a lance, at them. Another opens a door in a metal wall in front of him. Light floods through and he screws up his eyes and looks round him.

Luke holds up his empty hands to the guards. He helps David limp to the door, pauses on the threshold and half-lifts him through. They enter a windowless metal chamber with bunk beds screwed to the wall. A steel toilet squats in the corner.

Luke looks round.

'It's cool. We got inside the mill.'

David slumps down on the lower bunk and leans back.

The throbbing surrounds him and swallows him and he becomes a part of it.

Later Luke cradles him in his arms and lifts a spoon to his mouth and tilts it. Liquid runs down his lips and he sucks it in. It's a thick soup and it eases his throat. He is hungrier than he has ever been. He gulps at it and swallows the fragments of pasta and onion in it whole.

Luke whispers to him the whole time.

'There. Careful, take it down. You'll sleep better.'

He gulps at another spoonful.

'We're a team.' Luke murmurs. 'We'll find them, both of them, all of them.'

More soup. He clings to the spoon.

'Whoa. Just one more spoonful, OK?'

Luke tenderly wipes his lips and lays him back on the bunk. David feels the roughness of the blanket on his hand. As sleep consumes him, he thinks of Juno and Jupiter together in their stall, of Jeb and Annie and baby Mikey, and of Sarah, somewhere in the mill, perhaps the other side of this metal wall.

Boxer

David puts a hand to his lips and snatches it away. They're still swollen but the pain now comes in waves. He stands next to Luke in a row of women and men lined up on one side of a huge flood-lit chamber and swallows foul air and smells the reek of oil and sweat and hot metal. Somewhere in it is a leathery odour, like that of working horses. He sniffs but can't be sure. The throbbing pounds at them. Far away a huge furnace, the brother of the one in the first mill glares out at them, but there are no giant machines. He feels as if he is trapped in a cavern far under the ground.

The glare grows brighter. The furnace grins fire and gapes. Flame licks up from its gorge. The heat beats at him, even this far away. He shrinks back.

He glances round. He and Luke are in the front row of the squad, women and men, young and old, one resting her weight on two sticks. A woman dressed in spotless white overalls with long curly hair, scarlet lipstick and a porcelain complexion, a riding-crop tucked under her arm, strides towards them.

A Greenjacket pokes at him from behind with the butt of a cattle-prod.

'Eyes front!'

A rumbling roar with a rattle as of small stones grating together rasps out, like a heavy breaker crashing on a pebbled shore. Flames thunder in the giant chimney reaching up into shadow. The feed-wagon creaks back and the furnace maw grates shut. He shudders and holds himself still and stares at the scene before him.

The floor of the mill is crowded with machines, smaller than those in the first mill, the size of a kitchen range or a feeding trough. They're drawn up in ranks with alleys running between them. Artificers in white overalls, like the ones he and Luke wear, bend over them and service their needs. The contraptions are never still. They whine and bristle and chew. A shower of sparks bursts out from one. He hears distant shouts and the clash of metal thrown against metal.

He glances at Luke. How will they find Sarah – or Sam – in this?

Metal grates on metal somewhere on the other side of the mill. A roller-blind door, the height of a tall house, set in the end wall at the top of a grey concrete ramp creaks up. The light that slants down from above is daylight. They watch, barely able to breathe. A wagon moves towards the mill, hauled by women and men, yoked to the shaft. They're dressed in denim, corduroy, some of them in the once-bright colours of the Old Town, but faded and ragged. The woman at the front has wrapped grey cloths round her feet. Her head hangs down, mouth open. A guard stands on the bench seat, legs wide apart, and flicks his whip out over them, and snaps it down with a crack. The wagon jerks forward a yard. He brings the whip down again and someone screams and the wagon jerks again and reaches the top of the ramp.

The shutter creaks down and jams. A technician bangs at the edge of it with a metal pole. David squints and looks up past him and glimpses the huge wheels of a road-beast at rest on a roadway above them. He remembers how Sarah pulled him to safety when they crawled together under the beast at the castle. The shutter slams down and the throb of the mill echoes louder. He aches with tiredness. The Third mill is underground, under the others.

The wagon rolls down the ramp, towards the machines. The slaves brace themselves against the yoke to slow it and a brake squeals on one of the wheels.

'Eyes front!' snarls the woman in the white overalls. 'Welcome to Re-education. Here you will learn how to live as citizens of Market World. You are not permitted to fail. If you fail to learn the simple lesson, no pay without work, no food without pay, you will repeat it until you do.'

She points: 'The wagon team. They contribute brute effort, like horses, and earn their keep. You understand?'

The squad stares at her. David thinks of Juno, of Sarah holding out an apple to her, of how she taught him to fold little Mikey's nappy that day, and he started to think of a new life away from the City and the One Law and Market World.

The woman's eyes flick towards him.

'You understand?'

'Yes, Madam,' he mumbles.

She takes the switch from under her arm and steps forward and jabs it at him.

'What are you good for?'

He wants to say: 'Looking after babies.'

A rumbling crash resounds from the place of machines. The wagon cants to one side and the team sag from their harnesses. Metal angles and spikes and fragments are heaped against it, like spoil from a land-slip. White-overalled figures scramble and rummage in the pile. A memory from his childhood wells up: children in an orchard, rushing to pick over a pile of windfall apples.

He licks at his lips and forces out words.

'Horses. Good with horses. Luke, he knows horses too.'

The switch snaps across his face, hesitates and slips under her arm. His cheek stings, as from a hornet bite. He touches it and licks his finger and tastes rust.

'Stand straight! I decide what you're good for.'

He stares at the figures, the slaves harnessed to the wagon. The woman at the front raises her head and glances round, across the ranks of machines and their overalled servants, and her gaze passes over him.

He knows who she is, with certainty.

'Sarah!' he shouts out, 'Sarah! It's me, David…'

The Greenjacket clamps a leather-gloved hand across his mouth and pulls his head back. He twists his neck. The woman slumps forward in the harness, as if there is no strength left in her. He catches a glimpse of yellow cloth at her throat and shouts again, but the words tangle in his throat.

The woman in white glances at the Greenjacket. 'These two, get them out of here. Shed Three.'

Shed Three is built of grey sheet metal, shaped like a barn, larger than the others and newer. The rear section reaches up into the shadows of the cavern roof. Double-doors stretch the height of a house into the gable at the front.

The guard shoves David forward, his hand still over his mouth. Luke follows. The Greenjacket raps on a smaller door set in the side wall with his free hand. David notices dents on both sides of it, at chest height, as if punched out from inside. The metal is creased white at the peaks where it has been most strained.

Luke mutters:

'You got big rats in there.'

The guard ignores them.

'OK, wasn't funny.'

The door opens and the guard's fist slaps into David's back. He staggers forwards. Luke grabs his arm before he can fall. The door slams shut behind them and he hears the click of the lock. The rich, rank odour of well-used stabling fills his nostrils.

'That was Sarah. I'm sure of it.'

Luke squeezes his fore-arm.

'Yeah. We'll find Sam next.'

They stand to one side of a stable-block fit for a giant's palace. Awe fills him. Tack hangs from the wall beside them, bridles made of twisted leather thongs, straps as thick as three fingers, horse brasses like side-plates and a saddle that would take two men to lift. From the huge bins at the end he smells the bland, dusty smell of oats. Hay is stacked next to it, rick-high.

The eight stalls opposite are each wide enough to house a wagon. The massive hindquarters of a great black stallion, one and a half times as large as Juno, loom towards him. The beast swishes its tail and thwacks the stall and the structure shakes. A similar giant occupies the next stall and another next to it. The clack and shuffle of horses taking their ease fills the air, beneath it the throb of Franklin's mill. A stable-lad with a bundle of straw in his arms comes out of a stall further down, glances at them and bobs back into the next one. The stallion stamps. David's body shakes and he can't make himself stop. He looks up in wonder, a pygmy in a giant's world.

A voice floats down from somewhere above him:

'Impressive aren't they?'

Laughter and a young black woman smiles down at him. She perches on stilts, her feet level with his head.

'I'm Ruth and those beasts are mine. You don't have to gape at them.'

She has cropped hair and a red, green and yellow head scarf.

'They've got the road-beasts in the mill next door, and the riding beasts upstairs and we've got the Great Beasts. Much more fun. Road-beasts for the highway, but these are the beasts for cross-country work. Get yourselves changed.'

She points at a couple of grimy white overalls hanging on the end pegs.

The first task is stilt-walking. They start off half-size, leaning on the metal wall where the vibrations pulse against their shoulders and they shuffle and totter along. He takes a step away from the support, and then another, the stilts well apart, sways and tumbles backward and slams into the wall and slides down like a forsaken marionette.

Luke's hands stroke down his body.

'You OK?'

'Thanks.'

Luke helps him to his feet and he looks round for a mounting block. Luke grins.

'Watch me!'

He gives a twist of his body, leans into the wall with a knee bent and the stilt below him, wriggles and straightens his leg. He balances and reaches down and heaves at David's hand and David is up at the level of the stallion's back.

'You done this before,' says David.

'It's a knack.'

Ruth waves to them.

'OK. It's grooming, then mucking out.'

She strides off towards the end stalls, which seem even higher. They set off after her, wobble, and fight the desire to lean on each other.

They stagger along the wall into the shadows at the far end. The metal slats of an up-and-over door, hauled up by a cord like a well-rope, are set into the end-wall. He rests against it a moment and feels the pulse of the vibrations. Sadness grips him and he thinks of Sarah. How can he help her? Did she see him, did she know it was him?

Luke holds onto his arm and they set off, across the open space towards the stalls. Five paces.

Luke grins:

'You can really move on these things.'

He takes his hands off the stilts at each step and claps them together. David grimaces, lurches forward, totters, grabs at the end of the stall and crumples into it. He gasps out all the air in his lungs and takes in the odour of a well-exercised horse.

'Landed on our feet,' says Luke.

They edge past the hip of the great horse. David swallows and runs his hand down the massive flank. He feels the warmth of the body, the bristles of the coat coarse against his open hand. He breathes more easily and pats at the expanse of flesh in front of him. The stallion whinnies, very softly, and edges away from him. He moves forward between the flank and the timber of the stall, thick as the roof-beams in Old Town. The head swings round towards him and the huge eyes weigh him up. *You could crush me,* he thinks, *and it wouldn't even give you indigestion.*

The beast watches him. He has nothing to give. He wriggles under the overalls and slips out of his t-shirt. The planks at the end of the stall press into his back as he leans into them and reaches up to stroke the shirt down over the face, half as long as he is tall. His hand moves around the eye-sockets, follows the outline of the bone down the nose and gently over the lips and the mouth where the teeth are the size of piano-keys. He feels the shape of the colossal, subtle face, the contours of it under his fingers.

A name-plate hangs over the stall. *Boxer.*

'Pleased to meet you,' he says. 'I'm David. I know you. I wish you could meet Sarah, she'd approve of you.'

He caresses the side of Boxer's head once more and beckons Luke and hands him the T-shirt. He takes Luke's hand in his and guides him, stroking down and gentling the beast.

The brushes and combs hang on the wall above the manger. He starts work, brushing at the neck. When he gets to the shoulders he gives Luke the curry-comb and shows him how to follow on with circular movements. They work their way along the barrel of the chest and onto the loins, the thighs and the hind-quarters.

He crosses to the other side and asks Boxer's permission to squeeze by and they work their way down again. They've nearly finished when Ruth calls:

'Mucking out!'

She leans an out-size rake and shovel against the stall-post. They slide down from the stilts and start work.

Luke grunts:

'Some circus, this.'

David feels the soreness above his knees, where the muscles strain to keep balance. His body is somehow at ease despite this and the ache in his mouth. It is impossible to ignore the simplicity of the beasts about them. He knows he will sleep tonight as if in his own bed.

They shovel out the foul straw, scatter fresh and share out the feed along the row of mangers. Boxer lowers his head for David to stroke him again. When he takes his T-shirt back, it is moist and warm, with a warmth that reminds him of little Mikey's tummy.

He wakes as a voice calls out. Ruth. He's lying at the end of the stall propped against the wall next to the manger. Boxer's huge foreleg, the hair feathering over the hoof, is a few inches from his thigh.

'OK,' she says, 'Enough for today. Feed time for you, now. Wash up and follow on.'

The smell of bean stew wafts towards them from the enamel bucket Ruth places in the middle of the long table. She breaks a loaf into pieces and mutters something under her breath as she does it. She ladles the thick brown liquid into bowls and passes them round. Three stable-lads enter, all of them black. They carry brushes and cloths and other gear. Luke springs to his feet. The third lad drops his cloth and it flops down like an exhausted gull. He rushes forward and throws his arms round Luke and sobs. Luke reaches into the thick mane of hair on the back of his head and presses the lad's face into his shoulder.

'I thought I'd never see you again.'

The young man lays his hands one on each side of Luke's face and tilts it towards him and kisses him on the lips. Tears spill down both their faces. Silence. One of the others claps his hands together. Ruth joins in. The other lad pounds on the table with both fists, and David claps too, slamming his hands together so the palms ring.

After a long time Luke and the other lad look round, and it's as if light pours from their faces. They move towards the table, hand in hand. Luke beams with joy and shouts out, one word:

'Sam.'

David can't stop grinning at them.

'I'm so happy for you, both of you.'

I am, he thinks, but Sarah is not here.

They all crowd round, slapping Luke and Sam on the back, cheering. Sam has his fingers wrapped round Luke's forefinger.

'Stew's getting cold.'

Ruth leads the way back to the table. Luke pushes his bowl towards Sam.

'Wow! Thank you so much.'

Ruth shrugs.

'He's a good'un. Knows a bit about horses.'

David watches them together. There's a gentleness in

Luke's face, behind all the merriment, that he hasn't seen before. Sarah would notice that.

'Guess you've got a lot to talk about,'

He moves towards Ruth's end of the table and turns to her.

'Tell us about the set-up here.'

She looks down at her stew.

'Yeah, well. It's how you see.'

The stable-lad opposite, a young black man with a gold ear-ring and a broken front tooth, frowns.

'It's the other place.'

'What other place?'

Ruth lays a hand on the young man's wrist.

'Nathan, forget it.'

'But it's not right.'

'Nathan…'

Nathan bursts out:

'They take the horses through. They make them go, they don't want to. I hate it.'

Ruth sighs.

'Do you think any of us like it?'

'They send you to the wagons if you argue. "You like horses – try being one". But we'd be kind to the beasts, make it easier for them.'

He shivers and his face crumples. David looks from him to Ruth.

'What's that about the wagons? I don't understand, they send you to the wagons?'

'That's enough,' says Ruth. 'I make it good for you here, don't I? Keep your head down. Be thankful. Eat.'

Much later, the stable-hands stretch out on the straw at the end and listen to the comfortable sound of the beasts at their evening feed.

He asks Nathan:

'You from the Old Town?'

'Yeah. I was out with me mates and they picked us up on the street, said we were breaking curfew.'

The other lad, Ozzie, joins in. They can't be more than eighteen.

'They knew where we were. It was O'Connor. Remember how he looked at us. He said "You'll be OK, you'll hear 'em coming, you can hide in the alleys." Said he'd let us in the feast later. I remember that. He never did.'

David thinks for a bit.

'Remember someone called Sarah? Was she in here? From a village called Coneystone? Had a horse called Juno?'

The lads look at each other.

'Remember Juno in the Old Town,' says Ozzie.

'And Sarah?'

'Can't remember. I'm tired. Gotta sleep.'

He rolls over, away from him.

David lies there. After a while someone whispers to him. It's Sam.

'They know who Sarah is, they don't like talking about her. Someone said they brought her in a couple of days back and they sent her straight to the wagons. Don't know what she did. We're OK here, Ruth looks after us, we're the lucky ones. So now you know.'

He lies back and won't talk about it anymore.

Luke mutters:

'We can't do anything now. We will, we'll help you. You're like family. I promise.'

Sam lifts his head up.

'Yeah. Luke and me.'

Sarah and Franklin

Three days earlier, when the second of the great horses foundered and died in front of her at the place where the brambles narrowed the track, Sarah knew that she must escape. They'd kept a constant watch on her since her first attempt at the ford when they dragged her from the horse and she managed to smash a rock into that brute's eye-piece. Now her hands are pinioned behind her back and she's blindfolded, and slung over the loins of one of the great horse, the rods hissing into the cylinders below her.

The guard in front of her dismounts and she hears his footsteps and the thud, like a mattress dropped from waist-high, as he kicks something. There's silence for a second and then an electric crack and the smell of singed horsehair. The horse under her flinches and shies back. The Greenjackets all laugh and a whip cracks and they move off.

She's had no food since they took her. She keeps dipping into oblivion and she forces herself to stay awake. At last she hears the hollow sound of hooves on cobbles echoing from nearby buildings and sinks finally into sleep.

The room throbs. The floor she lies on pulses, the walls pulse, the air she breathes pulses. Someone rips the blindfold from her face and severs the bonds on her wrists but the room is in darkness and no-one speaks. A door slams somewhere far away from her and the pulse of Franklin's mill claims her.

Later, a hatch at the bottom of the door slides open and yellow light seeps in. Someone slides a tray with a cheese burger placed neatly in the centre and a plastic cup of water into the cell and the hatch closes. She eats the bread, which turns to paste in her mouth and sticks to her teeth, and the cheese.

Later a middle-aged balding man in an untidy suit peers into the cell. He reminds Sarah of the audit clerk in the courtroom long ago. He glances at the folder balanced on the pile of neatly-folded clothing in his arms.

'Ms Sarah Cordell? Good day. I'm Fortis Slocum, Mr Franklin's assistant. Important meeting. You must dress for the occasion.'

She groans and rolls away from him and Slocum drops the clothing on the bed. He tugs at Sarah's elbow but he has no strength in his hands.

'Please. You'll be late. You don't want to make a bad impression.'

Sarah turns her head and glares at him.

'Go away.'

'Please understand, we want to help you. If you do well, there's a chance they'll make you part of the team.' Slocum taps the golden balance pin in his lapel. 'I'll just step outside, while you change.'

Sarah fingers the clothing, a pinstriped business suit with a white poplin shirt and black patent leather shoes.

'I hate these clothes. Do I have to wear shoes like that?'

He's already gone. She pulls her grimy T-shirt over her head and the smell of sweat and horse-flesh surrounds her. The bruises on her arms are purple, like mulberries. She dresses and doesn't tuck in the shirt and winds the yellow and silver scarf round her neck and stumbles after him.

Slocum scurries ahead of her along a metal corridor, lit at intervals by yellow strip-lights. They enter a narrow chamber, like a cupboard, and he presses buttons on a pad in the wall. The chamber rises and the floor presses against her feet. She follows Slocum along another corridor with wood-panelled walls and a deep purple carpet. There's an emptiness in the air round her. The beat of the mill is gone.

He taps on a door and smiles at her.

'Good luck!'

The door opens and Sarah steps through.

Her first impression is of mess, as if the person who worked there never had the patience to put anything away. The drawers hang open on the filing cabinets, the desk is strewn with papers and files are stacked in corners and along the walls. A golden balance stands on a pile of ledgers at the corner of the desk.

Franklin looks up at her. His suit is grey, rumpled and in need of pressing. A paperback book with a picture of himself shaking hands with the President on the cover lies open and upside down at his elbow. The silver $\mathcal{F}$ sparkles in his lapel.

'Do sit.'

Sarah sinks into an armchair in front of the desk. She's tilted backwards and Franklin leers down at her with his wolf eyes. Tiny clouds blotch a sky of deep and luminous blue in the window behind the entrepreneur. She loathes the man.

He puts his hands together.

'I'm very glad you've come to see me. You nearly sabotaged my Programme for the villages, but I don't hold that against you. I'm sure we can come to an arrangement to mutual ..."

Sarah grasps the arms of the chair and drags herself upright. Her throat is constricted, she can hardly force the words through:

'I hate you. You hurt people, you don't care.'

'You know, you're your own worst enemy. Let me explain things to you. Once you understand, I'm sure you'll want to join my team. Who knows? You may even become my friend.'

He grins at her, showing a mouthful of teeth, and his eyes glint. Sarah realises that that is how he smiles.

'I hate you, I'll always hate you.'

Franklin blinks, but does not raise his voice. He sighs, as if he's said all this a hundred times before.

'Think of me as a farmer. Franklins have always been farmers. I farm the City, I farm the Old Town, I farm residence-blocks, shops and markets, I invest, I tend, I fertilise and I reap a profit – and I do it for the good of Market World. That's why people like me. The contribution of my generation of Franklins will be to farm Nature. What is wrong with that?'

Sarah grabs the edge of the desk and hauls herself to her feet. She cannot let this fat stupid man continue to spout nonsense, like a pundit on a newscast. She lunges forward, her face six inches from Franklin's, and screams:

'You poison the earth, the water, the air. Those poor people in the Secret Valley, they couldn't eat, they couldn't breathe. They died. Your work is devilment.'

'Ms Cordell, please. Everything I do is by the One Law. Nature is… recalcitrant.' He smirks at the word. 'My task is to fit nature to the market. The temporary environmental impacts you refer to are the price of progress. I offered people the chance to work in my enterprises, to buy oxygen masks, bottled water, tinned food. If they chose not to take those opportunities, that is their responsibility, not mine.'

Sarah glares at him, her mouth open.

'But…they died.'

'You are short-sighted. Think of future generations, they will have better lives because of what I have done, higher living standards made possible by economic growth. This is Market World. Markets mean progress.'

His voice flows on, the words swim round her and she feels giddy. She remembers the giant horse foundering in front of her and feels suddenly sick.

'Those horses… You kill them.'

Franklin pauses and looks down for a moment.

'Yes…my augmented horses. We bred the giant horses, but that is not enough. Don't you understand?'

His voice becomes urgent and he leans forward like a preacher.

'It's never enough. Always, we have to invest, to do better, to grow. That's the market. You've seen my giant horses, you've seen my mechanically assisted horses, always larger, stronger, better. Sadly we seem to have overtaxed the heart. I promise you, the next version will do better.'

He plucks a soiled linen handkerchief with the $\mathcal{F}$ in the corner from his pocket and wipes it across his mouth.

'Oh, I do want you on my team. You have such passion. If we could convince you, you would be such an ally.'

Sarah smashes both fists down on the desk.

'You. Are. A. Monster. I. Hate. You.'

The hatred burns pure within her, like a holy fire. She sweeps the papers to the side and everything cascades to the floor. The folders spill open and pour out sheaves of memos, charts and diagrams. She sees a pile of letters with the golden balance embossed at the head of the page and thrusts them away from her. She becomes aware of Slocum on his knees beside her, his hands pawing at the documents, muttering to himself.

'Oh dear, oh dear. I'll never sort it out, they'll all blame me, I know they will.'

Franklin smacks him, not hard, across the shoulder blades, and draws back his hand to smack him again as if he were a mule that refused to move forward, then grins.

'You're a fool Slocum, but you cheer me up. Now get that woman out of here, she understands nothing, we need her to learn. Re-educate her: full programme.'

He sweeps his hand towards her as if brushing away a fly. Sarah gathers the phlegm in her mouth and spits with all her force. The spittle flops out and dribbles down her chest. Leather-gloved hands seize her arms. She braces herself but can't break free.

Franklin screws up his eyes and laughs, a full-throated guffaw, showing all his teeth.

'You'll learn, nothing's for free, everything must be

paid for and if it doesn't come with a price tag, put one on it. And you'll pay for your education, one way or another.'

'You'll never win, you inhuman, greedy...'

Franklin nods to someone behind Sarah and a gloved hand clamps itself across her lips. She bites at it and tastes leather and the glove is jerked away from her mouth. She grimaces and licks her lips. The blood tastes salt on her tongue.

'They'll come, David, the Enforcers.'

She squirms in the guard's grasp but he drags her backwards.

Franklin sits back in his chair and grins broadly, like a shark that finds its prey amusing.

'The Enforcers enforce the market. They're on my side, Ms Cordell.'

The door slams in her face. The guard shoves her along the corridor. She knows she is nothing to these people.

'Wait! Wait for me.'

Slocum catches up with them. He leans against the wall, panting, and pushes his glasses up onto his forehead. He mutters to the guard and clicks wristbands with him.

Sarah glares at him and he fiddles with something he has picked up from a bench.

'Let us not part enemies. Would you like some coffee? I have a flask.'

She takes a plastic cup. The coffee tastes of burnt toast. Slocum's voice rattles on like a freight train over points:

'Expenses for attending the interview, plus recompense for inconvenience, minus escort, accommodation and clothing: 27 credits.'

He offers her his forearm, his sleeve pulled back, his face that of a chubby child anxious to please his teacher. She flips back her sleeve and he stares at her wrist.

'But you have no wristband? How do you live?'

'I have friends. We share things.'

'Oh, come on. You really do need to be educated. More coffee?'

They tramp along a metal corridor somewhere deep in the bowels of the fortress. The beat of Franklin's mill swells around her. She feels sick.

A grill across the corridor bars their way. Slocum unclips a large key-ring from his belt and sorts through it, murmuring to himself. He leans into the grill and clicks it open. They march on, pass through another grill and stop at double-doors with a metal spy-hole in them.

Slocum fiddles with his keys.

'Now I want you to look on this as an opportunity. Your first day on the job.' He blinks. 'It may not be everything you expected, but we all start at the bottom, well most of us. Do your best and perhaps you'll rise to office work.'

He peeps through the spy-hole and pushes one of the doors open. Cold air blows through. He pats her on the back.

'I knew you'd come good. I can always tell.'

He ducks back and the door clicks shut behind her. She is at one side of a large paved courtyard. She shivers and hugs herself against the cold. A yellow road-beast, smaller than the ones she saw on the highway, crouches in front of her, murmuring to itself. The rider, perched inside it high above, looks down through glass.

Iron-bound wheels grate on stone to one side. A wagon, made of wooden planks, moves slowly round the corner. A white-overalled man with a withered arm tucked in against his chest and a yellow helmet stands on the seat urging the team onwards. A yoke extends in front of the wagon and harnessed to it, in pairs, are men and women, twelve of them. At the front are a girl who can't be more than twelve and a grey-haired man. He hangs from the traces and gasps for breath.

The driver shouts:

'Put your backs into it. You're hardly moving.'

He tucks the reins under his arm and cracks a whip over them and brings it down, and a youth in the middle cries out and lurches sideways and regains his footing.

The team heaves at the yoke and the wagon inches forward and stops and jerks forward again. It's loaded with rubble, misshapen shards of metal, angle brackets and lumps of oily coal. The wagon passes in front of her and she sees how exhausted the team is, some of them hardly able to keep their footing, all of them bent forward against the yokes. The veins in their necks bulge and sweat drips from them. The youth staggers again. He has straggled black hair and a cut across his cheek from the whip.

The wagon moves slowly through a gateway to her left. It's dark inside the building but she can see a ramp leading down and the flare of a furnace somewhere below her. An engine rattles and a metal shutter rolls down.

'Welcome! I'm Adrian.'

A smart young man in white overalls, the double of the one on the recruitment poster in the Old Town, comes up to her, his helmet under his arm, his hand held out in greeting.

She stares at him.

'But… you have the road-beasts and the horses. Why do you use people, human-beings, to drag wagons like animals?'

'It's not your place to ask questions, we educate by experience, not discussion.' He pauses and narrows his eyes. 'You're new so I'll answer. Welcome to the Re-education Centre. The haulage team learns the value of labour. They work, they shift the ore that feeds the machines and we feed them. If we used horses or tractors, they'd learn nothing. You'll see, now it's your turn.'

He leads her round a corner to a bay with a loading platform where another wagon waits. The team are already strapped into the harness and most of them hang from the straps. They watch her as if sizing her up. One of them, a young man in soiled denims with a rip across the jacket sleeve, peers at her. She remembers him from the dancing after the feast, Rick. She raises a hand.

'Hi.'

The driver in the seat at the front of the wagon flicks his wrist and the whip slashes down across the back of her hand.

'No talking.'

Pain lances through her. She rubs at her hand. Adrian pushes her into an empty harness and straps her to the yoke, and snaps it shut behind her where she can't reach the fastening. The collar weighs heavy against her neck. She breathes deep and thinks: I can do this.

The driver stands on the seat and shakes the reins.

'Enough lounging about. We're off.'

The others all lean forward into their harnesses and push at them, the muscle swelling across their shoulders and down their backs and in their calves. Sarah heaves at the harness too. The straps chafe at her shoulders and the wagon moves forward a pace then lurches and stops. Behind her the whip cracks.

'Give it some welly!' shouts the driver.

She leans into the harness, her feet slip and nothing happens. Her heart hammers in her chest and the straps cut into her. She throws herself at it and the wagon shifts again, then they're through the gateway and moving down a concrete ramp with a brake squealing against the wheel. *How do we get back up?* she thinks. She's aware of a vast hall round her and the smell of working horses and the whir of machines and the hot breath of a furnace nearby.

She doesn't know how she gets through the day, or how many trips she takes. Getting the empty wagon up the ramp is worse than taking it down. At one point the driver gets off and walks alongside them, and swigs at a flask.

Later, the cold in the air sharpens and it grows dark.

Adrian releases them from their harnesses and makes a note on a clip-board and she follows the others into a shed at the side of the courtyard. There are mattresses on the floor and a bowl of something that stinks of grease and beans on the floor. They squat round it, elbowing their way in to scoop up handfuls of the stew and stuff it in their mouths. It tastes of sour fat, but hunger is like a wolf within her and she gulps it down. She thinks of David with Mikey on his lap and the milk dripping warm from his finger onto the rosebud lips.

Rick is next to her, shovelling the mess into his mouth.

'Hi. How long have you been here?'

'Keep your voice down. No talking. You only been here one day.'

'But how are we going to organise and get out?'

'Shhh.' An older woman grips her arm and the nails bite into her flesh. 'We've got enough trouble without you.'

The woman turns away. Rick has already moved off. She lies in the dark, alone, surrounded by the others, snoring, sometimes crying out in their sleep. Rick makes a sobbing noise and wakes and looks round and goes back to sleep. The image of David swims into her mind. The look on your face in that café. I was upset, but you did look crestfallen.

At first light, Adrian rouses them and orders them out. The patent leather shoes Slocum gave her have cracked and split. She kicks them aside and finds some cloths and ties them to her feet.

'You're late,' he grumbles as he straps her into the harness. 'Thought you'd do better. You can go at the front.'

The first journey seems easier, somehow the wagon runs better than before, but the second is impossible. They haul at the yoke but it's as if they are part of a sculpture, 'Wagon with Slaves'. In the end the driver gets down and they can just move forward. She gasps for breath and her lungs burn in her chest.

Somehow they manage it. The load is lighter for the third run but they're exhausted and the driver swears at them and smacks at them with the whip and can't keep a straight line. When they reach the unloading area, the grey-haired woman gives a little gasp and collapses, spittle dribbling from her mouth, and the wagon slews sideways into a dip and keels over. The cargo of coal and metal crashes out and she slumps onto the harness.

The driver bellows at them and workers scrabble in the spoil. The furnace roars very near to her and she smells ashes and hot iron and looks up and glances round. The hall she's in is huge and the machines the people work at surround her. Someone shouts out very loud and she seems to hear her name, but the only people she can see are busy among themselves. The tiredness overwhelms her and she sags down for the few minutes she has to rest.

She can't bear more than another day of this. She knows she will, she will conquer this because she has to, because Franklin is her enemy, because Dad and Annie and Mikey and David need her to stay alive.

Franklin's Horses

David seems to wake almost immediately he closes his eyes. The floodlights high among the roof-trusses glare down. The others are all at the table with a pot of tea and the leftover bread from last night. He takes the crust and puts half of it in his pocket. Ruth looks round at them:

'OK. Today, soon as everyone's fed and watered, we're going to clear out the tack room. I want all that leather dubbined so you can smell nothing but tallow in there. Make our horses proud of themselves.'

They nod and start ferrying the barrows of feed down to the stalls and sharing it out. The lads seem downcast. They answer his questions with a "Yeah" or "OK". The good feeling of last night, when Sam and Luke clasped each other in their arms and talked in whispers until the early hours, has faded like birdsong in a rainstorm. He's no longer sure that it was Sarah at the wagon.

Ruth tethers the beasts to iron rings set in the wall above the mangers. There's a plate over each stall with the name in copperplate: Boxer, Hero, Bellman, Samson, Evening Star, Copenhagen and a couple of others at the end.

'Don't want them wandering while we're busy.'

Nathan starts to say something, and Ozzie touches his forearm and he turns away.

When he's poured the feed mixture into Boxer's trough, David offers half his share of the bread from breakfast on his palm, the fingers flat.

'I know they say it's not good for you, but just a bit won't hurt.'

He feels the lips tickle against him and the tongue lick up the crumbs, strong as an eel. The stallion looks down at him and sniffs but he has nothing more to offer. He strokes the delicate face.

'See you later.'

In the tack room he sits himself next to Nathan and works dubbin into the leather of one of the huge saddles.

'Horses look pretty fit.'

'Yeah. That's the problem.'

'What do you mean?' He tries to keep his tone even, as if he was just chatting.

'Leave it alone, can't you?'

Nathan moves over next to Ozzie and squeezes himself onto the end of the bench, so no-one can fit themselves in next to him. David catches Sam's eye. The young man's face is set, his mouth stiff, almost as if he's stopping himself from crying. Luke has an arm round his shoulders.

A chain rattles and he hears metal grate on metal not far away, at the far end of the stable. Ruth raps out:

'Concentrate on your work.'

One of the stallions neighs, high-pitched, uncertain, maybe Boxer. David hears the shuffling of hooves. He gets to his feet and balances the tallow and the rag on the pommel of the saddle.

'I need a drink of water.'

'Stay here til you've finished.'

He opens the door. The horses are crowded against the side-beams of the stalls, towards him. They toss their heads and tug at the harnesses where they are tethered to the iron rings in the wall. The scraping comes from the metal hatch at the far end of the stables. It's halfway up and still rising. A figure, the body in tight green leathers, the head outsized, ducks through, followed by another. They hold cattle lances, point forward.

David feels the hairs on the nape of his neck prickle. The shutter creaks up. He can't see into the chamber beyond. He doesn't move.

The Greenjacket ignores him. She lifts the helmet off her head and sets it down beside her and shakes out a mane of red hair.

'I hate those helmets.'

She jabs the lance towards Bellman and then Copenhagen.

'This one. And this. That'll do for now.'

The other pauses and straightens his back. He holds the lance in front of him and advances on the end beast. He keeps clear of the hind-quarters and slides the tip of the lance between the flanks of the beast and the stall.

The woman folds her arms.

'Get on. He's tied up, he won't hurt you.'

The Greenjacket sidles past the hindquarters and slips in. Bellman neighs and tosses his head again and leans sideways. The guard squeezes himself past the huge belly and fiddles at the ring. He yanks at the tether to force the horse backward. Bellman bares his teeth and bridles and snatches the strap out of his hand and neighs like a trumpet blast. The guard throws himself flat and rolls under the manger.

The woman unfolds her arms, picks up her lance and jabs it into the horse. There's a crackle, like ice breaking. Bellman jerks forward, convulses and crashes sideways into the stall. David smells burnt hair. The other horses whinny and shrink away.

The Greenjacket gets to his feet and grabs the tether. He drags on it. The beast twists and backs out of the stall and follows him. The great head sags down, and the stallion staggers like a Saturday-night drunk.

The woman strides forward to the next stall and, without breaking step, rams the lance into the hindquarters of Copenhagen. The back arches above her and the head threshes from side to side, thudding against the end post. She jabs again and twists the lance. The stallion reels to one side and she untethers him and forces him out. David catches sight of the grin on her face as she tugs the horse towards the raised shutter. She's the boss and everyone knows it.

A hand grips David's wrist, so tight it hurts.

'I hate this. We have to do something.'

Luke edges along the wall. David checks the door behind him is shut, licks his lips, and creeps after him. The throb of the mill grows louder as they move towards the gate the Greenjackets took the horses through and peer after them. The metal of the doorframe presses cold on David's cheek.

The great stallions are lit up by spotlights. They're chained to rings at the far end of the chamber with their hooves clamped into metal frames. Guards with cattle-lances surround them. Masked artificers in white overalls bend over them with strange implements and yellow sparks shower out. They whinny and jerk at their legs but can't move.

A furnace, smaller than those in the mills, its gorge sealed, stands to one side, a metal pipe snaking across the wall and up. Smiths in leather aprons pound at something with great hammers.

The red-haired woman holds up one hand and whistles. They stand back and lift, some of them hauling on cables. The shape on the ground before them shifts, and they raise it up. David bites his lip. It's a red metal structure, a parody of a horse's flank and loins and hind leg. Something whirrs, like a drill. The leg moves towards the nearest horse and clamps itself against it. The horse shudders and snorts.

More smiths shift a duplicate of the structure onto the other side of the horse. They swarm over it, some with hot rivets, some with hammers, one with a great spanner as long as his arm. One of them raises tongs with glowing metal clasped in it and forces it down. The horse shrieks, so loud the whole building resounds. The woman forces her lance into him with both hands and the scream is cut off. The clash of metal scraping, pounding, grinding on metal echoes from metal walls. The great stallions slump their heads as if they lack the strength to stand.

Ruth's voice comes from above and behind them, whispering:

'Get back to your work. I don't want to call the Greenjackets.'

Luke stares at David, his eyes desperate, like a deer with the hounds after it, and they sidle back along the wall to the tack room. The door stands open. The others cringe, close together on the bench, their work forgotten, their mouths gaping, like criminals who know their punishment comes next.

David slams the door behind him and starts to speak. Luke cuts in:

'We care for those horses, we looked after them and they make them slaves. They break their spirits, they break their bodies. I hate them.'

Ruth claps her hands like a primary school teacher.

'Luke, David, Nathan. There is nothing we can do. Get back to your work.'

David ignores her.

'It's true what Luke says. I've seen it. The broken bodies of those horses lie across the trail from here to Coneystone. They work them to death. It's monstrous.'

The black lad who hasn't said anything so far raises his hand:

'We can't fight against cattle-lances.'

Ruth nods. David pulls the door open. His glance questions them, each of them, in turn.

'Who's with me?'

Three strides take him to Boxer's stall. The head swings round and he runs a hand along the beast's flank. Boxer wrenches at his tether and snorts.

'You and me, Boxer. You and me.'

He reaches up to unleash the beast. A hand covers his.

'And me.'

Luke stands next to him.

Sam and the other lads stand at the entrance to the stall. Behind them he sees Ruth in the door of the tack room. She steps back inside and pulls it shut. The up and over door rattles. A whistle sounds out in the workshop and hydraulics seethe like fat in a pan. He motions to the others and they all of them creep to the end of the stalls and lie down, under the mangers where they are out of sight. One of the stallions neighs and there is an answering neigh, much louder, from a great horse, and he hears the heavy tramp of hooves. Excitement twists in his belly.

He cranes round and gazes over the top-rail of the stall. The double gates in the opposite wall of the stables start to open. One of the great horses sniffs and stamps its foot. Softly he rises to his feet and looses Boxer. Luke crawls under the division and does the same to the beast in the next stall and he hears the clink of bridles as the others unleash their steeds.

He turns the horse in the stall, mounts bare-back, using the side-beam to lever himself up, and rides out. Over by the gates a great horse with the red-haired woman mounted on it dips its head and neighs and comes to a halt. The woman digs her heels into its flanks. A shudder runs through the stallion and it takes one pace and halts again. She kicks her heels into him and twists round and slashes at the hindquarters with a whip. The horse whinnies and rears up and kicks out with steel hooves against the metal wall with a clash that re-echoes like distant thunder, and stamps down. Silver rods flash under its belly. Another great horse comes up behind and the woman shakes the reins and she is through and the other horse follows her.

David shivers and glances from side to side. The Greenjackets will spot them any second. He jams his knees into Boxer's flanks and leans forward.

'Go!' he yells. 'Like never before.'

Boxer leaps through the double doors, past the great horses and on, down the alley between the machines, towards the ramp with the oblong of sunlight at the head of it. White suited figures scatter on both sides. One, an older man with a crest of white hair, stands his ground, amazed, and, at the last moment, throws himself flat and rolls to safety.

The wind of his progress, laden with the harsh smell of furnace-smoke, tears at David. Hooves beat the earth behind him and the other stallions sweep out into the cavern. Luke, Sam, Nathan and Ozzie crouch in the saddles. Further back whistles shriek and the great horses hiss and stamp and trample the ground.

Boxer smashes through the last barrier and slows as he starts up the ramp. A lance hurtles past David's head and rattles on the concrete and they're all on the ramp. A Greenjacket stands at the top by the door-shutter into the courtyard and fiddles with a control panel. A motor starts up, the shutter creaks down and the oblong of daylight narrows. Boxer bounds upwards towards the sunlight at full gallop. The muscles bunch and flow across his shoulders.

David catches sight of the wheels of a road-beast outside the portal. In front of them a team of wagon slaves struggle into sight, leather harnesses across their shoulders. They inch forwards and haul a wagon towards the ramp from outside. The veins in their necks stand out, their legs strain, and a whip cracks like a gunshot behind them.

Sarah tugs at the yoke dragging the wagon towards the gate. She stares at the great black horses as they race up the ramp towards her. Hope flares within her. Close behind them come others, ridden by Greenjackets with lances and whips, like a giant wolf-pack.

The shutter grates downwards above her. She recognises the lead rider, it's David, and she shouts:

'Pull, pull harder. We'll jam the gate. They'll get through!'

Around her the wagon-slaves throw themselves at their harnesses, they heave and brace their legs and shove. The driver shouts out:

'Stop! No, to the side!'

But they've made it. She throws herself sideways and Rick copies her, the yoke slews across and the wagon comes to rest on the lip of the ramp. The shutter crashes into it and traps it, and the whine of the motor rises to a scream and fails.

David shouts:

'They've jammed the door!'

Joy surges within him, like champagne, and the riders gallop past the wagon shouting and cheering. The guard by the door hurls himself backwards, stumbles, throws up both arms and drops over the edge of the ramp and onto the earth below.

The others are already in the courtyard. They cluster together and stare at him. The outside air cools his cheeks. He senses he is part of something that will be remembered, win or lose, when people tell stories at the feasts in the Old Town.

'I'm going back.'

He swings Boxer round, flattens himself in the saddle and bursts under the door. The Great Horses bound up the ramp, coming straight at him like tigers, the pistons hissing, the woman with the lance at their head. A riderless mount gallops behind them.

Blood pounds in his ears. He knows he can do anything.

He slips down from Boxer and pulls at the bindings of the yokes and they fall away. The warrior-woman is very near, crouched over the lance, and Boxer turns to her.

David comes face to face with the first slave and stands motionless.

'Sarah! I knew it was you.'

He rips the harness away and she slumps forwards and he catches her in his arms. Behind him there's a thud, like an axe splitting a log. Boxer grunts and squeals, as if sore wounded, and staggers sideways. The riderless horse careers through the gate. David swings round and Boxer twists away from him and falls, dragging down the woman from the great stallion by the lance she thrust into his side. His great eyes gaze up at David and he raises his head and whinnies softly, once, as if in farewell, and he dies.

Sarah grabs at David's hand and drags him from that place. He stares back through the gate at Boxer, lying so still, blocking the way. A Greenjacket tugs at a booted leg poking out from under the great barrel of his chest. The other slaves shrug off the yokes and tumble through the gap and breathe in great lungfuls of the outdoor air.

Luke scrambles up the ladder bolted to the road-beast and jabs his lance through the opening high up in the side. It gives tongue and jolts back against the gates and they crease and crumple, like cardboard, and fly outwards. The beast halts in the gateway and growls at them. Luke thrusts the lance into the heart of the beast and jumps clear, and it falls silent.

Someone whistles from beyond the shutter. They run, his arm round Sarah, and hers round him. He wants to live. He doesn't care what happens next.

The Battle in Old Town

Luke shouts:

'Into the alley – over there.'

Sam and the others rush after him, and the people from the wagon follow.

Sarah pulls at David. Her eyes glow like jet against ashen skin.

'Boxer's dead. We have to save the other horses.'

He calls out 'Hero!' and the nearest stallion looks round and bows his head. He strokes his hand down the side of Hero's face. The beast whinnies.

Sarah places her hand against the stallion's lips.

'Hero. You were a hero today.'

David cups his hands, she mounts and he swings up behind her. A Greenjacket whistles, others answer, and a lance hisses past, touches the cobbles and cartwheels down the street. Sarah shakes the reins and digs her knees into Hero's flanks and he plunges forward. The clatter of hooves resounds from the buildings on either side. David wraps his arms round Sarah's waist and they gallop on into bright daylight.

He slides down and stands by Hero's head in the main square. People gather round, dressed in the bright garments of the Old Town, chattering as if they're at a feast. A small girl in a pink corduroy smock comes forward, a greeny-yellow apple held out on the flat of her hand. The stallion bows his head, sniffs at it and takes it in one bite. She giggles with joy and the other horses neigh behind them. Sarah takes apples round to them.

'O'Connor!' he calls. 'Someone tell O'Connor I want him.'

People marvel at the black stallions and admire their size and strength.

'Greenjackets are coming, more than you have ever seen. Get O'Connor.'

A well-built man whose face is framed by a full beard and curly black hair comes forward.

'The Greenjackets only come out after dark. O'Connor made a deal.'

David raises his voice, as if he could get him to understand by shouting:

'The deal's over. Listen.'

Whistles shriek down towards the mills. Luke and the others spill out of a side alley.

'He's right. They're coming.'

The rasp of a bolt sounds from a doorway and O'Connor stands on his threshold in a fur robe. He glares at Sarah.

'You!'

And at Luke. 'And you! Making trouble. You want me to sort it out?'

He catches sight of Sam. His voice softens.

'And you, my nephew...' His mouth sags open and he folds and collapses on the ground. The bearded man crouches and slips an arm round him and talks gently to him. An older woman in a wool shawl who supports herself on a silver-topped stick kneels down beside him and touches his face. He opens his eyes. Sam squats and helps him to his feet.

Others rush past them. A young woman flings her arms round Nathan.

'I thought I'd never see you again.'

She runs her fingers down his face as if learning it for the first time.

Behind them other townspeople are claiming the wagon-slaves, throwing their own cloaks round them, leading them away. One man offers his son the flagon of beer that's in his hand. Another kisses a young man over every inch of his face.

David screams at them and Hero neighs, his tones rising to a bellow.

'Franklin's guards are coming. Take this man,' he touches O'Connor, 'Into his house. Everyone else, knives, whips, poles, hoes. We have to defend ourselves.'

Sam leaves his uncle and takes his place beside Luke, his face grim.

The tramp of many feet sounds out. Everyone turns and stares down, towards the mills. A giant black mare turns the corner of the street from the mill, a helmeted rider astride her. He grips a pennanted lance in his right gauntlet. Behind him the first rank of guards marches towards them, whips at the ready. They cram the street. Sunshine gleams on green leather from pavement to pavement. More follow behind.

A tremor runs through the crowd. People start to back

away. A young man in a pink jacket snatches up the child in the corduroy smock and runs towards one of the houses.

Sarah turns to the bearded man:

'And you?'

He is already gone, with O'Connor and the woman. The square empties out. Sarah on Hero, David on foot next to her, and Luke, Sam, Nathan and the others on their mounts line up across the street and Sarah looks round at them:

'OK. If you want to leave, now's the time. But please don't.'

No-one moves.

Franklin's horseman whistles and the force behind him halts, their whips at the ready. The great mare takes a step forward and stands still with a hiss.

He removes his helmet. He has the bluest of blue eyes, deep-set under heavy brows, and crew-cut hair, so fair as to seem white.

He raps out his words, staccato:

'My master, Franklin, instructs you to lower your weapons and surrender to him. You will be returned to the Re-education Centre. You have nothing to fear but the truth you will learn. The debtor always pays his debt.'

Sarah rides forward, holding herself erect in the stirrups. Hero's hooves ring out on the cobbles. She shouts, her voice high and clear.

'No! Go, back to your den below.'

The horseman sneers at her. He places the helmet on his head with the visor down and lowers the lance to point at her breast. David grasps the shovel tighter in his hands. He glances left and right. No one moves.

'Now!'

Sarah rams her knees into Hero's flanks and throws her mount forward. David dashes after her on foot. Hero's hooves strike sparks from the cobbles. Boots clatter all round him.

Hero halts, stiff-legged, jerks up his head and neighs, loud and long. The dark horseman's mount tosses her mane and replies, her whinny mirroring Hero's. Hero paces forward and bends his neck and nuzzles the mare's face. The mare whinnies low and licks at Hero's cheek.

Franklin's man shouts out and Greenjackets surge forward on both sides. He smacks the lance down on Hero's head, twists it and scores a red line across his face. Hero howls and the horseman's mount backs, shakes her head and rears up, teeth bared, on her hind legs. She stands tall, taller than David ever believed a horse could stand. The rider topples backwards and hurls his lance as he falls, and the frame on her hindquarters hisses like many serpents. He crashes to the street and lies still. His mount turns and plunges down with steel hooves.

Sarah throws herself forwards. The lance slashes along her side. It catches, sags, tumbles out and clatters on the cobbles. Terror coils tight round David's heart. Everything slows. The stamp of the foot-soldiers, the crack of their whips and the clash of metal on metal becomes background.

Sarah gasps and twists in the saddle and topples slowly, so slowly, and pitches sideways onto the cobbles. David rushes to her. Around him the riderless horses from the stables charge forward, neighing shrill and demonic. The soldiers flinch back, leaderless, trapped in the narrow street. A shop window shatters.

He crouches over Sarah and smooths the hair back from her face. The blood spills out through the rip in her T-shirt like a pan of broth boiling over.

Her eyes find his and she reaches up.

'It doesn't hurt.'

He jams the heel of his hand into the gash in her side. The blood wells warm as milk against his skin. He feels her pulse beat against his fingers. Tears prick in his eyes and his vision blurs.

A line of Greenjackets force their way between him and his friends. He sees Luke smack down, left and right, with a hoe. Nathan whirls round with a shovel, like a woodsman wielding an axe. The horses bellow and kick and stamp down and Franklin's guards slash at them with whips and lances.

Behind him a voice rings out: 'Forward' and he hears the tramp of booted feet. Troops in black sweep past him on both sides, visors down, whips at the ready. A gloved hand claps him on the shoulder.

'David Ashwood.'

He looks up. Adam stands over him.

'We happen to be on exercise in the area. We do not permit disorder.'

He glances to the side and raises his voice:

'Medic. At the double.'

A young black man with an armband squats beside him and prises David's fingers away from Sarah's side. Blood spills out and trickles onto the roadway. He has long deft fingers that remind David of an embroiderer. He presses a pad against the wound.

'Nice clean wound,' he tells her. 'Looks worse than it is. You'll be OK.'

Someone unfolds a stretcher and they lay Sarah on it, ignoring her protest. David peels off his jacket and lays it over her. She reaches out from under the covers and holds his fingers in her hand. The stretcher-bearers hurry down a side-street, turn left then right onto a boulevard and uphill towards the towers of the City. Other Enforcers spill out of alleys and form up on both sides of them. Two of them are wounded, one has a bandage over one eye and is helped along by a comrade.

He glances behind him. Adam is conversing in clipped military tones with a junior officer. Further back the peaked outline of the roofs of the mills is silhouetted against a reef of clouds, gold above and black below, lit by the setting sun. The glass-fronted atrium and the offices, the well-scrubbed, respectable faces of Franklin's mills, are turned up to the City, as if they had nothing to hide. The squad presses on, towards the Halls of Justice and Commander Ferris and President West.

Adam Mann

David knows he mustn't fall behind. He has to keep himself next to the stretcher, to keep Sarah's hand safe in his. She seems to be asleep. Someone drapes a jacket round his shoulders and he winces under the weight of an Enforcer's uniform. He is exhausted.

People crowd into the street as they get nearer to City Square. The Enforcers' helmets gleam in the light from the shop windows and the throng stands back to watch them pass. To his left a young man in a camel-coloured jacket claps his hands. Everyone takes it up, business people in suits, shoppers, tradesmen with their tool-bags, even an aproned shop-keeper with a walrus moustache in the doorway of his shop. Someone waves a scarf and people start to cheer. Adam, at the head of the column, keeps his eyes straight ahead, but others wave to the crowd and the lead stretcher-bearer puffs out his chest. Once David would have been part of this, now it's just a show, a parade to entertain the citizens.

At City Square, instead of marching up the main steps, Adam takes them to the side. They follow him, down a flight of stone steps, through a low arched entrance and into the Drill Hall. They halt and stand easy.

He removes his helmet. His glare ranges over them:

'This training operation is now concluded. You will not discuss the exercise or the injuries received with anyone. Anyone whatsoever.'

He pauses.

'You did well. You, you and you, accompany the stretcher and the walking wounded across to the annex. The rest, dismiss. Double rest period.'

The others start to file out and David follows alongside the stretcher. Adam slaps his thigh.

'Ashwood. I need to talk to you.'

He's no taller than David. David swallows.

'I've left the Enforcers.' Before he can stop himself he adds, 'Sir.'

'I hope, as a civilian, you are sufficiently grateful for the rescue to listen to me. Understand: that operation was an urban training exercise under my authority. The audit value of the exercise exactly matches the cost. Neither you nor the woman will be invoiced.'

'But…why?'

'Franklin sneers at Justice. The City will not act. Our duty is clear. We have the testimony of Ms Cordell, we have evidence that he traps people and compels them to work against their will.'

He pauses. His face creases and seems almost kindly. He touches David on the arm.

'It's late and you need to rest. Tomorrow we talk to the Commander and the President will interview you. You have done well, David Ashwood. Remember who your friends are.'

David rushes out of the building, across to the annex and flings himself into the sickbay. The three rooms forever smell of disinfectant. Sarah wolfs at a plateful of lasagne and peas, packing the food into her mouth by the spoonful. She's propped up on pillows in a bed in an over-heated side-room. She gulps at her water-glass, wipes her lips on the back of her hand, curls her wrist behind his neck and pulls him down and kisses him.

'So those are the Enforcers when they are feeling professional? Thanks.'

She grins at him.

'Sarah. I thought…It's so good to see you.'

'You want some lasagne? It's great. They've used chickpeas and cashews.'

'We're seeing the Commander and the President tomorrow. We have to persuade them to stop Franklin, to call him to account.'

She touches his cheek.

'You worry too much. There's more to it than the One Law and calling to account. He's done bad things. No-one trusts him and many people hate him. That matters.'

David holds her in his arms.

'The President won't listen to common sense. In Market World everything is about credits and profit and loss. Let's talk about it tomorrow.'

Later they lie side by side on the narrow hospital bed. He stares out over City Square to the Towers beyond. A band of light gleams in the sky at the eastern rim of Market World. Every window in Franklin's tower is bright and the figures inside scurry across them or stare out. Others stream into the main entrance or set off in the direction of the mills. Someone's thrust a pitchfork into the wasps' nest. He smiles.

Sarah curls against him. Her breath comes evenly. She sighs and shifts her body.

He wonders whether Luke and Sam know they are still alive, whether a rider could reach Sarah's friends in the Villages in time, whether Captain Mann can bring Franklin down.

President West rests her chin on her fingers. A brown folder lies on her desk.

'Proceed.'

Ferris wear his full dress uniform, gold braid on both epaulettes, the peaked cap gripped under his left arm. Adam Mann, in Captain's uniform, with the triple row of ribbons above his breast pocket, stands behind him. David notices a framed photograph of a young man in an academic gown with dark hair and a scroll held across his chest on the President's desk. He has the same cheek-bones as she does and the same set mouth.

'Madam,' Ferris clears his throat. 'You have already received my report on Franklin's activities. I have further evidence that you will wish to hear. A villager, Ms Sarah Cordell, and my agent, Mr David Ashwood, have both been imprisoned and forced to work against their will in his factories.

I submit that this contravenes the One Law. Franklin's account must face full audit.'

The President taps the folder on her desk.

'Mr Franklin is one of our most prominent citizens and our most successful Entrepreneur. He brings wealth and success. He is always careful to make sure that the other Entrepreneurs receive a share of the profits in his schemes. People, the people who count in Market World, like him. You came to me recently with allegations about breaches of the One Law in the villages and beyond in the valley. I'm afraid I cannot act on those claims. They are simply one person's view, Franklin will deny them and the City will be left with substantial legal costs.'

Sarah mutters:

'It's my view too. Don't I count?'

The President glances at her as if she were an impediment.

'Ms Cordell. I understand you were recently called to account for a major breach by Commander Ferris' Enforcers. That does not enhance your standing as a witness.'

David cuts in: 'But we have been to the villages, we have been to the Secret Valley, we have been his prisoners and suffered his tortures. The scar in Sarah – Ms Cordell's – side comes from his weapons. We have seen his crimes.'

The President holds up her hand.

'Crime is a word with consequences. Please refer to "Alleged misdemeanours and breaches" and please understand me. I am sympathetic to your position but you must understand mine. You are asking the City to take action against a man of immense wealth and impeccable standing on the word of a convict who contradicts herself and an impressionable young man who has fallen in with her. You will make me a laughing stock. I face an election in six months. I must be practical.'

She does not smile.

'Thank you for coming to see me.'

Ferris stands very straight.

'Very well. I believe heinous breaches of the Law are taking place. Just because a criminal is powerful does not mean he should be permitted to act as he chooses. I urge you to bring him to account. I shall continue investigations.'

'Be careful Commander. Harassment can entail heavy recompense.'

'This is nonsense.' Sarah has her eyes fixed on the President like a hawk on a rat. 'Franklin works his victims to death. He causes mayhem in the Old Town. He poisons the air, the water, the land in the Valley. He destroys villages and villagers die. You know these things. Your duty is to protect us. Shame on you!'

The President sniffs.

'Do you seriously expect me to answer that?'

'Madam.' A new voice breaks in, calm and deep, the same voice the man uses when addressing one person or a parade. Captain Mann takes one pace forwards and comes to attention.

'I have been an Enforcer all my life. I knew the world before the One Law, I lived through the Great Hunger. The One Law saved us then and the Law makes us strong. Franklin insults that Law. I have my savings. I will take a private action against him.'

For a moment no-one speaks.

President West stares directly at him and remarks:

'You may find it expensive to confront the richest man in Market World in open court.'

'Nonetheless. It is my duty.'

He flicks back his cuff to show his wristband.

'I have my savings. I will use them to uphold the law.'

Sarah folds her arms.

'I have many friends in the Old Town who will contribute.'

'I'll chip in.' says David, keeping his hand by his side. *Maybe someone'll give me a loan*, he thinks.

Ferris holds out his wrist and the noughts march across the tiny screen.

'I am not impoverished. I will contribute.'

Adam glances at him and, for one second, smiles.

Ferris adds:

'Madam, consider: suppose Franklin is convicted and people become aware that the City failed to act, it may damage your election prospects. And there is the matter of the tractor. That was clearly a gift to secure a contract, in contravention of the Law.'

The President glances at him and at each of the others in turn. No-one moves.

'Very well. The City will prosecute. The gift of the tractor is a clear Breach in front of witnesses, but it is a trivial matter. The balance between environmental penalties and economic gains from development is more … controversial. I will not authorise action in that matter. Best you stay out of it, Ms Cordell. You are a tarnished witness.'

Full Audit

David arranges coffee-cups, toast and marmalade on the tray. He balances a cut-out of an extravagant purple dahlia in a spare mug. It is the only flower he can find in the building.

He carries the tray through to the side-ward. Sarah rubs her hands together and her candid smile lights up her face.

'Lovely. Just what I wanted. You haven't got any eggs have you?'

'See what I can do.'

Later, when she's eaten and is dressed in borrowed jeans that don't fit and a spare T-shirt and has wound the yellow scarf round her neck, they talk tactics.

Sarah looks up at him.

'I'd really like to be called as a witness.'

'President West thinks you're a risk. They spent half the night telling me what to say.'

'Who cares what she thinks? Even if they win on this tractor business he'll wriggle out of it. Business as usual, that's all Market World wants. Maybe she just wants people to think she's doing something.'

He thinks of all the clever people in the courtroom, all determined to trip him up and watch him fall flat.

'I know. But what else can we do?'

'Yes, but if I can get him talking in front of everyone, he might just make a fool of himself. He's so sure he's right he doesn't care what people think.'

David gazes at her.

'Everybody likes him. He promises bigger profits and Market World loves that.'

'Don't forget I've talked to him face to face.'

'I have to go in a minute, or it'll be contempt of court.'

He puts his arms round her and they talk some more. Anyone watching them would think from their faces that they were discussing a business deal, and would be amazed at how they kissed each other on parting.

He walks out of the annex and into bright sunshine. City Square is already as packed as an ant-heap but people crowd in from all four boulevards. Still more flood in behind them, women and men, old and young, white and black, and the duty Enforcers marshal them into lines on either side of the main entrance to the Halls of Justice. There's a continual hubbub of bargaining and wristband clicks and a flurry of traded places up and down the queue.

David spots a troop of academy students in their dark-blue uniforms. The professor in the mortar board at their head clicks wrists with the duty Enforcer, who opens a path through for them. An Entrepreneur in a suit that fits like an eel-skin attempts to follow them, holding his wrist out to make a deal, but is rebuffed.

David has already unfolded his court summons to show the Enforcer when he sees a group from the Old Town, distinctive in their gaudy dress, clustered to one side of the square. A horse neighs and a figure mounted on a black mare enters the square behind the townspeople, followed by another. People open a space for their mounts and they lead the group forward through the press of people. David grins: good for the Old Towners!

The lead figure stands in his stirrups, scans the crowd, waves and pushes towards him. Luke, in a scarlet, green and yellow chequerboard pattern suit with lapels wide enough to touch his shoulders, is mounted on Juno. And that must be Sam behind him, well cut camel jodhpurs and a tweed jacket with a black velvet riding hat. He waves back.

Luke leans down and grasps his hand.

'David! So good to see you. Where's Sarah? I've got some decent clothes for her. And we've brought the old fellow.'

He gestures. Sam beams at him. O'Connor sits astride Jupiter, his feet grazing the cobbles on both sides. He smiles at everything, David, Luke, Sam, the crowd, Juno, the Halls of Justice and Jupiter, and hums to himself. David recognises a tune from the feast. The mayor wears a long, striped gown, which gives him an air of great age and wisdom, and a tricorn hat.

David laughs at Luke's costume.

'You look like you've gone up in the world. Congratulations!'

'Tell you about it later.'

David strokes Juno's nose.

'Wish me luck. I'm a witness.'

The mare sniffs at him and rests its violin cello head on his shoulder. Luke pulls on the reins and Juno backs away. David rubs her cheek.

'Give her an extra apple from me, and I'll see you soon. Sarah's great, she's resting back in sickbay, at least I hope she is. It's in that building next to the Halls of Justice. She wants to be in the trial. Franklin's going to get what he deserves.'

David sits on the wooden bench at one end of the witness room. It reminds him of his school-room. He stares at the picture on the wall opposite, an oil painting of a country market, long ago, like the one that used to hang behind the teacher's desk in his classroom. It shows Franklin as he made the first deal with a group of villagers. Their cart's behind them, piled so high with produce that the topmost apples would tumble off if you tried to move it. The horse rests docile between the shafts and reminds him of Juno. A younger Franklin, too slim to be the Franklin he knows, smiles as he clasps the hand of a full-bearded, open-faced villager in a brown leather jacket.

Slocum sits on a wooden chair next to the door into the courtroom and mops at his face with a large pink handkerchief. His glasses are pushed up on his forehead and he has the coffee-flask on the floor beside him. He avoids looking at David and mumbles something. The chair wobbles when he fidgets and the papers in the folder on his lap are on the verge of spilling onto the floor.

David calms his breathing: in through the nose on the count of five, out through the mouth on the count of seven. *Sarah, Luke, Sam, and you, Juno, and you, Jupiter,* he thinks, *I won't let you down. And you baby Mikey and Annie and Jeb. And all of you.* He ignores Slocum and remembers the body of townspeople pushing into the square, his friends in court. The file in his own lap has his witness summons and a couple of printouts from newscasts in it, and his report. Why is Slocum's folder so much thicker than his?

Slocum shuts the folder and opens the courtroom door a few inches. Warm air wafts through, carrying the rich tones of someone confident that their voice carries the ring of truth, because everyone knows it always carries the ring of truth.

'...I will now call the witness to Mr Franklin's negotiations with the villagers at the Pettiford moot.'

David takes a deep breath and gets to his feet. As he passes Slocum the clerk looks up and catches his eye and mutters something about the prospects for Mr Franklin's friends 'in the programme.'

David seizes his wrist and grips it.

'I've been to the Secret Valley. You should see it for yourself.'

Slocum shakes himself free and David passes through the door and into Courtroom One. His first impression is of the height of the chamber, as if he'd emerged from a burrow onto a hillside, and of the bright daylight, slanting in from the tall windows overlooking City Square. Next he becomes aware of the faces of the people who pack the courtroom all turned up to him, like a flock of sheep.

A young woman in a dark gown takes his sleeve and leads him forward to an upright chair with a wooden barrier topped by a brass rail in front of it.

The Assessor, a tall black man with a thin face and sharp eyes, sits on a high-backed leather chair behind an oak table on a raised platform. A wooden gavel lies by his right hand. Rachel West is on his left, still on her feet from her opening presentation of the case against Franklin. The chair to his right, the place reserved for the Guild-Master of the Entrepreneurs, is empty. The golden balance, emblem of Market World, stands at the corner of the table.

Franklin sits directly opposite David at a small deal table which resembles a schoolroom desk. It's too small for him and his belly sags over it. The mane of yellow hair sits like a beret on his head and the $\mathcal{F}$ in his lapel catches the light. He catches David's eye and winks at him.

David casts his eyes round the room as he is taken through a form of words he recalls from his Enforcer training: identity, affirmation, credit-worthiness. Courtroom One is packed. Entrepreneurs in suits, with their assistants behind them, fill the front rows, then there's a bench of students from the academy. A young woman quite openly offers a bag of toffees to her friends.

The rest of the room is crammed with ordinary citizens, women and men in dull blue and brown serge or corduroy. Some of them have brought their children, who sit with serious faces, their hands in their laps, not fidgeting. A knot of citizens from the Old Town brighten the room towards the back, continually in motion. He can hear the whispered conversations volleying back and forth among them from where he is standing.

The Assessor glowers at them and turns his gaze on David.

'Mr David Ashwood. Your witness, President West.'

The President smiles at him, thin-lipped.

'Mr Ashwood. I believe you were present at the moot in Pettiford.'

He looks up at the townspeople at the back and spots Luke, and his heart leaps like a salmon. He raises his voice, as if to address Luke alone.

'I was. I was there with Ms Cordell and her family.'

His voice seems over-loud in the silent courtroom.

The President nods.

'Good. Please just confine your answers to the question. Now, did Mr Franklin make a gift to the villagers?'

'He did. He announced it immediately after he lost the debate with Ms Cordell. It is my belief that...'

The President claps her hands and cuts in.

'Thank you.' She's no longer smiling. 'Did Mr Franklin ask for anything in return for his gift?'

The Assessor frowns at him. He's doing well.

'No, Madam. Ms Cordell believes it was a bribe...'

'Objection.'

An older woman with white hair and a thin, seamed face, dressed in a black silk gown, a white ruff at her throat, is on her feet. She glares at him with glittering eyes. He tries not to wince.

'The court is not enquiring into the actions or beliefs of Ms Cordell.'

The Assessor speaks as if fatigued.

'Sustained.'

President West allows her gaze to range across the courtroom.

'Very well. We have demonstrated that Mr Franklin made gifts to the villagers in direct contravention of the Law. Perhaps he thought of them as simple people who would not suspect the artifice in his actions.'

She sits and the Assessor murmurs:

'Your witness, Ms Jarman.'

The white-haired woman addresses him in a pleasant voice.

'Mr Ashwood. You resigned from the Enforcers earlier this year, I believe. Why?'

He hesitates. His mind is as empty as a blown egg. He sees a movement in the shadows under the balcony. Adam Mann stands there watching him, with an expression on his face that is almost as if he were praying.

'I…I felt unhappy with the direction my career was taking.'

'Perhaps I can clarify things for you. The statements of earlier witnesses,' she gestures to a folder on the Assessor's desk, 'show that you met senior Enforcers and the President and alleged that Mr Franklin had abducted Ms Cordell. You requested that the Enforcers should call Mr Franklin to account, which they quite properly refused to do. Ms Cordell was lawfully undergoing re-education in the programme operated for the City by Mr Franklin at the time. You also presented a report on the pilot work for Mr Franklin's Development Proposal, prepared together with Ms Cordell, which makes further libellous allegations against Mr Franklin.'

Her voice hardens.

'It will not surprise the court to learn that the City did not act on your report, either. You then became emotional and resigned from the Enforcers. You entered into a conspiracy with others to use violence against Mr Franklin's employees, break into his factories and sabotage his operations. President West was present at these meetings. I understand she does not dispute these statements. Mr Ashwood am I right?'

The President shakes her head. The Assessor taps his gavel against the stand.

'Please. I'm sure I don't need to remind you that the charge concerns the alleged gift of a tractor. Once again, please direct your questions to the matter in hand.'

The Counsel bows to him.

'Thank you, sir. I merely wish to establish that this witness is prejudiced against Mr Franklin and that the suggestion that he might speak with the authority of an Enforcer is highly misleading. No further questions.'

'I note the points you make. Mr Ashwood, please sit. We may need you later. Mr Franklin, have you anything to say before I arrive at my determination of the case?'

David sits and watches Franklin as he pushes the desk away from him and heaves himself to his feet. His feral eyes sweep across the courtroom and rest on David for a moment before returning to the Assessor. He addresses the court in a voice rich with the assurance of many credits.

'Sir, may I save the court some time? I plead guilty without reservation to inadvertently failing to secure proper paperwork for the transfer of the tractor. I am ready to pay appropriate costs and recompense for what is a purely technical breach. The villagers are an undeveloped people, who do not grasp the importance of the market, although I have attempted to introduce them to the benefits of trade on many occasions. I was simply seeking to expedite an arrangement that is clearly in their best interests. I apologise to the court for my impatience. I am sure many people will believe I did the right thing.'

His gaze ranges round the court-room and the Entrepreneurs wave their papers in applause. Someone calls out 'Franklin!' and another starts to clap.

The gavel smacks into the desk with a sound that reminds David of a mallet striking a tent-peg.

'Silence. This court is not a music hall.'

Franklin holds up his hand.

'I apologise. I am a popular man and my friends can be over-enthusiastic in their support. But may I submit, sir, that proceedings this morning indicate the need to consider two further issues? First, my Development Programme. I believe the matter of the tractor falls into insignificance alongside the opportunities that the programme offers. Secondly, Ms Cordell. I am surprised that the City has not summoned her as a witness. I understand she participated in meetings with the others who instigated this audit. She is a close associate of Mr Ashwood and is better placed to comment on the issues than he is. We cannot assess his testimony without introducing her to the court.'

He smiles, showing his teeth. The Assessor regards him and tugs at his ear-lobe.

President West rises to her feet.

'Sir. These are not material issues. This case concerns a straightforward breach of the law to which Mr Franklin has already confessed. Whatever plans he may have and whether others support them has nothing to do with it. Ms Cordell was not called as a witness because her testimony is irrelevant to the case and we did not wish to waste the court's time, in consideration of the costs that would then fall to Mr Franklin.'

The Assessor glances from President West to Franklin. A murmur roves round the courtroom and he scowls at the public benches, directing his glare particularly to the townspeople at the back.

'Very well. Mr Franklin, I admit both your requests. Please bear in mind they may cost you a considerable sum of money. President West. If Mr Franklin establishes that the gift of the tractor was essential to progress his Development Programme, that is a material consideration. The court is required to take context into account in assessing actions.

Ms Cordell is clearly at least as cognisant of Mr Franklin's activities in Pettiford as Mr Ashwood is. I regret your oversight in not declaring her presence at a recent meeting between you and other key litigants to the court. I believe she is in the care of the Enforcers. Court-Serjeant! Require her immediate attendance.'

The Old Town group crane forward in their seats. David watches the official bow and bustle out of the doors at the back of the court and licks his lips.

The Assessor glowers at the court:

'Ms Jarman: proceed.'

Franklin's counsel is already turning to President West, a lapel gripped in each hand, when Franklin intervenes:

'Sir. I am best placed to discuss my own programme. Allow me.'

Ms Jarman sits and stares down at the papers in front of her.

Franklin continues.

'We are Market World. Trade is our heritage, trade is our destiny.' He glances at the Entrepreneurs. 'I have already brought many opportunities for trade to the City. If we wish to go further, for our future to outshine our present, we must expand. We have no choice. We must enable the Market to grow until it embraces everything in our world. My programme offers the next step towards that goal.'

Someone touches David's sleeve. He becomes aware that Sarah has been brought into the courtroom and is seated next to him. He can't help grinning at her. He feels a burden slip from his shoulders.

'Well done,' she whispers and squeezes his hand.

Franklin's gaze sweeps over the court.

'When did you last see an apple tree with a price tag on its fruit? When did a coal seam last charge you when you drove a mineshaft to it? When did the river present an invoice for fresh water or the sky for fresh air? Fruit, fuel, water, air – we cannot trade these goods without prices. My task is to put those prices into place and that requires us to ensure that someone owns them. I will bring all of Nature, everything, into the Market. Then trade can expand without limit into the world that our children and our children's children will inherit.'

He pauses and the Entrepreneurs and the city benches are loud in their applause. The townspeople sit grim-faced. No-one cheers at the back of the hall.

'Thank you. That is what my plan will do and what these villagers, ignorant of their own interests, oppose. But I see Ms Cordell is now with us. Let us proceed to cross-examination.'

The Assessor sighs.

'Of course, Mr Franklin.'

Sarah rises to her feet and grips the rail. Franklin fixes his wolf's eyes on her.

'Ms Cordell, I believe we have met before.'

She stares back at him. Her voice is steady.

'Yes, on two occasions. Once when I out-argued you before the villagers at the moot in Pettiford and once after you revenged yourself by kidnapping me and enslaving me in your mill.'

Franklin glances at the Assessor. His expression is that of a bishop explaining a diocesan matter to the deputy arch-bishop.

'Sir, these statements are highly tendentious. Ms Cordell attempted to disrupt the moot. She committed various offences of violence, was arrested by my security guards and purchased necessary re-education at my Centre between the Old and New Towns, which operates under contract to the City. The relevant contracts and affidavits from multiple witnesses are in your folder.'

The Assessor nods and a gasp echoes round the courtroom. Franklin fixes his eyes on Sarah.

'Ms Cordell, I had occasion to explain my programme to you, I believe?'

'Yes. You devastated the Secret Valley, now called the Broken Land. You talk of putting prices on everything, but you poisoned the air, the water, the earth. People can no longer live there. You talk of growth but you have made it a desert, all for your greed.'

Franklin watches her and says nothing.

She raises her voice.

'You trapped me, you made me a slave in your mill, you treated me worse than an animal.'

294

She pauses for breath and he remarks:

'Most criminals see their lawful gaolers as oppressive. They cannot see beyond temporary environmental issues to a bright future.'

He speaks more slowly, with emphasis, and there is a slight echo to his voice in the courtroom.

'Now we come to the heart of it. I stand for progress, I stand for a future of investment, of trade, of growth and of profit.'

He pauses for the cheers from the Entrepreneurs' benches to die away.

'Those who oppose me are trapped in the past. They want the old ways to continue for ever. Ms Cordell has demonstrated that she is a ring-leader among them. She stands convicted for breach of the One Law. She lies and schemes to subvert my programme. I am all for young love, but I am afraid she has turned Mr Ashwood's head. For her, he has cut short a promising career in the Enforcers.

What is more she has been convicted of major breach and he paid her recompense in direct contravention of the One Law. The records from Courtroom Three and a certified statement of his account from the central computer are in the folder. I suggest the court takes these points into account in evaluating Mr Ashwood and Ms Cordell's testimony.'

Someone cries out: 'What?' The murmur of many people talking at once ripples round the hall. The gavel hammers into the stand and the noise dies away.

Franklin smiles at his audience and inclines his head as if acknowledging praise.

'Remember, I stand for progress and a rich, bright future for us all. Those against me stand for reaction, for decay, for the past. I operate within the spirit of the law.

What's more, the people of Market World recognise my contribution whether this court does so or not. This is an election year and I am the most popular citizen in this City. I rest my case.'

He sits, and a tumult of applause thunders forth from the Entrepreneurs' benches. The Assessor's gavel slams into the stand three times and the balance quivers at the corner of the desk. David gazes at the townspeople at the back of the hall. It is as if a shadow has passed over them, despite the sunlight. He realises that their faces are cast down and no longer visible. Some of them are already leaving at the back of the chamber. The applause is confined to the Entrepreneurs and the richer citizen of Market World.

Sarah remains on her feet

'But...'

The Assessor bangs his gavel down again and the clamour subsides.

'Any more disruption and I shall clear the court. President West, do you wish to cross-examine?'

The President glances at Sarah and David and at the Entrepreneurs, who sit silent, their faces set and turned towards her and at Franklin. She shakes her head.

'But...'

'Thank you, Ms Cordell. You have given your testimony. I will now determine the case.'

Words flow from his mouth. Sarah sits and David takes her hand and her fingers grip tight on his. He longs to throw his arm round her. A rustling, like the sounds made by bats flying from a cave, rises in the courtroom. The Entrepreneur's assistants are whispering into their communicators to place bets on the outcome.

The Assessor concludes:

'I find the defendant guilty as charged. Major breach.'

The clerk hands him a slip of paper. He glances at it.

'In view of the excessive court time that this case has occupied and the additional demands on Enforcers and on the City, including substantial disruption of trade for today, I fix recompense at one million, two hundred and three credits, subject to interest and due from Mr Franklin. Court will rise.'

He stands and draws himself to his full height.

'Never have I been present at an audit hearing where the public has behaved so abominably.'

He leaves by the door through which he entered.

David follows Sarah from the room. He glances back. Franklin has gone but President West remains in her seat, her face covered with both hands. He can't guess at her expression and he couldn't care less.

The door swings shut. Sarah turns to him, her face as open as a summer sky, and a delicious joy capers through him.

City Square

They sit side by side, close together, on the bench in the empty witness room. The din from the crowd passing through the lobby next door fills the room.

Sarah stretches herself.

'I'm worn out. Let's wait a bit.'

David slides an arm round her and she rests her head on his shoulder and he thinks they could stay like that for ever and no-one would mind.

'That was what you wanted?'

She looks up at him, innocent and mocking at the same time.

'Yes. The Entrepreneurs love him, but did you see how Franklin's schemes went down on the Old Town benches? I couldn't really see, I was too busy, but I think it was OK.'

'You are very, very clever. The fewer credits people have, the less they like Franklin's scheming when they hear what it really means. The townspeople liked it least of all.'

'You have to trust ordinary people.' She fixes her eyes on his. 'And no-one ever told me you paid my fine all that time ago, and I love you for that.'

She takes his head in her hands and kisses him for twenty seconds or half an hour, he doesn't know how long. He feels as if a charm of finches is soaring up within him.

Images flash into his mind, Sarah leaning against the shaft of the apple-cart with the Enforcers surrounding them the first time he saw her, Sarah confronting Franklin at the moot, Sarah with little Mikey in her arms, teaching him how to bathe the baby, Sarah leading the way into the forest, Sarah, lit up by the fires of Franklin's castle, throwing herself between the wheels of the road-beast in the Secret Valley.

She takes her lips from his and holds him at arms' length.

'We're not finished yet. Come on.'

'Yes. And I love you too, Sarah Cordell.'

A little later, he opens the door into the lobby. Their friends, the townspeople, who were seated nearest the doors, have already gone. The people filing out of the building now are mainly families from the City, some with children bundled into dull smart clothes.

The doors leading to the front of the courtroom are flung open from inside and everyone looks round. The Entrepreneurs who sat on the padded benches at the front emerge and their assistants push the others aside for them to stride through and exit into the square. Two of Franklin's guards in their plainclothes green overcoats follow them through the doorway and stand one on each side, their whips coiled in their hands. One has a slight limp and David remembers him from the mill.

Franklin advances into the room. He smiles and raises a hand, as if surrounded by well-wishers. One or two of the City folk try to raise a cheer, but most nod to him without enthusiasm. Some of the children wave. David watches a girl in a denim suit, perhaps eight years old, poke her twin brother in the side and jerk her hand back. She thinks her parents can't see.

Slocum scurries after Franklin.

'This way sir.'

The Enforcer at the reception desk looks up. David recognises Jan. She regards Franklin as if he were an animal of a species unfamiliar to her. He puts out his hand.

'Good to have you with us. Have you come far to be here? A very special occasion. We will all grow rich together.'

She raises both eyebrows.

'Sit down, please.'

The clerk rubs his palms together.

'Sir, an official matter. The recompense.'

Franklin frowns at him as if he can't quite focus.

'Oh, I see. Yes, of course.'

He flips back his cuff and sweeps his wristband across the reader twice. The clerk squints at the window.

'Sir! That's too much.'

Jan purses her lips.

'Refund applications are via the accounts section. Open tomorrow, seven to eight a.m.'

Franklin shrugs and waves again to the crowd.

'Put it in the benevolent fund. I must greet my people.'

He waddles off towards the main doors. The clerk scuttles past him, the folder abandoned, and pulls them open. Outside, the square is still packed with people. The Old Town group, much larger now, more of them on horseback, pushes forward and the contingent of Entrepreneurs waiting at the front starts to applaud.

Franklin raises both hands in triumph and a tumult of cheering and shouting rises up to greet him with a roar like a river cascading over falls. He takes his stance at the head of the staircase, like a conqueror returning to his people.

'My fellow citizens. Today justice has been done. The path to the future, the golden path of progress is clear before us! I congratulate you all! We will...'

A blond young man, dressed in the best fitting suit David has ever seen, embraces him. A woman with a black leather briefcase grips his hand and shakes it warmly. Others queue behind them to congratulate him.

Franklin continues:

'I promise you, all of those who invest in me will receive great returns. I offer you the finest opportunity you will see in your lifetimes. All you have to do is follow me.'

He looks out over the square, beaming at the citizens of Market World. On the far side the bright colours of the Old Town glow against the drab clothes of the City. More and more of those from the area beyond Franklin's mills pack themselves in. Franklin looks out over his people for the last time and proceeds down the steps, both hands held out in greeting. He plunges into the crowd still smiling, still waving, still declaiming, but David can't make out the words.

Sarah leads David to the top of the steps. They gaze out over Franklin's progress. She presses his hand:

'Pride comes before a fall.'

She slips her arm round his shoulders. He sighs, half in contentment, half in weariness.

'Look at them. He's more popular than ever... It's as if

we went through it all for nothing.'

'The Old Towners aren't cheering. They're nearly half the square now.'

'We'll go away somewhere, maybe we'll see the sea. We'll take little Mikey, and your Dad. We'll take Juno. We promised Annie an adventure'

'Yes, we'll do that. Later.'

He kisses her.

When they look up, Franklin is far into the crowd, his arms just visible above the heads of the mob. The guards force their way after him, but people don't make a path for them as they would for Enforcers. Slocum is doing his best to follow them, David can see his bald head bobbing among the bright colours. The folk from the Old Town press forward, more of them with every minute. The colours, yellow, red-gold, pink, suffuse into the crowd, like sunrise behind a cloud-bank.

David feels that it is all far away from him, as if he has done what he could and he is no longer part of the City and the squabbles in the Halls of Justice.

Luke and Sam come up with paper bags of food in their hands. Luke mutters something to Sarah and hands her a wrap of humus and coriander and cauliflower and passes another to him. He bites into it and the creamy texture fills his mouth.

'Thanks, this is good. Can you see what Franklin's doing?'

Luke glances at Sarah.

'Not really. He pushed his way right across the square.'

They sit together at the top of the steps. Sam squats next to them and hands them a flagon.

'That's Old Town beer. Only beer worth drinking.'

He passes it to Sarah and she takes a swig and wipes her mouth with the back of her hand and gives it back to him. It tastes bitter and sweet at the same time and something else, almost nutty. He looks out, over the turmoil in City Square, past the towers of the Entrepreneurs, past the residences, to where he can just make out the green of the forests on the hills beyond the fields, where the villages are.

He passes the flagon on to Luke.

'We've been there. As far as you can see and further, much further. No-one else in this square can say that.'

The sun is low to the west and the air grows chilly. He takes another swig of the beer. People are starting to leave. A voice shouts out quite clearly above the hubbub:

'Where is he?'

The Entrepreneurs at the front are starting to leave. They stride towards the Boulevards as if they'd been reminded of meetings that required their presence, with their assistants clustered behind them chattering to each other, like starlings. Some of the Old Towners gather round the horses, others press towards the exit on the south of the square. A patch clears among the crowd some way distant and grows larger. David watches a father holding his daughter up to stroke the nose of a bay mare on the edge of it. He feels a gust of warmth towards the man.

The guards have reached the clearing in the crowd now. They cast round them, and jab their whips at people on the edge of the multitude and the broad-shouldered one with the limp shouts:

'Where's he gone? Where's Franklin?'

A young woman spreads her hands and the guard

pushes her to one side. The crowd thins, melting away. The sun is setting to the west and, as the shadows of the Towers fall across the square, more and more people leave.

Slocum has reached the empty area. He rubs at his head and says something to the guard. David senses a change in the mood of the crowd and stands to see better.

'Slocum doesn't look happy.'

Sarah takes his hand.

'That's one good thing. Look, that's Juno over there. They've brought her over. It would be rude not to say hello.'

Luke hands him a bag. It's full of apples, yellow-gold, bright as lanterns.

'We ought to get back. You hang onto Juno for a bit, she likes you. See you soon, in the Old Town.'

Aftermath

David would have known where he was blindfold. It isn't just the fact of the voices around you on the street, they sound different, somehow more musical, it's the range from child to adult to older person, and they laugh more. You can feel their pleasure at greeting each other, at hearing the local news, at the goods in the shops and the sun warming your face. Above all, it's the smell in your nostrils, sharp and heavy at the same time, compounded of wood-smoke and fresh bread and well-groomed horses and people close to each other and everything about the Old Town. He knows that today they really have to make a decision.

Sarah wraps the cloak Annie gave her at the Pettiford moot round her shoulders and takes the oil-lamp down from the shelf by the door. She leads the way down a squeeze-gut alley between two tall houses, across a small square with a rowan tree in the middle and a timber yard to one side and along a narrow street. She stops in front of the double doors of a stable while David catches up with her, and lights the lamp.

'Ready?'

He nods and she pushes one of the doors open and they enter together.

David blinks at the darkness inside the stables. He smells clean straw, but no horse sweat or urine. Sarah lifts the lamp and the figure in the end stall grasps at the side-rail and pulls himself to his feet and stumbles forward. A chain runs from his ankle to a ring-bolt in the wall behind him.

He croaks a few words, then says, quite clearly:

'Please. Please let me out. I have an important meeting.' He holds out his forearm and the golden wrist-band catches the light of the lamp. 'I'll pay, anything you ask.'

He falls back against the side of the stall.

David glances at Sarah. He keeps his voice low.

'What are we going to do with him? There are Enforcers everywhere, they're bound to come looking round here soon.'

'That's not the only problem. Luke came round yesterday. The others want to…deal with him the way he treated the villagers in the Secret Valley. They don't know we've hidden him in here, but they'll find out.'

She looks at him and his heart goes out to her.

'We thought he might change, he'd learn to be a different person when he saw how we treated him, when he thought about his life and all the misery he had caused. That he'd be sorry, that he'd want to do something for someone else.'

They stare down at Franklin. He picks up a handful of straw and fumbles with it. He polishes his wristband and wipes the screen again and again and stares at the tiny numbers as they scroll past.

David gazes at him and at Sarah, then back at Franklin. He thinks of everything he's seen, of the woman from the forest with the sores on her body and Mikey in her arms and how she saved him, and the flames whirling up above her. He thinks of everything Franklin has done, of the steel castle in the Secret Valley and the devastation around it, of the wagon-slaves in the mill, of the giant horses and how they died. He thinks of Sarah, of how she held him after he had fought the road-beast, of the fire in her eyes when she shouted 'Shame on you' at President West in the Commander's office, of the smile, mocking and ardent, on her lips the first time he saw her, leaning back against Juno's flank with her ankles crossed, when the Enforcers stormed towards her.

'There's no other way. Wait here.'

He's back within five minutes. Franklin squats in the same position. He seems to be plaiting the straw round his wrist. David takes a step towards him and holds the axe out and hefts it in both hands and swings it up. The light glints from the blade and he smashes it down. Franklin screams, a high wailing cry. It takes a second blow to sever the wrist. He falls back moaning and cradles the stump against his chest. Blood spatters into the drinking water.

David kicks the dead hand with the blood seeping out of it like the juice from a fresh steak. The jerk activates the tiny screen and numbers march across the window. He brings the blade down a third time and the device shatters into glittering fragments.

'I'm truly sorry, Mr Franklin.'

Blood spurts from the stump like the jet of water from a hand-pump. He drops to his knees, unfastens his belt and binds it round Franklin's upper arm and the spurt slows to a trickle.

'That should hold it. We'll get you to a doctor. We'll pay.'

Sarah doesn't move. Her eyes are large with horror. She grips his arm.

'Why? Why did you do that?'

'There was no choice.'

'But….'

'I did it for the villagers, I did it for the wagon-slaves, I did it for Boxer, and Sam and Mikey, I did it for you.'

She looks down and nods.

'Juno's stabled in the next street. Let's go and see how she's getting on.'

In Market World "Street-trader" is really a nice way of saying "beggar". Charity is a serious breach of the One Law, both for the donor and recipient. That's why the people who crowd onto the bottom rung of society, who huddle in grimy blankets on cold evenings along the boulevards in the richer parts of the City, don't ask the well-to-do for money. They always offer to trade a meagre stock of sweets or matches or second-hand toys with the wheels missing or a few misshapen vegetables for enough credits to keep body and soul together for one more day.

The street-traders are not hard-hearted. They'll look out for each other. When one of them has made a good deal they'll buy something off the others, spread it around.

The fudge-seller, his name is Jerry but hardly anyone uses that, is perhaps the leader of them. He does a bit better than most of the others. The truth of it is that his mother helps him. She always had hopes for him. In the early morning, before first light, when you can slip down the alleys to the streets around the Pit and no-one will know, he makes his way back to where she still lives.

There's a place in the end wall, a cavity with a stone across it. He waits and after a while he slides the stone, it's easier than it looks and someone's put a pad of cloth there so it doesn't make a noise. There'll be a bag of fudge there for him, still warm from the kitchen. It's a secret, no-one must know. He touches it and thinks of the man who came to live with them, when he was young, and shudders. He knows that the man's gone. He doesn't have to take the fudge and go away. They'd be a place for him, but he can't just yet. Maybe he will one day.

He has his hopes, that in the time to come they'll be a guild of street-traders recognised by the City, with badges and a code of conduct and designated areas to ply their business in. Maybe they'll have pitches where they can keep their blankets and sleep if they can get warm enough.

It falls to him to have a word with the new arrival. The others mutter but no-one will do anything. Besides, you have to keep standards up, otherwise there will be trouble with the Enforcers and all his work will be undone.

When evening falls and there aren't many citizens about he goes over and squats by the new man. The other sits, hunched up on the pavement, staring at something he holds cupped in his good hand. He wears a crumpled suit, stained with what looks like porridge on the lapels and with a rent across one sleeve and the other pinned up to hide his missing hand. Close up you can see that it was once high-quality, pure wool, with a pin-stripe. He doesn't look up.

'You can't keep on like this. You've got to get a trade, find something you can sell, doesn't matter what.'

The new man mutters, as if to himself.

'Don't you know who I am?'

He sounds hoarse, as if he's not looking after himself and the cold is getting to him.

Jerry strokes his ear-ring. He prides himself on his reasonableness. It never helps to be aggressive.

'Doesn't matter who you were, we're all the same here. Try and live without trading, you'll make trouble for all of us.'

The beggar looks as if he is about to burst into tears.

'They stole my wristband. I'm Mr Franklin, everybody knows me. I own all this, that tower, all the stores and market-halls, half the residence blocks they're all mine. People like me, why don't you like me?'

Jerry never judges anyone. He speaks gently.

'You've got it mixed up. Don't you remember, it was all over the newscasts: Franklin's gone, the account's closed, the Tower's locked up and the City's auctioned everything off? That's how the market works, people go up and down, maybe our turn next.' He scrutinises the beggar. 'You can't be Franklin, I've seen him on TV. He's a big man, hands like joints of meat, a rich man's belly. You look as if you haven't eaten in weeks.'

He glances round. He shouldn't do this.

'I've got a couple of sandwiches.'

The other looks up. There's something about his face, but it can't be him, can it? He's holding a trinket, a lapel pin with a silver-coloured $\mathcal{F}$ on it in his hand. He could say he's selling that.

'Here, peanut butter. Not bad?'

A bit later the Enforcers come round on their patrol. Jerry edges away and pulls his cap down over his forehead. He likes to smooth things over, but sometimes you can't do anything, you just need to steer clear.

The Enforcers stop, as he knew they would, in front of the new man. He could at least have kept at the back, out of the way. One of them flashes a torch in his face.

'Excuse me, sir. What are you trading? Show me your wristband.'

Jerry huddles himself down. This kind of thing always upsets him. The man with the lapel-pin starts in his rasping voice, as if he has a permanent head-cold.

'I'm Mr Franklin. Take me to your superiors. Commander Ferris knows me.'

The nearest Enforcer has a small black moustache. He touches it and growls back at the beggar.

'Yeah, and I'm President West. Withered arm, eh? That's no excuse. You've got a wrist, you should have a wristband. I'm not asking again.'

He grabs the beggar's left hand and flashes the torch on the wrist. He slides his other hand along the bony forearm, then steps back and reaches for his notebook.

'We'll take you to the Halls alright. You can explain yourself to the Assessor tomorrow.'

But then something happens Jerry has never come across before. The other Enforcer touches the arm of the nearest one.

'Haven't you read "Orders of the Day"? This one has a charmed life. Don't know why. Special bulletin, signed by Captain Mann himself. "Street-trader, no wristband, lapel-pin with the letter F, calls himself Franklin: report all sightings, take no action. By order." It's this one's photo, I'm sure of it.'

The torch snaps off. Jerry hears the boots tramp away and, very softly, the sound of someone weeping to himself.

He rolls himself up in his blankets. He's done enough kindnesses for one day. And, in Market World, no-one ever says thank you and means it.

An extract from *Blood Ties*, a novel by
Peter Taylor-Gooby, Troubador, 2020

Crossing the Road

London, where justice stands blindfold on a pinnacle and
stockbrokers jostle money-launderers in the fat lands of the
City. London, mother of parliaments, where tourists shove
against anti-terrorist barriers in the shadow of Big Ben,
where wealth is smeared over poverty like jam on stale bread.

It's no good preaching at people, it's no good telling
them it's not fair that other people are wretched when they
aren't. Nic and Jack, my wonderful children, understand
many things, but not that. They campaign tirelessly for
refugee rights, with little success. In my world of brands
and promotion and image-building everyone knows what
to do: make it fun, make it theatre, make it new, and people
will listen. That's what I'm doing.

It only took two weeks to set everything up. I
assembled the gear, found the right phone number in the
Parliamentary Security Department and alerted some of
my contacts. Tim will tip them all off as soon as I'm on
my way.

I wait by the crossing at the Parliament Square end of Whitehall. The sun's hot on my neck. I lick my lips.

The lights change and the green figure strides forward. Jaunty bugger. I shuffle out, head down. The iron collar chafes at my neck, my arms stretch out to the cuffs that clamp my hands to the yoke and the chain between my legs clatters on the tarmac. People are already taking photos. A group of Americans, their backs to me, snap selfies with the weirdo. Performance art – you get a lot of that around in tourist London.

My knees are already bowing but I keep going, the breath harsh in my throat. The green man flashes and I know I'm not going to make it. Sweat runs down my back, my trousers stick to my legs and my feet ache. The last of the crowd streams past, a woman in a yellow jacket drags a child who stares up at me, an ice-cream fast to his mouth.

Engines rev up and a motor-bike shoots past in front of me, followed by three cyclists, two in pink and white lycra and one in a pinstripe suit, with the whirr of an electric motor.

'On your bike,' he mutters out of the side of his mouth.

I take another step. The iron ball on the chain between my legs rumbles after me and the anklets scrape at my skin. A car hoots and I catch the uneasy howl of a siren. I'm doing well, nearly half-way and the taste of rust in my mouth, but I'm still moving. Vehicles squeeze past in front of me, a taxi, a dustcart, a bus. The sweet smell of biodiesel keeps me going for another stride. On the other side of the road a man with a London Dungeon sandwich board cheers. People line the pavement and point at me. They hold up mobile phones and clap and shout advice. They think the chains are plastic. They aren't.

Big Ben chimes the hour and all the faces jerk upwards. Five pm on a Tuesday in early September. Rush hour, start of the parliamentary term – maximum impact. I catch sight of Nic in the crowd, a huge grin on her face, her hand raised in a thumbs up. I try to grin back, but it's not Nic, it's someone else, holding up a placard to the cameras:

"Kill the Anti-Immigrant Bill. Welcome to the World".

I drag myself forward another pace, lift my head up so everyone can see my face and fall to my knees and then flat out. My chains crash onto the tarmac. For an instant I feel an immense luxury, lying there. The wrapper from a Paradise Bar blows past, right in front of me, absolute colours, black and white and red. I could do with one right now.

I force myself up off the road and drag my body forward, my knees scraping on the tarmac.

'Stag night was it, sir? Don't suppose you've got the key?'

I twist my head sideways. A helmet, blue eyes and a moustache. I shake my head and the iron collar bites at my neck.

'Alright, get his other arm, someone take his legs. We'll get you out of everyone's way and then we can have a chat.'

Cameras flash from both sides and the crowd makes way. About time someone showed up from the real media. A woman I nearly recognise in a blue suit with neat blonde hair leans down towards me and holds out a microphone.

'Why are you doing this?'

A younger woman in jeans stands behind her, a TV camera clasped to her shoulder.

Brilliant! I told you I've still got contacts.

Another policeman in a flak jacket with a submachine gun slung across his chest is forcing his way through the crowd towards the camera. He's not your ordinary copper and he's going to slap his hand over the lens. One chance.

'Britain needs immigrants!' I shout and start coughing, my throat as sore as if I'd run five miles.

I spit.

'Make criminals out of refugees, you drive them into the hands of people traffickers!'

Another officer, this one wearing a steel helmet, with goggles pushed up on it and a mask like a visor across his mouth, stands between me and the interviewer. He pulls the mask down under his chin with a gloved hand and grasps the interviewer by the elbow.

'Madam, you are obstructing the pavement. There will be a statement later.'

Tim timed the call just right. They've sent the terrorism squad and Parliament's in lock down. My heart's pounding but I haven't blacked out. Everything is going splendidly.

'Mr Morlan. What exactly did you think you were doing?'

We're in a windowless room with four chairs and a table, but it's not the same as you see on TV. There's no one-way mirror, no recording device and no surveillance camera. The furniture is scratched and the air smells clammy, as if it's been breathed too many times before. It reminds me of an all-night café at 4.00am. My shoulders are as sore as if I've been carrying a sack of cement. Pain stabs at me like a blade when I shift my arm.

The officer who brought me in sits across the table. He's wearing a grey-blue pullover with three-star epaulettes stitched onto the shoulders. His hand clenches into a fist, relaxes and clenches again. Next to him is a large balding man in a grey suit with a Brasenose College tie. He stares directly at me for the entire interview and says very little. They've taken my shackles.

'Modern slavery flourishes, now, here in London, hidden in plain sight. The Repatriation Bill plays into the hands of the people-traffickers.'

'I see. Time-waster.'

'I have a right to protest.'

'Not near parliament. Not without telling us first. You're looking at a five thousand pound fine. Minimum.'

I could argue with him. I have a right to see my MP.

'I'm sorry. I don't want to waste police time.'

'First one I've had in here who's said that.' He lays his hand flat on the table and looks down at it. 'I get demonstrators here every day – "Real Jobs with Real Pay", "Kick Out the Illegals", "Britain for the British", "Welcome to the World". Half of them want to start a fight and blame the others for it. Somewhere among them, hidden in plain sight, the shy young woman with the suicide vest or the schoolboy with the knife.'

He lifts his face and stares at me.

'We've got race-riots in Dagenham and officers injured. Britain is a divided nation and it's my job to police it. You don't make it any easier. Get it?'

Someone raps on the door. The man in the suit opens it and goes out. When he comes back he looks at me, as if memorising my face, and says

'OK. You're out.'

'I'm free to go?'

The terrorism officer looks at him for a moment, shrugs and stands up. He grasps me by the upper arm and escorts me from the room.

'Good-bye. Come back and I'll … don't come back.'

He slams the door and it quivers in the frame. I rub at my arm and look round. I'm in a large tiled lobby, rather like the entrance to my school, with the bustle of the reception area off to the side.

A figure in a pinstripe suit strides in through the street doors in a gust of cold air. He holds out his hand, then hugs me.

'Jack!'

'Dad! Sit down for a minute.' He pauses. 'You know you really shouldn't be doing these things.'

'Thank you.' I hold him. He's my brilliant son and I don't see enough of him. I don't care about the ache in my shoulders. He's wearing his City suit and I smell the aftershave. 'It's wonderful to see you. Let me buy you lunch.'

'It's Adam you should thank. My solicitor. He's a friend of Thomas's.'

A lean man who can't be more than twenty-five stands next to him. His suit is immaculate and his tie smells of Oxford. I thank him. He does not return my smile.

Jack takes my arm.

'Thomas?'

He grins.

'Tell you later. Now listen. My party can't be linked to extremists and we don't do stunts. Why on earth did you do it? They might have shot you.'

He watches my face closely. He needs to be sure I'm telling him the truth.

'I want to help. Get you and Nic some publicity.'

'Well you did that alright. Listen, I have to get back to the House, it's the Select Committee for the Immigrant Repatriation Bill. Can I drop you somewhere?'

He raises his hand and a taxi appears as if it had been waiting for him. I'm about to say 'yes' when my phone rings, so I wish him good luck. I'd rather sit in a café, anyway. Preferably the all-day breakfast, maybe leave the fried bread.

I shout:

'Thanks again – you're a star,' and thumb the button on the phone.

'Mr Morlan? I'm Adeline, BBC *Overview*.'

I sit down where I am, on the steps of New Scotland Yard, and give her my full attention. *Overview* gets five million viewers on a good day and I'm going to tell them the truth about modern slavery. For once I'll have done something that will impress Jack and Nic. I'm feeling good.